Northfield

By
Jerome A. Kuntz

© Copyright 2008, Jerome A. Kuntz

All Rights Reserved.

No part of this book may be reproduced, stored in a retrieval system, or transmitted by any means, electronic, mechanical, photocopying, recording, or otherwise, without written permission from the author.

ISBN: 978-1-4357-5131-6

Cover photograph of the Iron Bridge over the Cannon River to Mill Square in Northfield, Minnesota. Photo courtesy of the Northfield, Minnesota Historical Society. Circa 1876.

For purchases contact Lulu.com

Introduction

Searching for family heirlooms and keepsakes was the last thing on my mind that blustery September day in 1987. It was only a family obligation to complete, and then we'd be on our way home for an adult beverage before dinner.

The Compton family estate had sold the family farm located on the outskirts of Northfield, Minnesota. My great, great, great grandfather, Harlen Compton, purchased it before the Civil War. The last farming-busted Compton moved away a decade ago, and we no longer considered keeping it economically sensible.

Successive renters had occupied the farmhouse, but one room in the attic was padlocked and off limits, and even our family appeared to have little interest in the contents. Soon after the sale, we knew we had to clean it out. There was no key, so we hacksawed the lock.

Stale musty air wafted out as we slowly wedged open the warped door. At first there appeared little of interest: Christmas decorations, moth-eaten clothes on hangers, boxes of books—McGuffey Readers on top, ladies hats. That's about what we expected. Then we uncovered the wind-up phonograph, the kind that played cylindrical records. A nice find. Several records were also stored in their original cardboard containers, none of the artists familiar to us. We moved it all out and down the attic steps, sneezing and commenting on how we'd throw everything away except the phonograph with records and the books.

A redbrick chimney passed through the room before disappearing into the roof boards. That must have helped keep things dry. Behind the chimney and wedged between slanting rafter planks is where we found the padlocked steamer trunk. Aye-yi-yi, what do we have here? With excitement mounting, we dragged it out where the light was better. This lock appeared manufactured in the 19th century. Without a key, we again had to use the hacksaw.

I can best describe it as a communal family gasp as we slowly lifted the creaking cover. Two Colt revolvers, still in their leather holsters and wound in individual cartridge belts lay on top. The leather was cracked and dry and the guns speckled with rust. Cartridge belt-loops were full—the Comptons were ready to defend their home.

Below them were twenty-four notebooks of various sizes, thickness, and manufacture. We had no clue as to what they contained. Pushing for space like piggies at a trough, as brothers and sisters are prone to act, we each got one. Mine was off the top, labeled Chapter 1, and I found it covered in longhand writing by Custer Compton, our great, great grandfather and oldest son of Harlen Compton, Civil War veteran, that I already mentioned as the original owner of the property.

At first I wasn't impressed as it appeared to be a description of the famous Northfield Raid by the James/Younger gang. I knew several non-fiction books were already available on the subject. Then everyone got excited, jabbering like loonies. We read succeeding chapter numbers; they made one complete story! It was obviously a memoir and each notebook contained one or two chapters. We couldn't believe it: good Lord, here we had a Compton family memoir from the 19th century—our family memoir! My sisters began tearing up, and I wasn't that far behind. Below the notebooks were dozens of little cardboard boxes of ammunition of various calibers.

For reasons still not clear to me, my brothers and sisters assigned me the task of typing it in the correct order. The writing was in both pencil and ink and greatly faded by passing years. Grammar, well, rules were different in those days and I doubt if I found all the mistakes. Same applies to punctuation, but I only made changes where I thought clarity was called for. Other than that, it's the exact story Custer wrote over one-hundred years ago. I figured it was his memoir, so why mess with it.

It isn't possible to date the writing except for the Epilogue. It's obvious he wrote that when he was quite old (1930s), his wife passed on, and their children moved away. That particular notebook was in the best condition. Another statement of his caught my interest: in the Epilogue, he said he began writing the story on the train back to Minnesota. Can we assume he started with the robbery in Chapter 1? If so, that notebook could date from 1876. Amazing, isn't it? How easily it could have been lost forever.

Of course, I was soon to learn the value of the Colt revolvers and trunk of ammo. Custer only described them as Colt six-shooters, but two of his other statements seem to verify the authenticity of the weapons. In Chapter 25, he stated, "I saddled Monty and Cowboy, and tied Buck's few belongings on his saddle, along with his pistol and belt. It was about the only thing of his I carried back to Northfield." If he brought Buck's Colt home, he certainly would have brought his own. Again, in Chapter 25, he included in his description of returning to Cheyenne, in search of Jasmine Bodecker: "I found out, cowboying was a weedy row to hoe. I had to punch new holes in my gun belt." One of the gun belts does have two added buckle holes, but no, they're not punched. Someone cut them with a knife, which would indicate a job done on the prairie without access to proper tools. There's little doubt; the revolvers belonged to Custer and his younger brother, Buck.

The trunk with ammunition is likely one that Custer mentioned in the story. In Chapter 15, he told us in reference to his fear of Indians after the Sioux Uprising of 1862: "Long after the time of the Compton posse, almost to the turn of the century, Pa stored Grandpa's old steamer trunk in the house, filled with hundreds of rounds of ammo for every gun we owned." We're sure it's the same trunk.

We'll probably donate the guns, holsters, trunk, and ammo to the Northfield Historical Society Museum, but for now anyway, we can't bear to part with them. Besides, have you ever tried to get an entire family to agree on something?

After typing Custer's frontier memoir, I made several copies for the family, but people continually encouraged me to publish. It wasn't until I retired that I had time to find an agent and publisher.

It would be pointless to explain what this memoir means to the Compton family, as you will easily guess that after reading it. I was impressed by Custer's accuracy for historical events and dates, and I can only conclude he related his entire memoir with an honesty characterized by how he handled himself in everyday life on the frontier. He was scared and so alone, but he stood like a man.

Byron Elgin Compton
Cody, Wyoming 2005

Chapter 1

I froze like a cottontail when I heard the shots. Northfield, Minnesota was normally a coonhound-sleepy town. Even as far back as 1876, the drowsy dirt streets seldom echoed with gunfire. A small war must have broken out.

Mrs. Hollins' classroom was not the place to spend a beautiful Indian-summer day, so I was playing hooky along the Cannon River west of town. I raced toward the shooting, completely forgetting my unexplained absence in school. If there was bloodshed, I intended to see it firsthand.

Running lickety-split across Division Street and up a back alley, I came out on Fourth Street. The action was on Division in front of the bank and in Mill Square. A stairway reached up the outside of the Dampier House Hotel on the corner of Fourth and Division. That's where I hid. It reeked from cat pee and mouse turds, but by lying on my belly and poking my head out around the end of the bottom step, I could see all of Division and the Square.

I'll make this quick. I can only tell you how I saw it. Everyone there appeared to have seen something different. When I told people who weren't there, they didn't believe me—maybe because I'd gabbed some stretchers in my day. You'll fine plenty of history books that maybe have it straight.

Mill Square wasn't safe. Bullets whined and crackled across the Square before slamming into buildings or ricocheting off concrete structures. Wisps of blue smoke floated lazily overhead.

The First National Bank's windows were shattered, and men blazed from all directions. I knew it was a bank robbery; I just wasn't sure at first who the robbers were. Four men on horseback thundered across the Square, all firing six-shooters. One big lunker swore a blue streak and fired at everything that moved. Weeks later, we learned he was Cole Younger. Two local men hiding behind Lee & Hitchcock's dry-goods store sniped at the mounted men. The deadly roll of gunfire sounded like the Fourth of July. Plate glass windows exploded out of several buildings across from the bank.

Jerome A. Kuntz

Some fool ran out from Wheeler's Drugstore and headed toward me. It was Henry Wheeler, a medical student and son of the drugstore's owner. He sprinted into the Dampier House. The outlaws continued to race their horses around the Square, shooting and driving everyone indoors.

Minutes later, a shot crashed from the top-floor window of the Dampier. It was Henry, not much older than I, blasting down at the outlaws. A robber tumbled off his horse and lay face down in the street. One down and four to go, I thought, according to my count. I had no idea there were three still inside the bank.

The big outlaw (Cole Younger) ran to help the man in the dirt. Then he spun around like a child's top, shot in the hip. He jumped back on his horse and shot a local man coming from a basement saloon. Another robber tumbled from his horse. Two down! One of the robbers' horses screamed in pain, staggered, then collapsed into the dirt. Old Henry was having a field day; he shot another man in the elbow.

Cole ran to the bank's front door, blood soaking the side of his pants. "The game's up," he shouted. "We are beaten." Then he raced back to his horse. I heard another shot in the bank. Three robbers came out, cursing and shooting in all directions, daring people to poke their head up. Two looked familiar. Before I could identify them, they mounted up except for a man wounded in the shoulder. He begged not to be left behind. Cole Younger turned back and swung him into the saddle behind him. Then all six outlaws pounded across the Cannon River Bridge, still shooting back into Mill Square as they fled town.

All was quiet now. Quiet as any Sunday morning when old Homer Fennie stops pulling the church-bell rope before services. It seemed no one wanted to be first to enter the Square. A mixture of blue gun smoke and dust floated above the streets. I read later that the shooting lasted only seven minutes. Even arriving late, it seemed much longer to me.

Elias Hobbs, the town marshal, came out first, walking as if stepping on eggshells. Other men followed, crouched and still pointing their guns. A little group silently gathered in front of the bank and looked through the broken windows. A few of my classmates, pale-faced and silent, had arrived. Two older ladies made the sign of the cross in front of the bank. Inside, the bank's cashier, Joe Heywood, lay dead on the floor. Sadly, the robbers had blown part of his head off. It must have been the last shot I heard before they fled the bank.

Then we spread out, everyone looking over the carnage. Doc Coons—white shirt, black suspenders—knelt down next to another local man wounded in the head. He frantically dug in his black medical bag for something.

Along with the dead horse, two thieves lay crumbled in the dirt. Doc wouldn't be able to help them; they looked graveyard dead and their stick-up days were over. Great pools of blood soaked the ground around the bodies. I was wondering how one person could hold all that blood. Someone grabbed my shoulder.

"Custer! What are you doing here?" I spun around to find Pa eyeing me suspiciously.

"All the students are here," I blurted, as if that explained everything. Buck told me later Mrs. Hollins screamed bloody murder as my classmates bolted out the door when the shooting started. I guess we shared a common belief: any excuse to skip school was a good one.

Just then, Uncle Roy, Pa's brother who was Rice County sheriff waddled over. He pulled Pa's arm and off they went. "Go home and tell your Ma we're all okay," Pa called over his shoulder.

Phew! That was close. I only hoped he hadn't seen me coming from the north instead of the schoolhouse.

I couldn't figure why adults always harped about school. I had all the education I needed to go out West and be a cowboy. Both Pa and Uncle Roy had worked in Nebraska and Wyoming territory after the war. They hauled freight as far as Fort Laramie. When the time was right, I'd be on *my* way, and my parents knew it; certainly I'd told them enough times.

Buck and Sadie, my brother and sister, were in the crowd and gawking at everything as if a circus had come to Northfield. They were fraternal twins and two years younger than my seventeen.

Freckled towheads, not dark-haired like me. Granny Sikes, from Pequot Lakes, recited endlessly, "Land sakes, you put those two in a gunnysack, shake um up, pore um out and you couldn't tell one from t'other."

Buck hated that. He didn't enjoy looking like a girl, so he kept his hair short in contrast to Sadie's ponytail. Like all the boys then, he wanted to be a man, not some snot-nosed kid in short pants.

Naturally, seeing them every day, I knew there were big differences between the two: Sadie was outgoing, drawing other people into her merriment. Buck was quiet and reflective, content to live life within his own thoughts.

Even though a pain at times, Sadie was the smart one in the family, and, as far as I could see, it had little to do with school learning. She'd already made up her mind to be a schoolteacher. Oh, she could get on our nerves—proving she was right about things and we held a cold deck.

Buck wasn't much help in arguments either. Living in a schoolhouse wouldn't change him. He claimed to hate school, but he still read every book he could get his hands on, long as he didn't have to buy it. He was more interested in hunting and fishing, and living in Minnesota, there were plenty of opportunities for both.

"This had to be the one day I didn't have my squirrel gun," Buck said, shaking his head sadly. He hardly went anywhere without his rifle, even taking it to school. So did other country boys, so they could bag game for the table on the way home. They stashed them in the cloakroom during class. Like Pa, Buck figured it was better to eat wild game than butcher your own stock.

"Buck Compton, you would have run like a chicken with its head cut off if Jesse James shot at you," Sadie said, pointing her finger at him. She rarely wasted a chance to make Buck look foolish or faint of heart.

"Why did you say Jesse James?" I asked, before Buck could counter with his usual wisecracks.

Sadie rolled her eyes. Egad, that was an annoying habit, and I hoped she would soon outgrow it. "Didn't you hear, Custer? The James Gang tried to rob the bank, but Pa and Uncle Roy stopped them."

That's why I recognized the last two men coming from the bank. The James brothers! Their pictures had appeared in the *Minneapolis Tribune*. I never expected to see them in Northfield, so I didn't make the connection.

Along with my classmates, I enjoyed following the exploits of outlaws and heroes alike. We loved the Beadle Westerns, especially the Ned Buntline novels of Buffalo Bill and Wild Bill Hickok. Unfortunately, Jack McCall had murdered Hickok in the Number Ten Saloon in Deadwood, Dakota Territory, one month earlier, August of 1876.

"Pa had a gun?" I asked, unbelieving. The only time he carried a rifle was for hunting.

"Uncle Roy tossed Pa a pistol when the shooting started, and they saved the bank's money," she said proudly.

"Ah, there were a lot more'n Pa and Uncle Roy shooting at the crooks," Buck said. "Half the town got in a few licks...except me, of course." Again, he wagged his head in frustration. "Damn it to hell, I wish I'd taken my rifle today." It appeared Buck considered shooting outlaws as much fun as deer hunting.

"Buck Compton, I'm gonna tell Ma you were cussing again," Sadie said, pretending to be shocked. She could act mighty hoity-toity for someone who knew as many swear words as Buck and I together.

Sadie went off with her friends. Buck and I hung around to watch them flop the two dead outlaws on stretchers and head toward the funeral parlor. A local reporter from the *Rice County Journal* hurried back and forth, trying to interview as many people as he could before they left the Square. I listened in stunned amazement; they all sounded like sharpshooters who had saved the day. I couldn't help thinking they only cashed in two robbers. Six rode out, more or less alive.

We slowly walked out of town, heading for our small farm half a mile away. "Uncle Roy's getting up a posse," Buck said.

"Oh, of course. That's his job...and I'm going with him," I said. "After all, I saw the James brothers and can identify them."

"Really?" Buck said in surprise. "You saw them?" As usual, that boy never believed anything unless he heard it twice. But then again,

Jerome A. Kuntz

I'd laid some almighty whoppers on him in the past so he was naturally suspicious.

"You bet, and they're going to need me." Actually, this cockeyed idea just popped into my head. How many times would I look back to that day and wish I could change everything!

"I'm going too," he said, with that stubborn look I knew so well.

"Now wait-t-t a minute, Buck. What's good for the goose might embarrass the gander. Who's going to help Ma and Sadie with the farm?" It was a weak argument; they'd handled it before when we went on hunting or cattle buying trips.

We had 80 acres on the edge of town, a few chickens, pigs, and milk cows. A small operation, but it kept us in beans. Pa wasn't much of a farmer anyway and seldom fancied steady work. He hired out to neighbors if we needed money—provided it didn't muss his plans for hunting and fishing.

Buck ignored my question. "Goose, gander, meander, flander, I don't care. Either we both go, or I'll tell Pa you were playing hooky again."

There it was. He always said just what was on his mind and didn't waste time about it either. I'd blundered by talking to him first. If Pa found out, I wouldn't have a lame coonhound's chance of going. When it came to skipping school, girls, coarse language, and tobacco use, he treated us like 12-year-olds.

Actually, I wanted Buck along, but now I'd have the extra rigamarole of getting him included. Even though he was quiet, he had a bone-dry sense of humor, and was fun to have around. A happy-go-lucky kid with many friends in Northfield. You'd have liked him.

Chapter 2

As usual, Buck and I found things to explore on the way home, and we forgot the time. A large slough, choked with cattails, bordered the dirt track leading to our prosperous holdings. Frogs bragged of their beauty, bluebottle flies glided along its green cow pasture shore. Mallards, geese, and mud hens quarreled endlessly over property rights. Border disputes teetered on violence. Ill-tempered seagulls skimmed our heads to drive us off until everyone peacefully settled on their little homestead. Of course, we knew that day would never come.

Buck told me what happened in school. Oh, did we have a laugh! I *almost* wished I'd been there. It was the day for Buck's grade to stand and speak or read in front of the class. The purpose of this unusual cruelty was "to prepare oneself for public speaking." I'd gone through it myself. The schoolmarm cautioned older students to "pay no attention and continue your studies."

It came off without a hitch until Frightened Freddy took the podium. Everyone braced for merriment. He was small for his age with curly black hair, serious as measles, and ears swinging off the side of his head like open haymow doors.

Purposeful ear wigglers in school could even get Saints and teacher pets into hot water, but with an innocent wiggler like Freddy, you might as well lock the door and go home.

He began to read. Sadly, he reached a trapdoor in the text sprinkled with obscure words that had dozed for decades, and they probably shouldn't have been disturbed. Not to be outdone, Freddy struggled mightily to pen up those stubborn syllables and slam the gate.

Then it happened: his ears wiggled and the fox was in the chicken coop. Thirty students clapped hands over their mouths to keep from laughing. Some didn't make it. Giggles squeezed from between tight fingers. Mrs. Hollins looked around with alarm.

Danged Freddy wouldn't give up. Ears fanning, the dictionary continued to read and appeared not to notice the ruckus. Students

Jerome A. Kuntz

choked with laughter as they bowed down to hide behind desks. Teacher's face reddened. The signs were there: she was a rusty boiler about to burst. No one could stand much more.

Then came the shots, cracking like thunder through the walls. Everyone jumped up and pounded for the door. They had to get air. Mrs. Hollins bellowed threats at the top of her voice, but nothing could stop them. Books and tablets were knocked off desks and skidded across the floor. Out the door they raced, two or more at a time as they headed for the shots, same as I'd done from another part of town. Oh, would she lay it on the next day!

Sadie had beat us home. By the time we arrived, Ma seemed to know more about the robbery than we did. In Sadie's customary story-telling fashion, she had filled in information gaps with outrageous guesses as to what actually occurred. Truth for her was merely a flimsy foundation to construct fairy tales for everyone's enjoyment. Ma had listened good-naturedly while bustling about the kitchen preparing a fried chicken and mashed potato supper. She was used to Sadie's imagination. Pa would be home soon with something more closely resembling the facts.

Ma was making milk gravy as Pa banged through the front screen door. She seemed to be in a rush to get things done. The cook stove, filled with wood, threw off more heat than a steam locomotive. Even with all the windows and doors open, it was almost too hot to enjoy eating. I said *almost*. Ma was the best cook in the county, and her apple pies never failed to win first prize at the Rice County fair in August.

We soon gathered around the kitchen table. A huge platter of chicken and a mixing bowl of mashed potatoes made our mouths water. There were cold sliced tomatoes and cucumbers too, spiraled around on a clear glass plate. With Ma's garden, we ate well even when money was tight. We only waited for the gravy before digging in—and Ma, of course. We knew better than to start before everyone found a chair.

Pa brought us more news, and we excitedly chipped in with our own version of events. He and Uncle Roy had scouted around until they picked up the outlaws' trail. Roy wanted to go right after them, but they were losing the light, and Pa sagely advised starting out tomorrow at dawn instead. Besides, it was suppertime and it wouldn't look right not to show up after the wives had worked so hard. That was all it took. Uncle Roy weighed 300 pounds and didn't generally make a habit of missing meals. Neighbors considered his wife, Aunt Millie, the second best cook in the county, and Sheriff Roy's ample girth was proof enough.

The big rush was over and we leisurely enjoyed our apple pie. There was little room left to store it so we ate slowly. I figured the time had come to make my move, and I had one chance to do it right. "Say Pa," I said, feeling my way like a tightrope walker, "I saw the James brothers leave the bank and can identify them."

"That right?" he mumbled, convincingly pretending lack of interest and not looking up from his pie. I had my work cut out.

"Yeah, that's right. Thanks for asking. A while back, the *Tribune* printed their picture. Jesse was the last man out of the bank, and more'n likely, he was the one who shot Joe Heywood." I knew I sounded a lot more confident than I felt. In other words, I skated on the slippery edge of a lie.

"Hum-m-m," I think he said, but it could have been a belch, nose still in his plate. Yeah, he was impressed. Skinning a cat would be easier than this. I hoped I wouldn't have to beg—always a last resort. I glanced at Buck. He watched closely, daring me to exclude him. I threw caution to the wind.

"Pa, Buck and I want to join the posse. Without me, you and Uncle Roy could well ride past the James brothers and not even know it…and Buck's the best shot in the family."

Finally, he took his eyes off his food and looked at me. "Wha-a-a-t? What about school?"

"Well now, I'm glad you mentioned that, but we both feel confident we can make it up when we get home. Shucks, we did it several times after deer hunting. Besides…Buck and I carefully talked this over, we need money for the extra schoolbooks Mrs. Hollins is always carping about." I had crossed the line. Buck and I both enjoyed novels, but schoolbooks were on the bottom of the list of things we'd buy.

Jerome A. Kuntz

I heard a choked-off giggle. Sadie had both hands over a face as red as a turkey wattle, and her body shook like Ma's plum jelly. "Pa, you can't help but catch them with General Custer along," she managed to squeak out between giggles.

I gave her my meanest look to shut her up. Fortunately, no one paid her any mind. I'd better explain. Both Pa and Uncle Roy were Civil War veterans and great admirers of General George Armstrong Custer. Ma called me Matthew or Matt until Pa returned from the war. Then he started calling me "Custer" and everyone else took it up. Even in our large family bible, which the folks bought after Pa returned, I'm down solid as Custer Compton.

Three months before the bank robbery, June of 1876, the Sioux and Northern Cheyenne wiped out General Custer and the Seventh Cavalry on the Little Big Horn. The newspapers portrayed the general as brave but reckless and foolhardy. I had already decided to go by Matthew again after moving out West.

Ma started to look cross. "They're too young," she said flatly. This is what I counted on. If Ma said one way, five'll get you ten Pa would take the opposite side of the road. That was just his way.

"Now, Jenny, don't you worry none about that," Pa said. Being a firm believer in superstitious signs, or any danged thing else that brought luck, I crossed two fingers on my left hand. I'm sure Buck did the same. We needed our right hands for eating pie. "We won't get near those outlaws before they're caught by another posse ahead of us," he continued. "It pays two dollars a day per man, and, if they do get over the Iowa border, the wages continue on the ride back to Northfield. It'll be more like getting paid to go on a picnic."

I was to think back a hundred times on Pa's little speech in the months to come. Never before had I found him so wrong about something.

It got very quiet. Ma slowly looked around the table until her eyes rested on Buck. "Well—? What do you say? Cat got your tongue?" Buck knew enough to keep his mouth shut.

"These boys might get killed," Ma said, pointing her fork at Pa. "You we can spare, but I won't have my boys shot up." She was a large, dark, forceful woman and few people got the better of her. Pa was skinny, fair-haired, sleepy-eyed and didn't appear to have a chance. Even *we* felt they were a funny looking couple; I don't know what the neighbors thought. That's not how things generally worked out though: Pa normally got his way.

"Roy already looked for men to ride," Pa said impatiently, ignoring Ma's little stab and assuming his righteous look. "Anyone willing to go has already ridden out with one of the other posses. Who's left but those stool polishers from the Exchange Saloon?" He forgot to mention that was also *his* favorite hang-out. "Besides," he continued, "I honestly feel American citizens ought to be willing to uphold the laws of Minnesota before it becomes another Missouri."

Boy-howdy, was I learning how to grease the skids!

Ma sniffed at that whopper. "Best I can remember, Harlen, you never upheld a law in your life. Most of the time you're inclined to break them." In polite company, Pa was what might be called a social drinker. Moonshine mostly. I'm sure he knew every still around Northfield—and it was definitely illegal.

"Keep in mind, Jenny, that's six dollars a day for the three of us."

"I think I'm capable of such difficult arithmetic as you are," she fired back, volume turned up, "but I'm telling *you,* it won't do you any good to come home if these boys are hurt, 'cause I'll shoot you myself."

The three of us cracked up pretty good over that one until Pa gave us black looks. No one took her seriously; she'd been threatening to limit Pa's days on Earth since I could remember, but he still enjoyed finger-lickin' good fried chicken with the family.

Before we ate, Ma had used the red pump over the kitchen sink to fill a pan of dishwater. It bubbled softly on the stove. Pa made himself scarce as chicken lips after supper, saying he had to get Sheriff Roy's okay for us to join the posse. The rest of us reluctantly cleaned the dishes. Then Buck and I went to the barn to make sure our saddle horses and Pa's mule were well-fed and ready to travel.

We didn't worry about Uncle Roy turning us down. Pa had a way of handling his younger brother even if he was sheriff of Rice County. It was something to watch; he'd assure Roy—as the high sheriff—that he had a bank-full of answers, and then Pa would began chipping away the foundation.

Jerome A. Kuntz

We got precious little sleep that night. It was all too exciting: the Compton family riding off to capture the famous James Gang! Pa had ridden with Sheriff Roy before, mostly chasing penny-ante horse thieves or cattle rustlers. This would be the Compton posse's first real manhunt. Anything was better than sitting in Old Lady Hollins' classroom, listening to her drone on about nouns and verbs. We already spoke English. Why bother to keep studying it?

Chapter 3

It was barely daylight when a horrible commotion erupted in the front yard. Buck and I watched out the barn window as Uncle Roy, chock full of energy, galloped up to the house. Snowy leghorns scattered in every direction, squawking their fool heads off.

Even our two bloodhounds, Bubbles and Mr. Moses, bayed alarm to prove they didn't sleep around the clock. In hot weather, that's exactly what they did. After recognizing an old friend, they lazily staggered back to shabby rugs on the roofed front porch, content with their performance. Both were splashed brown-and-white and appeared wracked with grief. Any stray happy thoughts were closely guarded. Only the prospect of coon hunting brightened their spirits. Every day was Saturday to them.

We rode Prince and Jack to where Roy impatiently waited on his horse. They were our farm team, but they still made pretty fair saddle horses. No speed of course, but they could stay on a trail from light to dark. Just trying to be nice, we had also saddled Jenny, Pa's mule. Ma was still hot over Pa naming the mule after her but he refused to change it. I doubt the mule cared one way or the other; she just wanted to stay home and doze under the pasture oak.

Roy fairly bristled with guns. Two 44-caliber Colt "peacemakers" hung from his belt, and two more nestled in holsters either side of his saddlebow. He picked up that habit in the Civil War. "When things get tight, you don't want to fool with loading—best to carry more guns," he said many times. We couldn't follow his advice if we wanted to. Pa was lucky to afford the 1866 lever-action Winchesters the three of us used. Long ago, Indians named them "yellow boys" because of the brass receivers. Nothing fancy, but they were good enough for us. Still, being we planned to tackle the James Gang, I thought having one of those six-shooters would be handy in case things "got tight."

Northfield residents declared Roy carried everything on his saddle except a hangman's rope. True enough. He'd had several brass rings installed to hold his handcuffs, leg irons, short pieces of chain, and padlocks. Sounded like a tumbling hardware store when he rode. I never could figure how he kept all the keys straight that jangled from his belt.

"Where's that husband of yours, Jenny?" Roy called as Ma stepped out on the front porch. I assumed long ago that Roy and Ma both agreed she hadn't found the best mate. They'd given up trying to change him.

"Claims he can't find his pants, and I can't find them either."

Pa stuck his head out the door. "I'm not going to ride out after a bunch of outlaws half naked," he said, modestly. He still wore his shabby green bathrobe.

"Ohfergodsake," Roy said, using his favorite expression.

"Oh, you saddled Jenny, Custer?" Pa added. "A man ought to saddle his own mount." I thought that was an odd thing to say. Pa always had us saddle Jenny when we went hunting. It looked like he was in a contrary mood this morning.

"Just put on your good pants, Harlen," Ma snapped. "Can't you see Roy's ready to go?"

Pa stared at her with astonishment. "You mean my church-going pants? No-o-o, ma'am. I want to keep those nice for Sundays."

Buck and I tried not to laugh. We both knew he had married Ma in those pants, and they still looked store-bought new.

"You might as well come in for breakfast, Roy," Ma said, giving a long-suffering sigh. "His pants have to be somewhere in the house."

Uncle Roy groaned as he carefully eased his great bulk down off his horse. He was every bit as fat as Pa was skinny. It amazed us how they could be brothers.

Truthfully, Roy didn't seem all that put out. I don't recall him ever turning down one of Ma's fine meals. Buck and I realized it had been a spell since we ate breakfast, so we all tramped into the house and placed ourselves around the kitchen table. Pa joined us, still wearing his bathrobe—his lost pants seemingly forgotten.

Ma dropped a dozen eggs into one frying pan. In another, she laid thick strips of bacon. She then cut several slices of homemade bread and browned them on a metal rack on the cook stove. They would taste swell smeared with butter and Ma's strawberry jam. It was plain silly to go traipsing after outlaws on an empty stomach.

Darn the luck, Sadie was up and helping Ma build a mountain of venison sandwiches for the trip. She was just full of the devil. While the adults were busy with conversation, she'd catch Buck's eye and pretend she was shot, strangled, or ghastly maimed. It made me a little uneasy for some reason. She'd clutch her belly, bug her eyes out, and stare at the ceiling. Other times, she'd loll her head to one side with her tongue sticking out, and roll her eyes up in her head like a crazy person. Both hands were reaching for the ceiling as if clutching a hangman's rope.

Normally, Buck would act mad, but now I noticed he couldn't stop grinning. This was high adventure for us both, and nothing was going to spoil our day. Of course, we were already spending the money. We always did when we chanced upon any, which wasn't often. Yes sir, two dollars were already as good as in our pockets.

For some reason, Pa couldn't stop telling all the stupid or funny things that happened to him in the war. Normally, he had little to say—maybe grunting a few times over stories we told about school. The kitchen wind-up clock steadily marched on, and I wondered when we'd leave.

Finally, every speck of breakfast was gone—plates clean as a coonhound's bowl. We had Sadie's sandwiches stashed in the saddlebags, canteens filled. Now surely, we'd be riding out. That didn't seem to be the case. Oddly enough, Pa recalled no end of little jobs that needed tending before one could, "reasonably leave the farm in the care of two helpless women." It didn't make a lot of sense; Sadie was almost as capable as Ma was when it came to chores, so I wondered whom he was referring to. It was a safe bet Pa wanted the posse money, but had little interest in capturing the James Gang. Uncle Roy even lost interest and appeared content to smoke his pipe and digest breakfast in the shade of the front porch.

I never realized how we had let the place go to rack and ruin. The pasture gate was catawampus and dragged the ground long as I could remember—now it required jacking up and the ropes tightened. The chicken laying-boxes desperately needed fresh straw, a leaky hog trough needed patching, and we even had to board up a hole in the doghouse. I figured if those coonhounds wanted more fresh air, who were we to argue?

Luckily, Pa located his pants by the time the work was done. He even found time for a couple of drinks while we worked on the gate. From his past posse work for Uncle Roy, he knew there was no drinking on the job. Roy was a stickler about that. He would send Pa home immediately if he drank, and then the pay would stop. I'm sure Pa rationalized it was his last drink for several days and the actual job didn't start until he climbed on Jenny.

Finally, we gathered in the yard by the horses. Roy assumed his official look and said, "It's time to make this legal."

With Ma and Sadie watching from the front porch, Sheriff Roy swore the three of us in as Rice County deputy sheriffs. Pa looked sleepy and unimpressed. I thought Buck might pop his buttons. Being the older brother, I held up my hand and took the oath as if standing in a court of law—calm and professional. I had a duty to act in Northfield's defense. Sadie leaned against the porch post, giggling helplessly. Then Roy handed out sheriff's deputy badges, which we promptly pinned on.

I was already rehearsing the victorious story I'd tell classmates when we returned...if we returned, that is. Even in Minnesota, we knew members of the James Gang were ex-Confederate soldiers and a salty bunch. After all, in 1863 Jesse and Frank rode with William Quantrill's cutthroats to Lawrence, Kansas, where they murdered 183 people and burned half the town.

Uncle Roy finally crawled aboard King, his huge sorrel stallion. The poor horse staggered sideways, trying to keep its feet. King snapped his head around and rolled his eyes up to see what was crushing him. He tried to bite Roy's boot, but Roy kicked his nose to keep from losing his toes. It was too much. Buck and I buried our faces in our coat collars and rocked with silent laughter.

We said goodbye and swung the horses out of the yard. "Buck, can I have your room if you don't come back?" Sadie called, teasingly. Like I said, she had a million ways to tweak her twin brother's nose.

Northfield

"Hush now, Sadie," I heard Ma say as we rode away. It was glorious September in Minnesota, my favorite time of the year—a slight breeze sighing in the box elders, robins and sparrows calling hello, and brilliant green sunshine. The scent of Ma's late-summer flowers surrounding the house followed us: hollyhocks, marigolds, geraniums, and mums.

Every time I looked back, Ma and Sadie waved from the porch. Ma was religious. I wondered if she was waving goodbye or blessing us. Already, I felt homesick and uneasy about bracing the James brothers. I looked at Buck. He had found something mighty interesting in his horse's mane and never turned around.

It's how I forever remember that day—Ma and Sadie waving endlessly. I can't explain it, but even then I knew I wasn't merely waving to them; I was waving goodbye to my youth.

Chapter 4

Uncle Roy referred often to a shabby Minnesota road map he carried. It must have been badly outdated, because we found several trails looking like the main road that weren't even on the map. At times, we'd find ourselves in someone's shady, mosquito-buzzing farmyard and we'd have to retrace our steps, searching for the through road southwest. People must have graded new farm roads without consulting the county.

We planned to follow the Old Indian Road to Sioux Falls, Dakota Territory, and then turn south. Roy figured the James Gang had enjoyed enough of Minnesota and would take the fastest and easiest means home: the Missouri River. If we later learned they'd gone southeast instead and boarded a train for Chicago, we'd wire the Pinkertons, and then return to Northfield. That idea didn't please Buck at all; he was itching to shoot his first outlaw.

Minnesota roads in 1876 were mostly dirt trails winding through mosquito and wood tick infested thick woods. Potholes filled with water spanned the entire track at times. People traveled only if they had to. In places, road builders had cut down trees without bothering to pull the stumps. Not so bad on horseback, but danged slow going for people with wagons. The only gravel road I heard of in the state ran from Minneapolis to Fargo. That would be something to see.

Supposedly, years ago, people saw an Indian walking alone down this road, and they named it the Old Indian Road. Being naturally curious, I asked around Northfield if it was the Indian that was old or the road. The question seemed to irritate folks so I dropped it. People seemed to think it was risky poking too deep into things. I always felt the opposite; why not straighten the kinks before you find yourself knee-deep in mysteries? Even in school where you'd think solving problems was the goal, it still got me into trouble.

We heard a crying baby just north of Mankato. Pa's face creased with concern. "We better stop, Roy," he said. "Sounds like trouble."

"Ach, babies always find something to cry about," Roy snapped. "That's why they're called babies." He had reason to be in a touchy mood. A big man like him suffered more than average from the heat. His shirt was almost as wet as King.

"Yeah, I guess you're right," Pa said, "It's probably nothing, but what if those killers wiped out the family and that baby is alone? I wouldn't want that on my conscience." I didn't say it aloud, but I doubted Pa was unduly plagued with a guilty conscience. Of course, Buck and I envied him of that acquired skill.

Roy was in the lead, and, without a word, turned his horse up a slippery road toward the crying baby. Pa had his way again. We followed behind, keeping a sharp eye out for outlaws. Don't you know, trouble knocks when no one's home.

A shabbier place would be hard to find. We just sat on our horses, watching wood smoke slowly twist from a sooty house chimney. Chickens in the front yard dusted themselves in the lazy afternoon sun. Sleepy non-descript farm dogs had shaded up under a spreading pin oak, not even bothering to bark. Guess they figured there was nothing to steal. Mourning doves lamented their hard life in the nearby woods. The baby continued to screech. There was only a flat-roofed cabin and a leaning, swaybacked barn. A rotting split-rail fence slouched around behind the barn. Chinking had fallen out from between the logs of the cabin and someone hadn't bothered to step outside to spit. Tobacco juice dripped from the logs.

Ma often pointed out, "Only a cow needs to chew a cud, so you can tell the quality of a man chawing tobacco." That never stopped Pa or Uncle Roy; they'd been spewing brown juice since we left home. Buck and I were not allowed though. It might stunt our growth. Only adults seemed immune to side effects of the simple pleasures of life.

Finally, a young man in baggy overalls shuffled out of the cabin. He was thin, bowed, and he matched the buildings. We introduced ourselves. Hennessey was his last name; he didn't bother with a first name. We told him why we were down here, but he claimed the James Gang didn't worry him. They were a piddling thing compared to his troubles now. "Makes a body feel guilty, hogin' all the bad luck in this ol' whirl," Hennessey said, dismally. He made our bloodhounds look giddy.

Jerome A. Kuntz

We followed the forlorn man into his house. "Custer, are these people too poor to have two names?" Buck whispered. I couldn't tell if he was serious, so I didn't answer. The boy didn't talk much and his humor was as dry as dust bunnies.

The house consisted of one large room and a small bedroom in back. Kitchen, dining, and living room were combined. Coats hung on a wall near the door. A couple of rifles leaned in the corner. Nearby were two saddles with bridles, piled on the floor. A clothes tree stood near the kitchen stove. I could guess what that was for; plenty of diapers were on the way. In the corner sagged a davenport with so much stuffing poking out, it reminded me of the scarecrows we optimistically placed in Ma's garden in Northfield.

This traveling was educational; already I'd met people poorer than us. In fact, I felt guilty over our vulgar wealth and wasteful way of life. Even though we only scratched a living on the Compton Estate, we at least dined high on the hog. Our host seemed to be doing even worse.

Hennessey showed the squalling new baby. Mama had given birth recently and was ailing in the bedroom—too exhausted to worry about the kid. A chicken bubbled in a large pot on the woodstove. No matter what the illness, Minnesota always turned to chicken soup. Someone's sick? Not to worry. Toss a chicken in the pot. It's the same way today.

Uncle Roy seemed bothered no end by the situation. He had a sheriff's star custom-made for him when he took office, claiming, "Normal badges look sissy on a man of my stature." Now it fairly danced on his chest as he excitedly stomped around on the hardwood floor. "Consarned, it man, why haven't you fetched a doctor?" he shouted, looking hard at Hennessey.

The sad-looking farmer protested in a high-pitched whine, "Then who would care for the baby?" Truthfully, I wondered how the baby could get less care with him gone.

"But don't you have any kith or kin to help in a situation like this?" Roy shouted again. I couldn't understand why he kept yelling. Hennessey was about addled already.

Northfield

Pa was a picture of calm and commonsense. He knew exactly the right course of action. "Roy," he said, dropping into a comfortable rocker. "You better ride to town and get the doc. Me and the boys will hold things down here."

Roy looked at him open-mouthed. "Get the doc? Ohfergodsake, we're on a manhunt!"

"What you say is absolutely correct, as usual. I also think part of good law enforcement is to care for citizens who are generously paying taxes to support our efforts." Ma always said Pa was honey-tongued as a meadowlark. He would someday talk himself out of hell and be swapping stories with Saint Peter.

"Paying taxes?" Roy said, his face turning red. Government official hate being reminded who pays them. "Oh, all right. I'll get the doc, but don't none of you get too comfortable. We don't want the trail to get cold."

I didn't say it, but it seemed to me the James Gang would have ample time for sightseeing before shuffling down to Missouri—maybe even make a surprise visit to northern relatives. A blind mule could see what Pa was up to: he'd been wasting time since we started, hoping the outlaws got away and we wouldn't get into a messy shooting scrape. Our wages were all he cared about.

After Roy left, Pa became a model of efficiency. He put me to chopping wood for the cook stove and told Buck to unsaddle Jenny, Jack, and Prince. Hennessey showed Buck where the hay and grain were located.

When we got back to the house, Pa was still polishing the rocker and had his big pipe stoked. This added to a room already smoky from the stove. It was getting dark so Hennessey set a yellow-glowing lantern on the kitchen table. The place was feeling downright homey.

When Doc Paulson arrived in his black buggy, he picked up the baby, hurried into the bedroom, and shut the door. He was an older, dignified man wearing a dark suit and string tie. His black, gambler moustache twitched as he talked. He certainly didn't look like the kind of doctor who would take chickens for payment instead of cash. Ten to one, Roy would have to foot the bill.

Jerome A. Kuntz

Hennessey busied himself over the stove making supper. He didn't seem keen on getting involved with his wife's illness. After a bit, Doc stuck his head out the bedroom door and ordered a bowl of the chicken soup. Fortunately, the baby had stopped screaming. A good meal worked wonders with that little grasshopper.

There was an irritating pest in the house. Hennessey was the first person I'd ever known to have a pet duck. Lester was black with white tail feathers, and eyes like bitty chips of coal. He spent his time picking food tid-bits off the floor. Nothing seemed to please him. He either wanted more food, thought we were in his way, or were sitting in his chair. Never knew ducks were that hard to please. Now I don't mind dogs in the house; they can be housebroken. Once you cross that line and share the house with farm animals, you might as well live in the barn.

Hennessey fried pork chops. That explained the peculiar odor when we rode up. I saw no pigpens, so he must have let his hogs run wild in the dark woods. Likely, when he needed meat, he hunted them like wild game. A cheap way to raise pork provided black bears generously overlooked a few.

After Doc finished, we all sat for supper. Mother and baby would be fine. It was dark by them, and, as usual, the food bag was on and all urgency of the chase drifted away like smoke up Hennessey's chimney.

Besides the chops, we had sauerkraut, mashed potatoes, baking-powder biscuits, and even deviled eggs—food that'll stick to your ribs. Could that Hennessey cook! Never saw a *man* prepare deviled eggs before.

Would you believe that damn Lester took to flying over the table! Only Buck and I seemed concerned over what could happen. I tried not to worry, but being raised on a farm, I knew what passes for fowl hygiene. Pa, Uncle Roy, and Doc barely noticed. Likely, they'd seen worse in the war.

Ma wouldn't tolerate such nonsense. She'd invite Lester for dinner, if you know what I mean. Pa was likely to take a softer tone in such matters. "When in Rome, do as the Romans do," he liked to repeat, even if it didn't really apply to the situation. From what I'd learned about those danged Romans, they weren't people with habits I'd care to pick up.

We washed dishes after eating. There wasn't enough food left over to feed a house mouse. Posse work sure gave you an appetite. I doubted Hennessey could afford to have us for houseguests very long. He retired early to the bedroom and we didn't see him until breakfast.

Doc's next patient was farther down the road, and, it not being urgent, he decided to spend the night. His horse was already getting acquainted and mooching supper in the barn. We passed time listening to his hair-raising experiences as a Civil War doctor with the First Minnesota Volunteers. Pa and Uncle Roy added a few of their own horror stories, most of which I'd heard before. Doctors were scarce in battle and frequently more dangerous than the wound itself. Some soldiers, having never been to a doctor, were in the habit of caring for themselves. Many carried a "housewife"—a pack of needles and thread and a thimble for clothing repair. However, they used it for other tasks: sewing up shot off fingers, ears, and other superfluous appendages.

Before long, yawning like Rip Van Winkle, we crawled into our blankets on the floor. The snoring was horrible! When Pa sucked in, Uncle Roy blew out like a bull elephant. How could Ma and Aunt Millie stand it? Buck and I counted sheep for hours, and then we counted them again to make sure. It looked like our next night's sleep would be back in Northfield.

Somehow, we finally dozed off and then all of us overslept. Hennessey pouring milk in the kitchen awakened us. There'd been a gulllywasher during the night, but now bars of sunlight streamed through the kitchen windows. He'd already milked, fed the cows, and fired up the cook stove. If those outlaws doubled back for breakfast, they could have wiped us out. I guess I was the only one who considered that.

It all worked out. Doc Paulson continued his rounds after Roy paid him off. Hennessey had cooked a meal and put us up for the night (in a manner of speaking), so Roy used that saved taxpayer money to pay Doc's bill. Everyone was happy.

Jerome A. Kuntz

After consuming a huge breakfast of pancakes, syrup, and black coffee, Pa bravely led the way on another guilt trip. "We should help this poor unfortunate family," he solemnly repeated. I knew what was coming next. Uncle Roy didn't complain; he preferred to let his breakfast settle before he tried arguing with King again.

Jobs were everywhere. We fed the small amount of stock Hennessey owned, spread out a bunch of corn for the wild pigs, and then the split-rail fence desperately needed repairs. Pa even devised a makeshift method to brace the barn. Slapdash as all get out, but better than nothing. We then grabbed sickles and proceeded to cut ferns and ugly nettles that threatened to overtake the front yard. Not wanting to interfere with anyone's personal habits, Roy merely advised Hennessey to plug those openings between the cabin logs; winter was coming. I began to think camping out would be easier than working for board and room.

Still, Pa had been right: posse work was mostly a lark, but that could change almighty fast if we got careless and overtook the James Gang.

Chapter 5

Bright sunlight warmed the world by the time we again shuffled down the Old Indian Road. Steam curled from drying land like smoke from a smoldering grass fire. The trail was soup; our mounts slipped several times, almost went down. For hours, we followed the meandering road through thick woods, trees branches entwined overhead. Mosquitoes as large as Shield nickels tried to kidnap us. I breathed deeply of wet earth, fern, thistle, and rotting leaves.

Buck and I were secretly grateful for Pa's appreciation of comfort. Camping out in last night's downpour would have built needless character. Even on hunting trips, he could nose-out a warm hearth faster than a house cat.

West of Faribault, we overtook a small family in a buckboard, sunk to the axles in the slop of the "road." The distraught father popped the reins and shouted as if his team was deaf, trying to get the tired, mud-splattered horses to pull harder. It was a no-go. They lunged into the traces and then backed off in distress when they couldn't pull out.

"Hold on there now, mister. You'll tear that wagon in half," Roy called, in his usual take-charge fashion. It's no wonder Rice County voters elected him the grand pooh-bah sheriff for three consecutive terms. He began spouting orders like a track-crew foreman. Without dismounting, Buck and I tied ropes from our saddle horns to the wagon pole-ring. Jack and Prince gamely pulled ahead—an easy job for them. Soon, the buckboard stood dripping on solid ground.

The father said his name was Teddy. He didn't give a last name and didn't bother to introduce his wife or family. He kept rubbing his jaw and casting anxious looks down the road.

Oh, were they dressed spiffy: two young boys in back wore new overalls, and the shy mother appeared worried she'd spot her new dress. I noticed an 1873 Winchester carbine on a blanket in the wagon bed—price tag still attached to the trigger guard. All this seemed to peak Roy's curiosity. "Been to a church meeting, folks?" he asked blandly.

Jerome A. Kuntz

"Shucks no, this ain't Sunday," Teddy said. "I sold sandwiches and apples to a couple of swell fellows passing through. Then we went to town for supplies." He was tall, thin, and his head listed off the side as if suffering the effects of uneven gravity. His Adam's apple fairly danced when he spoke.

Roy remained silent for a moment, eyeing them closely, getting that cagy look I knew so well. "You say there were only two of them? By any chance, did they have a family resemblance? Did they look like brothers?" he asked. He was thinking of the James brothers; we didn't learn until weeks later that the three Younger brothers were also in the holdup.

Teddy scratched his stubbly jaw and looked off in the distance. "Well, could be kin. Why? Somebody you know, are they?" he asked.

"Oh sure…sure, probably men from our town. Fine neighbors," Roy lied smoothly. Buck and I kept straight faces and our traps shut.

Roy stifled a massive yawn. Like I said, cagy. "Still, Teddy," Roy continued, "it seems you bought some pricey stuff after only selling a little grub."

Now the man looked scared, blinking his big eyes like a high-noon owl. After all, he couldn't help but see our badges. "Well, shore 'nuff," he said. "Sold a couple of saddle horses and they left their tired nags. Likely, they're wealthy, out-of-state horse buyers. In case you haven't heard, there's a sale in Mankato."

Roy's head spun around to look down the road to the southwest. "Hum-m-m, yeah I guess that would explain it. How long ago might that be, if you don't mind my asking?"

Teddy stood up and snatched the reins as if anxious to leave. I suspect he knew all along that the deal was a little too sweet. He was probably worried his two new horses might be confiscated. "Last night, just before dark," he said, his Adam's apple bobbing. "Thanks again, but we gotta get home for chores."

One of the boys jumped from the buckboard before his frowning father could leave. Now he had to wait. The boy trotted over and handed me a book, shy-like and not making eye contact. He ran back

Northfield

and his brother gave him a hand up. I guessed he wanted to pay us for pulling them from the mud.

"Which way were they headed?" Pa asked.

"Didn't see. Told you it was getting dark. Giddy-up!" He slapped the reins and they trotted off at a good clip, trace chains jangling, mud spinning off the wheels.

"Thanks for the book, kid!" I remembered to shout after them.

"Uncle Roy, aren't you going to stop Adam's Apple?" Buck asked. "He helped the James brothers escape."

"Nah. He's pretty shook up. Most likely if he didn't sell those horses, the brothers would have taken them at gunpoint. I don't grudge him for making a few dollars. I will say you boys sure come up with strange names."

Long ago, our folks gave up chiding us for naming people as to how they looked. In fact, they laughed at some of our inventions. We had descriptive names for all our neighbors in Northfield. They were just easier to remember, using that method.

Pa smiled indulgently, not a care in the world. Likely, with fresh mounts, the outlaws would now get away. Six dollars a day was his main concern.

Banks are of piddling concern to people who seldom use them. In fact, we didn't need much cash money to survive: we churned butter, canned vegetables and dill pickles from Ma's garden, butchered beef and pork, rendered lard, grew bushels of potatoes, and gathered eggs. We turned plums, chokecherries, apples, rhubarb, and gooseberries into jams and jellies; milked cows and separated cream, and wore home-stitched clothing. Neighbors lived about the same.

I looked at the book. *Don Quixote.* We had discussed the novel in school but never got a chance to read it. Our favorite author was Mark Twain. *Tom Sawyer* was his latest. What young boy doesn't dream of skipping school and gliding down the Mississippi—never knowing where you'll stop for the night, or who you'll meet. It could just as easily be a new friend or a rogue you'll have to flee to save your skin.

Buck didn't seem too put out either by the outlaws acquiring fresh mounts. "I thought you wanted to shoot an outlaw," I said.

"Well, they were pretty nice to that family. Maybe they're regular fellows."

"Ah-h...Buck, they probably haven't worked since the war, and any Confederate money they had was useless. Likely they're now using stolen money," I said patiently, wise in my superior age.

"Ah, just some bank's money!" he snapped back. "They got plenty."

I watched him closely. He was tough to read, mostly joking I figured. One thing was for sure, I wouldn't be able to change his mind.

We rode toward Mankato, taking it easy on the tired horses. Other travelers on the road looked as if they too had recently come into a little money. When we questioned two strangers riding to Sioux Falls, they lost their tongue, pretending to have no notion as to whom we were seeking. Roy didn't push it. It was probably the first real money some of these folks had seen in a while. Maybe there was some truth in what we'd heard about the James brothers: they stole from the rich and gave to the poor.

By this time, the outlaws' reputations had notched up in Buck's estimation. That worried me a little. If we found them, he might want to shake hands and ask for a loan instead of shoot. I eased my mind, telling myself we'd seen the last of those killers.

I watched Pa closely, seeing how he'd hold up. Normally, he brought along at least a pint of moonshine on our hunting trips. If he ran out, he'd buy more. Even on the farm, it wasn't unusual for the twins and I to find bottles stashed in the cow barn, haymow, granary, or corncrib. Ma would have thrown them away, but we knew enough to keep our hands off. He seemed a bit shaky, but so far, he hadn't complained. He sat straighter in the saddle too, even helping Roy stay on the right road. There were several splits and T's, so they had to watch carefully. Either somebody had pulled up the road signs or they had never existed.

Without any interesting sights along the road, I had time to read. It appeared Don Quixote was a traveler much like us—except that he was chuckleheaded and we were, more or less, sane. We missed being knight-errants by a mile, but we had done a few good deeds along the

Northfield

way. It was gratifying to recall how we had helped Hennessey and Adam's Apple, so I better understood Quixote's desire to rescue the unfortunate.

Darkness was creeping in by the time we reached the Speckled Loon Inn in Mankato. The trail had turned as cold as catfish the last few miles. No one had seen strangers on the road, or so they claimed.

The Speckled Loon was a two-story, false-fronted building of rough-sawed lumber. The owner certainly wasn't dumping profits back into his business: the paint job was even worse than our house back in Northfield. The hotel looked plumb enough, but the swaybacked rear stable leaned twenty years into the past. Kitchen and dining room were on the first floor. A narrow creaking staircase led to rented rooms on second floor.

A horse sale was taking place at the fair grounds, just like Adam's Apple claimed, so Mankato was crowded with people looking for that buy of a lifetime. We were fortunate to find a hotel, but still, putting four in a room with one double bed was a bit over the line. Buck and I could only hope we'd fall asleep before Pa and Uncle Roy started bellowing again.

Luckily, we were on time for supper. Ten of us crowded around a scarred oak table with long wooden benches on both sides. White crockery cups and a large black coffee pot were on the table. The only light came from a kerosene lantern on the table, causing spooky shadows to jerk across the walls. We were all strangers so everyone conversed in low tones as we waited for food.

I stared at a Western picture on the wall over the table. It was a longhorn stampede in the dark of night with cowboys trying to turn the herd. A thunderstorm raged. Lightning splayed across a black sky. Gray storm clouds, swollen with power, raced for the horizon. Likely, you've seen that picture or another just like it. One hung in the Dampier House Hotel in Northfield. I think they were in half the hotels in Minnesota—probably still are. That was the life for me and it wouldn't be long now. Still, I think it fair to say I was a bit scared to go out West. Trouble was, I'd jawed about it for so long, that now I had to go.

Roy had us hide our badges earlier, thinking it'd be easier to get the drop on outlaws if they happened to stay at the Loon. Now I wondered about the wisdom of that, being he was the only one armed anyway; he carried two pistols concealed under his coat.

"Beans and stew, biscuits too," called the owner and cook in a singsong voice, as he waddled in carrying a huge metal tray. "Plenty of coffee besides. Just help yourselves. If you want anything else, we ain't got it." He was a fat, bald man with a goatee beard just like a billy goat and a moustache that reminded me of bicycle handlebars. A spotted white apron reached below his knees. He lived with his wife behind the kitchen. It was a simple meal but plenty of it, requiring two more trips for steaming bowls from the kitchen.

No one wanted to be the first to dig in, so we waited, staring at the food with our hands in our laps. Finally, Billy Goat sat and reached for the biscuits. The bear was in the pantry. I never saw such a grabby bunch. We soon got the hang of it and heaped our plates. It wasn't as good as Hennessey's cooking, but then again we didn't have that damn Lester winging over the table.

Uncle Roy was all business—jumpy as a cricket, as we used to say. Normally, if grub was in reach, he was too busy to talk. Not that night! He eyeballed everyone and pestered them with questions as to where they were from and what was their business in Mankato. Most didn't want to talk and stared suspiciously at him. Those men were hungry and didn't care to answer fool questions.

Buck and I exchanged a look. I was the one who had claimed to recognize the James brothers, and told Pa he needed me to capture them. Now, I doubted I could identify them even if they were sitting in the same room.

So far, the men appeared to be what they claimed—horse buyers from around Minnesota. Then Roy got to the two men across from us. They were thin, hard-looking, sunburned, and had a family resemblance. Their clothing looked new.

"So are you guys looking for horses too?" Roy asked, smiling.

The youngest fixed Roy with a hard gaze. "You're askin' a lot of questions, stranger," he said, continuing to eat. "Suppose you tell us what you're doing in town."

"Oh, I don't mean any harm," Roy said, laughing. He pointed at Pa. "This is my brother, Harlen, and his two sons, Buck and Custer. We're from Rochester and hope to find good horses for our road building business." I thought it smart of Roy to pick a town east of here instead of up north where we would be more likely to have heard of the robbery. The two strangers didn't bother to introduce themselves or even look at Buck and me. By this time, everyone stopped talking and ate in silence.

Roy forged ahead. "What kind of horses are you two looking for?"

Again, the youngest answered. "Well now, tubby, maybe that's none of your business."

If the reference to Roy's bulk bothered him, he didn't let on. I know I wouldn't dare insinuate he was packing extra lard.

Billy Goat's head glistened in the lamplight and deep furrows appeared over his eyebrows. Uh-oh, he was staring daggers at Uncle Roy. I was afraid it would come to this. "Now, mister," the landlord growled, mustache puffing off to both sides. "I won't have you harassing paying guests of the Speckled Loon. Maybe they don't want anyone knowin' which horses they plan to bid on. Did you ever think of that?"

Roy shook his head and his fat face melted into his sorry-but-I-didn't-mean-no-harm look.

"I didn't think so. Now, let's eat in peace."

"I do apologize," Roy said. "Tell you what, if I see you men at the sale, I'd like to buy you a cold one."

They didn't answer and continued to eat in silence. I figured Roy had lost his marbles. Why would outlaws spend the night at the Speckled Loon when they could be running for the Iowa border? Then again, maybe they figured other posses would think the same and not look for them in a hotel this close to Northfield.

Supper was over and everyone lit up—excepting Buck and me, of course. Too dangerous. Billy Goat cleared away dishes. Pa and Uncle Roy packed their big pipes as if the planet's future depended on a good burn. It wasn't hard to figure what they were up to: they were waiting to see if anyone flew the coop, and, if not, which room the two sourpusses occupied. Soon, a gray fog of noxious fumes obscured the ceiling.

The hours dragged. A few of our fellow diners were shameless windbags, plain and simple. Their horse stories simply wouldn't hold water. There were tales of bad years where horses ate the neighbor's saddles; horses swimming across fabled lakes of infinite vastness; and even agile horses that climbed trees in a flood. Luckily, Billy Goat saved the night by loaning us his stereoscope and a large box of stereo cards. Several were of important buildings in Europe and mountain ranges we'd never even heard of. The best were Paris street scenes where well-dressed people with time on their hands seemed to stand before our eyes and stare back at us.

I knew Pa and Roy wouldn't go upstairs until the two suspects went first, no matter how late the hour. Buck and I could have gone to our room, but, if fur-and-feathers flew, we wanted to be in on the chase, not sleeping like hogs in a hay pile. It looked like a long night. If the men turned out to be the James brothers, there was little hope of taking them back alive, and we'd better be ready.

Chapter 6

I thought those men would never tire of talking horses (more like horse apples). The hours dragged and interest in the stereoscope wore threadbare. I dug *Don Quixote* from inside my shirt and began to read. Every few minutes, Buck would poke me, wanting to know what new trouble the foolhardy knight and his lackey squire had gotten into. The writing wasn't as obscure as Shakespeare's *Julius Caesar,* but it sure wasn't the kind of English allowed in Mrs. Hollins' classroom. The story seemed to follow our own travels. I told Buck how the hapless wanderers stopped at an inn for the night and "took a bad drubbing" in a case of mistaken identity.

Finally, those fibbers stood, stretched, and rubbed sleepy eyes. Billy Goat had set out short candles in star-shaped tin holders so people could navigate the creaky staircase and find their rooms. The two suspects were last to go; Roy was right behind them and we were on his heels. They entered the room directly across from ours.

We pretended not to notice and followed Roy into our room. He set the candle down and waved us into a tight circle, keeping his index finger on his lips. The sheriff had a plan. "Now listen carefully," he whispered, dark eyes rolling back and forth between our three faces. Buck and I were suddenly wide-awake. Pa looked bored and sleepy. "I think those two living across from us are the James brothers. Neither your pa nor I got a look during the holdup. How about it, Custer? Are those the two you saw come out of the bank?"

All eyes were on me. Uh-oh, the chickens were coming home to roost...or maybe to roast. Either way I was in trouble. "I-I can't be sure," I stammered. "They came out so fast and mounted up, but these guys do look about the right size." Boy, did that sound lame. Even Buck was shaking his head in disbelief.

"Custer," Pa whispered, "I know you skipped school that day. If I'd called you on it, your ma would never have let you go. Just tell Roy anything you remember about them."

So he knew all along. "One thing's for certain," I said, "they bought new clothes somewhere along the way. Even their hats are new and not the ones they wore during the holdup—if they are the James brothers. Still, the styles are about the same. The youngest brother wore a flat crown, flat brim, and the older guy had his turned up on the sides. That's about the best I can do."

"Why didn't you arrest them, Uncle Roy?" Buck asked.

"Ssshhh, not so loud." Again, the finger. "Two reasons. First, they might be horse buyers as they claimed," Roy said, looking at each of us in turn. At home, adults seldom collected our two-cents worth, so now it felt cozy to be included in the plan. "Second, if they are the James brothers, they won't be taken alive and we can't have gunplay in a full hotel. No, we'll watch them all night. We'll keep our door cracked open in case they make a run for it. Guard shifts will be two hours. Harlen, you can take the first watch, then Buck and Custer after him. I'll take the morning shift until breakfast. If they leave in the night, wake everyone else up and we'll go after them together. If those men are okay, we'll only lose a little sleep, and I'll question them further in the morning." Roy silently waved us toward our blankets and blew out the candle. Pa took his position next to the slightly open door. Now, this was the excitement Buck and I had waited for.

I didn't think I would ever fall asleep. Of course, Roy jumping around on a noisy corn-shuck mattress and his loud snoring didn't help matters. That room was tiny. I slept on the floor next to Roy's side of the bed. Buck was next to me, my Winchester on the floor between us. I wanted to be able to find it immediately if things got tight.

It seemed I lay there for hours. I could hear men in other rooms talking, laughing, and roughhousing. Pipe smoke and the all-too-familiar sweet odor of moonshine drifted into the room. It had to be tough for Pa; three days without a drink was probably tying him in knots. I'm not saying he was a drunk. Usually, we couldn't be sure if he was drinking or not, but then again, we might have just gotten so used to it. Now he was stiffening his spine and doing what it took to make our six dollars a day. I didn't fool myself into thinking he would give it up permanently.

I began to think about home. Ma and Sadie were probably making plum jelly now. The farm was a great place to grow up, and I knew

I'd miss it out West. In early summer, provided we weren't adding to several rock piles scattered around the farm, or chopping quack grass from potato rows, we searched for bantam chicken nests and new families of kittens. We kept bantams for the joy of watching mama and a dozen balls of fur scurrying around the yard, making a living from wild seeds and scads of grasshoppers. It was Bubbles' job to keep marauding foxes and badgers away from our pets and Ma's laying hens.

We didn't expect Mr. Moses to trouble himself. He was getting on in years and required a full night's sleep, meaning at least 12 hours. During the day, he slept in the shadow of our front yard oak tree. He would shift position as the shade moved. Ma enjoyed watching him through the kitchen window; she liked to joke about telling time by where Mr. Moses dozed.

The kitties were the most fun. A kitten's color usually determined its name—Whitey/Snowball, Blackie/Midnight and so on. A calico cat was orange, white, and gray and always highly prized. When we discovered the tumbling family, friendly arguments began concerning their ownership: "You got the calico cat last time. Peaches is mine!"

"Okay, but only if Marshmallow and Tom belong to me!"

"You guys do what you want as long as I get Melody." And so it went. At day's end, every cat had a name and owner. The world could again rotate on a greased axle.

I drifted off eventually, but it didn't last long. "They're leaving!" Buck yelled. I jumped three feet off my soft bed on the floor. Some people were pounding down the stairway. I looked at the door. It stood wide open and Buck was gone!

"Buck! Buck!" yelled Uncle Roy. "Come back here!"

I frantically scrabbled for my Winchester. It was gone too! That danged Buck must have taken mine by mistake. "Where's Buck's rifle? He took mine," I whined. I was feeling the floor when Roy stomped on my hands. "Ouch! Damn, Uncle Roy, you're stepping on me!"

"Custer, please watch your language," Pa said, sleepily.

"Sorry, boy. Didn't know you were so close."

"Where are my boots?"

"I can't find mine either."

"Ow! Get the hell off me, Uncle Roy!" He had stomped on my leg.

"Custer, I won't have you speaking disrespectfully to Roy," Pa said, a slight edge creeping into his voice. I thought it a helluva time to be teaching manners.

Pistol shots exploded in the quiet of night; then came answering rifle fire. Cripes, ants raced up and down my spine. Buck was alone in a shootout with the James brothers!

"Can't someone light a candle?"

"Candle, hell! You got my boots. What the dickens am I supposed to wear?"

"Hold the damn noise down!" some guy down the hall bellowed.

"Who the devil is shooting?" another asked. The neighbors were getting irate. No need for stealth now; everyone in the hotel seemed awake.

"How's a body 'sposed to get any sleep around here?" someone else asked in a groggy, whiney voice.

"Ouh-la-la, Pa!" I said. "That was a girl's voice."

"Ah...ya, someone must have gone for his wife."

I assumed that was for Buck's benefit, but who knows? Like I said, he treated us like we were both twelve. I had finally located Buck's rifle and was struggling with my string work boots. "Damnit, Roy!" I yelled. Now he was mashing my toes. I'd had enough. It was as if a farm bull was tramping me into the floor. I slid into a corner and continued lacing my boots, not worrying about being fully dressed.

"Will you guys shake a leg! We gotta back that boy!" Roy said as he ran out the door and down the stairway. Imagine, three hundred pounds stomping down those rickety old steps. I thought the building would come down on our heads.

More pistol shots! Then rifle fire. Little Buck was holding his own. Like Sadie, he had spunk to spare.

"Come on, Custer! Stop horsin' around. Buck's alone!" Pa needlessly reminded me and then he was out the door. I was right behind him, not wanting to lose them in the darkness.

Northfield

My head cracked into the floorboards before I realized what happened. Panicky as I was, I didn't point the damn rifle into the hall, but jammed it crosswise in that stupid narrow door. I had flipped over the top and landed on my head.

"Quiet, you inbred bastards!" a grouchy guest squawked. More foul language erupted from other rooms. I guessed mine wasn't the only aching head in the hotel. If Sadie was there, she could have added some priceless cuss words to her bawdy collection.

By now, I was as frazzled as an egg-stealing fox, trapped in a chicken coop. The only safe way to descend that black stairway was on my butt; my head wouldn't stand another knock. I reached the street and chased after a dim figure ahead, assuming it was Pa. The night was black as a coal chute and raining hard. Farther ahead, Uncle Roy bellowed Buck's name.

"I'm over here!" Buck shouted. "Don't shoot!" We all reached him about the same time. He was crouched behind a tree stump, peering down his rifle barrel. We hunkered down beside him. Roy began firing questions. "Where are they, Buck? Did you hit anyone? Are they on foot?" He soon got his answer. We heard the mud-splashing hooves of hard-ridden horses. It wasn't tough to figure what that meant: they'd left saddled horses close by while Jenny, Prince, Jack, and King peaceably dozed in the comfy hotel stable.

Poor Buck. Even in the dim light and rain, his face looked as pale as milk. "Th-there they go. I guess they tied their horses in this vacant lot after checking in at the Speckled Loon."

"Do you think you winged 'em, son?" Pa asked.

"Naw, I didn't want to wound their horses or hit one of those houses." He was calming down pretty fast for a boy caught in his first shootout.

Pouring rain soaked our skimpy longjohns and we quickly turned toward the Speckled Loon. Uncle Roy put his hand on Buck's shoulder. "You did fine, Buck," he said, "but sometimes, lawmen have to shoot horses from under fleeing suspects. It's a dirty business but can't be helped." We walked a bit in silence before he added, "Remember this too men, from now on shoot to kill. As you saw in

Northfield, Confederate vets don't respond to wounds. Most been shot and stabbed any number of times."

Billy Goat waited with a lantern under a rickety roof reaching over the hotel's front steps. Buck and I chuckled over his long white nightgown and floppy nightcap. He looked like Scrooge from Dickens' *The Christmas Carol*. Other men crowded behind him in various stages of undress. There was no sign of the girl whose voice we had heard in the night. It was just as well: most of us were dressed rather bold.

The men acted afraid and I couldn't blame them; they had no notion we were lawmen. "I figured you people were up to no good," Billy Goat said, accusingly.

"Consarned it, man," Roy said, "I'm the Rice County sheriff and these are my deputies. Those men you were so blasted careful to protect are the James brothers. They robbed the Northfield bank and killed a bank clerk three days ago."

"What-t-t-t? Jesse and Frank James were here at my hotel?" he asked, shaking his head in wonder.

"The very same. Now we need to pack our gear and leave immediately. I figure they're headed for the train station in Sioux Falls, Dakota Territory."

"Pa's already saddling the horses," Buck said. That Pa. We were seeing him in a new light. Actually, he was the only one who had found his pants. Things were heating up; finally it looked like we were getting serious about this manhunt.

"Well, you can't leave before breakfast," Billy Goat said. "Anyway, your room charge includes two meals." I couldn't help thinking he was gossipy and didn't want to miss the robbery story.

"Breakfast?" Roy said, a smile stretching across his fat face. Uh-oh. Remember, I told you Roy was done at the mention of food. He was like a pup coonhound when a rabbit crosses his trail. With all the excitement, he must have burned through last night's supper. Imagine keeping that man in groceries.

"Hell yes, I'll have coffee, pancakes, sausages, and eggs, all ready in no time. If you want anything else, we ain't got it."

I crossed my fingers while idly feeling the knot on my head. It did seem foolhardy chasing killers down a strange road in the dark and rain. Worse yet, riding out with an empty belly. Roy looked us over and nodded his head. The cook headed for the stove, and we all tramped back into the Speckled Loon.

It didn't take long to put on dry clothes and bring down our meager belongings. The rain stopped and we carried our rigs outside, where Pa had the horses tied. Minutes later, other tenants, now fully dressed, joined us at the dining table. They were probably too excited to sleep and hoped to hear more of the robbery. The men who swigged 'shine would probably sleep it off. The gray light of dawn was fast approaching as we waited for Billy Goat to bring food.

"Buck," I said, "what's wrong with your cap?" We both wore the same kind—the top snapping down on the bill. He pulled it off and poked his finger through a bullet hole. A sick look spread over his face like a slow sunrise.

"Whew! That was close," he said. "Wait till Sadie sees this."

"No, son," Pa said. "I'll buy you a new cap on the way home. Your Ma will skin me alive if she sees that."

The landlord brought in breakfast and it was a repeat of last night's supper—you had to be quick. Those men gobbled food like Vikings. The tenants had a hundred questions about both the robbery and the sequence of events in the night. Buck was the center of attention and enjoyed every minute of it. As in the past, the urgency of the chase disappeared like a hobo with a job offer. We ate our fill and sat back to relax. Buck passed his hat around so everyone could poke a finger in the bullet hole, soberly shake their head, and tell him how lucky he was. Pa and Uncle Roy carefully packed and layered their big pipes again. I knew it'd be a spell before we ambled down the road.

Last night these men didn't know Buck and I were alive. Never mind that I would be eighteen in just nine months, I was still a kid in their eyes. Now that we'd pinned badges on, they realized we were sworn deputies and couldn't stop staring at us, especially Buck. Surprising how a shootout with the notorious James brothers enhanced our reputation. Of course, we pretended not to notice.

Jerome A. Kuntz

The sun was topping the horizon when we gathered in the front yard of the hotel, and still no one seemed in a hurry. I was getting used to the pace and didn't care when we left. Besides, it appeared the James gang wasn't moving any faster than we were.

Several tenants and the landlord came to see us off, shaking our hands and slapping our backs. They seemed to think we were on a grand adventure—not something they'd be interested in, thank-you very much, but a rollicking good time just the same.

Before mounting up, a reporter and photographer from the *Minneapolis Tribune* arrived, wanting our story and picture. Coincidentally, they were in town to cover the annual Mankato Horse Auction. Pa wasn't interested; he didn't want Ma and Sadie to read about the shootout. The rest of us, foolishly as it turned out, were only too happy to oblige the snoopy newsmen.

Uncle Roy had his king-sized star prominently displayed while he told the story again. The reporter acted terribly impressed by our courageous actions, and begged for more details. Buck and I piped up now and then when we could make it more exciting. Already, we revised the exact sequence of events: hours of boredom magically evaporated and continuous action seemed a normal part of our day. Sadie wasn't the only member of the family who could tell a ripping tale. We had to repeat various incidents because the excited reporter couldn't keep pace scribbling in his notebook. All of us seemed incapable of relating what happened the same way twice, much less three times. But then, what fun would that be?

Finally, the Compton posse story wore thin and we mounted up. The horses bobbed their heads and stamped their feet, anxious to see some country. That's when the photographer took our picture. If you ever see a copy of that newspaper, the Speckled Loon's in the background. It would be two days before we'd see the interview in the *Tribune*. By then, it was too late to wring that smart aleck reporter's neck.

Chapter 7

Our horses tired long before reaching Sioux Falls, slowing our pace. There was little doubt the James brothers aimed for the train depot. That's where the showdown would come. If they caught the train before we could head them off, they were home free. Uncle Roy led the way on his powerful stallion, holding a fast walk as we struggled to keep up. All his chains, padlocks, leg irons, and handcuffs rattled like a tinker's wagon. It took all of four days and we slept our first nights in the open since leaving Northfield.

By mid-afternoon of the first day, it had turned bright and sunny. Steam rose off the wet road, and it was like passing through a thin cloud. I continued to follow the exploits of the brave but loony knight of La Mancha, and his potbellied squire. I didn't *know* Sancho was overweight, but don't you think he just had to be a short, potbellied man riding a donkey named Dapple? I thought so.

I was getting a little tired of Buck's questions each time I started reading, but after all, he too had a hand in pulling Adam's Apple from the mud hole.

"What's Donald doing now?" Buck started his grilling.

"Donald?" I murmured absently, not sure who he meant.

"You *know*, the knight from the novel. Wuddayacallhim?"

I looked at him without expression. "*Don* Quixote and his squire, Sancho Panza."

"Yeah, him too. What kind of trouble they got into now?"

"He's attacking giants with his lance while at full gallop on Rozinante."

"*Giants!* Is Sancho holding his own?"

"No, he sensibly decided to sit this one out."

"Hum-m, that's strange. Then again, Don can probably handle them easy. I've yet to hear of a giant that wasn't a pushover. Still, Sancho's lacking in get-up-and-go if you ask me."

"I wasn't asking," I said, turning back to the book. Silence for a spell while I continued to read. I knew Buck couldn't curb his curiosity for long.

"I never heard of giants in Spain. What kind they got? How many?" he began again.

How could I resist? "Oh, they're made of iron, thirty feet tall, and they have long spinning arms. There's about a dozen of those rascals."

"Like our windmill back home?"

The boy was clever for sure. "They are windmills!" I said. He stared at me with his mouth open.

"Catching flies again, are you?" I asked.

"You mean he's—"

"Didn't I tell you he's sun-stroked?" Buck was wagging his head in disbelief while I related the rest of the episode. It was so funny; you should have seen this. Before I finished, Pa and Roy had crowded their horses near ours so they could hear the story too. This happened several times on our travel to Sioux Falls. I have to say, we had a lot of fun with that novel. Pa had often reminded us that good deeds are repaid in doubles.

We found a clearing surrounded by oak trees and safely off the road where we could spend the night. After camping so many nights while hunting, we all knew our jobs. Roy pulled out a small bag of beans and another of rice and we soon had them bubbling over a small campfire.

Supper over, I asked Roy about something that most likely was bothering all of us. "If it's only the two James brothers up ahead, where's the rest of the gang? There were eight. Two kicked the bucket. Six ran out of town. Where are the other four?"

He slowly drew on his pipe before answering. "They could be anywhere. Might still be in Minnesota, running in circles trying to avoid the posses. Don't forget, we're pretty sure the other four are wounded. That's bound to slow them down…if they can move at all."

"All we can do is keep an eye on the newspapers," Pa said. "It's the biggest news in the state, and you can bet reporters are spreading out hoping to get the story—better yet, photographs of dead outlaws, like they did in Northfield."

"What newspapers? I haven't seen one since leaving home," I said.

"Don't worry, the *Minneapolis Tribune* is sold in both Dakota Territory and Iowa," Pa said. "We'll keep an eye out for it in the general stores."

"I only hope they haven't made plans to meet where we're headed," Roy said. "They'd be too strong to capture, and I don't know where we'd turn for help. Most of these little towns only have one lawman."

"Pinkerton detectives?" Buck suggested. "We could send a telegraph. You know they'd love to get their hands on the James brothers. They've been trying for years."

"Well, maybe," Roy said, "but in the past it's never worked for the Pinkertons to be notified when the gang was spotted. In Missouri anyway, the gang always scattered like pigeons. They got too many friends there—locations where they can hide until it's safe to pull another holdup. Even hiding, they move from place to place. Besides, gang members change quickly, so the law is never sure exactly who they're looking for. Only the two James brothers remain constant."

"Are you saying we haven't a chance of capturing them if they make it to Missouri?" I asked.

Roy considered that for a moment. "If they reach Missouri we might as well go home," he said. "There's no way we can smoke them out on their own ground. Another thing, lawmen in Missouri won't take kindly to us pursuing crooks in their state. Reconstruction has about ended, and you can bet the South is glad to get rid of Yanks. Missouri stayed in the Union, but a good percentage of its soldiers fought for the CSA."

"The Pinkertons are looking for them there," I said defensively.

"True, true, but they work for Federal. Got more horsepower than we do."

As it turned out, two weeks passed before the four other members of the gang were either shot or captured in Minnesota, just twenty miles south of Northfield. Every paper in the country carried the story. Only the James brothers got away and we were still on their trail at that time.

Like back home, wolves and coyotes howled just at falling darkness as if to notify each other of their location. That was our signal to turn in.

The second day we reached Jubal's Merchandise, a small general store just before crossing into Dakota Territory. Roy had brought plenty of Rice County funds to cover expenses. If he spent his own money, the county would reimburse him. Jubal placed items on the counter as Roy and Pa ordered. Several boxes of 44-caliber rimfire ammunition for our Winchesters were part of the purchase.

"Yes sir, gonna have to stock more ammo," the storekeeper said innocently. "You're the second bunch that's ordered today."

"Is that so?" Roy said, showing little interest while he idly looked over a counter containing shoelaces and gloves. "About what time was that?"

"Huh? Say, are you lawmen? I heard about the Northfield Raid. A couple of other posses stopped here in the last couple of days."

Roy just looked at him. "What time did you sell that ammo?"

Jubal looked carefully at Roy's king-sized badge. He pulled off his cap and scratched the top of his head as if to stimulate his memory. "Well, before dinner...'bout ten o'clock. You think they were part of the—?"

"What'd they look like?" Roy snapped. "Did they have a family resemblance?"

"Yea-a-ah, sort of."

Roy described them just as they looked at the supper table in the Speckled Loon two nights ago.

The storekeeper was sure they were the same men. The James brothers were just six hours ahead. Now we were certain their destination was the Sioux Falls train depot. We needed to get there before the train pulled in—any train for that matter.

We soon mounted up; there was no time to lose. I remember another two days of hard riding, and a drizzling rain dogging us the entire final day of travel. Our last camp was as miserable as any I can remember. More than once, we'd taken a wrong turn and had to backtrack.

Northfield

The poor horses couldn't have gone much farther. Frequently, they'd snatch a mouthful of grass as we walked along. Kind of annoying as it broke their stride, but they were hungry from fast traveling. It was long after dark when we reached the depot—wet, cold, and miserable.

Instead of putting our mounts up at the local livery, we tied them in thick woods not far from the depot. A bad decision as it turned out. The livery was in town a mile away, and it would have meant walking back to the depot. We were frantic to take control before the James brothers arrived. Grabbing our blankets and ammo, we raced to get in position.

You've seen plenty of those old wood depots—wide soffits, shake roofs, painted either all white or green with red trim like the one in Sioux Falls, and corralled by heavy, scarred-plank platforms. It had two rooms—the ticket agent and passenger waiting room, and the freight office, separated by a solid oak door. The freight office held the stove. Oh, did that pot-bellied stove feel good! We were soaked to the skin and as cold as a winter pump handle.

Only one old man was on duty. Tony Casson, the ticket agent, had a deeply grained face, wooly white hair, steel-framed glasses sliding down his nose, and he wore a Northern Pacific railroad cap. If nerves were part of his system, they were on vacation. His job was to operate the telegraph key and sell tickets. The ticket booth had a chicken-wire-mesh window over the business counter.

The next train was due at nine o'clock. No strangers had tried to buy tickets. The James brothers should have gotten here first. We guessed they were afraid we'd trap them in the station, so they decided to jump the train in the dark like a couple of hoboes. Plenty of men were doing that in those days. We doused all but one lantern immediately, so likely they knew we controlled the station. One nail-biting hour to kill.

Buck and I would hold the freight office while Pa and Roy guarded the ticket area. All four of us carried rifles, and Roy had his four Colt pistols. We stacked ammunition near the windows, and then paced the room like zoo animals, taking occasional peeps into the night. The polished wood floor creaked ominously under our heavy muddy boots.

Tony sat on the floor next to our one dim lantern and read the paper as if a possibly deadly shooting siege was a normal workday. We couldn't send him home; the James brothers would likely blast anyone stepping onto the platform.

This depot was farther out of town than normal. Abandoned stock corrals separated it from houses on the west; the thick woods where we had tied the horses stretched to the east. Even though the building was a heavy wood structure able to soak up lead, the windows would be dangerous. Suddenly, Mrs. Hollins' classroom in Northfield seemed as cozy as a kitten's nest.

Nine o'clock and no train. Nail-biting tension. With one dim lantern and no moonlight, we paced in darkness. No need to watch the tracks; we'd hear the train a mile out. "Sometimes it runs a little late when the weather's bad," Tony remarked dryly. What was that supposed to mean? Why would rain slow the train? If the damn tracks washed out, it wouldn't be coming at all. Stay calm, I ordered myself for the tenth time in the last hour. I found it peculiar that my teeth chattered even after drying out.

Nine-fifteen. A feeble glow reflected on the wet windows. A pistol shot cracked in the direction of the woods, followed by the sound of pounding hooves. The outlaws must have found our horses and were scaring them off. Minutes later came the faint "ka-chunk-ka, ka-chunk-ka" of the approaching train. O-o-oh, Katy bar the door!

"Get ready, boys," Pa said calmly. "They'll try to drive us from the station and force their way on the—"

A bullet crashed through the window. "Stay back!" I screamed needlessly. Glass sprayed across the freight office floor. Damned thing missed me by inches. Flying glass had cut both our faces. I flattened against the wall, sleeving blood off my face. Another came from the opposite side, smashing part of the window frame into the room. They had us surrounded!

"Only shoot once, men; they'll be waiting for your muzzle flash!" Roy bellowed.

What the hell were we supposed to shoot at? Buck was already blasting into the darkness, spent shells jangled and bounced across the floor as he jacked in new rounds. That little devil had been waiting for

Northfield

this. After the narrow miss, I was too frightened to peek out. This was my first gunfight. Buck acted like an old hand.

Not wanting to be a scared-sister, I fired at a flash in the dark, and instantly a bullet came from the opposite side of the depot. "They're working as a team!" I warned. "If you shoot at one flash, the brother takes his shot!" With everyone firing, I doubt they heard me. I could see muzzle flashes move after every shot, both in the stockyards and trees. Those outlaws knew how to night-fight. Several bullets slammed harmlessly into the outside of the building. Dark as it was, they probably couldn't make out the windows.

While hunting, Pa always cautioned us to use cartridges sparingly. Amazing how fast both of us could fire now with taxpayer ammunition. The metallic slams of the Winchesters were deafening. You think a rifle shot is loud in the woods? Try four people shooting at once inside a building!

Remember how I had told Pa that Buck was the best shot? It was the truth. At home, he barely aimed before hitting targets. A gun in his hands seemed as natural as a hammer for most men, including me. He had to be scaring hell out of those outlaws.

I could clearly hear the train now. The engineer must have been hanging on the whistle cable.

"Tony, can you signal the train not to stop?" Roy called.

I heard a muffled answer. Tony must have been on the floor in his ticket booth. "Be my guest, Sheriff," he said. "Normally we set a lantern on the outside signal order board and show red or green so the engineer knows whether or not to stop. Hopefully, if you swing this green lantern out the window, they'll keep on going."

Just than a slug spanged off the stove. The entire stovepipe clattered onto the floor, smoking-hot soot spewed out where the sections separated. Choking black smoke now curled to the ceiling.

"Auk-k-k, I can't breathe," Buck wailed.

"Breathe, hell, I gave up that luxury long ago," I said, trying to act brave despite my voice shaking as if I was sitting on a block of ice.

"I'm getting out! Come on!" Buck yelled. He backed toward the ticket office, so he could keep shooting out the window. I followed his lead and we slammed the door behind us.

Jerome A. Kuntz

Buck and I then fired out opposite ticket-office windows while Pa and Roy prepared the lantern.

Pa smashed out what was left of the window over the platform. Roy crawled over with the burning lantern. The train was getting close. We flattened onto the floor. Roy crouched below the platform window and waved the green light on the end of his rifle barrel. Bullets whined through the window like angry bees before thunking into the opposite wall.

We waited, not daring to breathe. The train got louder, angry sounding: KA-CHUNK-KA, KA-CHUNK-KA, KA-CHUNK-KA! Still louder and the floor vibrated. Buck and I yelled at the same time. "It's not stopping!" In fact, it was picking up speed. The engine roared by, tophat-stack hammering billows of black smoke into the night sky. Flames leaped from cracks in the firebox. Steam snarled against the depot. The building shook like a colicky horse. Minutes later, the train faded into the distance.

We waited. Incredible silence. Was it finally over? No more shots came.

The depot was a disaster! Spent shell casings and shards of glass littered the floor, black coal smoke snaked from freight office windows, and the inside plaster walls were pockmarked with outlaw lead. (For years after, people visited that old cattle-shipping depot before they tore it down and built another closer to town. They gaped at damage done by the James brothers' bullets. The Comptom family posse, forted up and under siege, was only a footnote to the story. People wanted to hear about the famous outlaws.)

Even in the stillness, we continued to shout. Our hearing wouldn't return to normal until noon the next day.

"I need to go," I said. Everyone looked at Mr. Casson. Only a fool would waltz around in the dark looking for the outhouse.

"I keep a thunder jug here in the cabinet," Tony said, getting up stiffly to retrieve it. "Use it myself when the weather's bad." He pulled it out and we all took our turn in the corner.

We'd been lucky. Other than several cuts on our faces and knuckles from flying glass, we were all unhurt.

It was a long cold night, crunching around in total darkness and keeping an eye out for another attack. Fortunately, we had blankets and were able to take turns sleeping.

The long-awaited light of dawn came and we ventured out to survey the damage. Just as expected, our horses were nowhere in sight. We got our first look at Sioux Falls. It was galling to walk downtown knowing the outlaws ran our horses off, but we did find a swell breakfast at Mother Mabel's restaurant. People kept walking over to ask who was shooting at us. Where were they last night? Some relief would have been welcome after the train passed through. Curiosity must only bloom in daylight. I'm afraid we weren't very sociable. We were tired, hungry, and mostly interested in coffee and pancakes.

Later, Pa and Buck rented horses at Dakota Livery and picked up the trail of our mounts. In the meantime, Uncle Roy and I tramped around town checking to see if Frank and Jesse had found another Teddy (Adam's Apple) and bought fresh mounts.

They must have been desperate; a local man had a couple of nags stolen in the night. He didn't seem too put out, claiming the two left behind were better than what they swiped. Lucky our horses were tired out, or they would have taken them.

Finally, we could relax—the outlaws had left town and we might get through the day without ducking lead. I found that wears thin after the first slug.

It's a mystery Pa and Uncle Roy didn't go on alone. They could have sent us back to Northfield, but I guess they figured we had to grow up (or die trying) soon. Don't judge Pa too severely. Looking back, I find that time strange, but life was short and most parents expected kids to mature quick and get on with their lives.

You're probably wondering why Buck and I didn't fabricate our own excuse to leave. I doubt we even considered it. Don't assume we were brave. Our parents had always taught us to finish something once started, and I suspect that carried into the manhunt. I suppose it was the right thing to do—probably the last time I overly worried about doing the "right thing."

Jerome A. Kuntz

I'll warn you early on; we should have turned tail for our carefree home in Minnesota.

Now we had to take the outlaws' trail before they found faster mounts. Worse yet, they could double back to the depot.

Chapter 8

Sioux Falls was a busy settlement on the edge of the frontier—the streets crowded with people driving buckboards and Conestoga covered wagons. Many were newly arrived pioneers preparing to claim homesteads on the vast grasslands of western Dakota Territory. Tinny piano music rolled from busy saloons. Horses stood hipshot beside hitch rails, hides rippling and feet stomping as they shook off blowflies. After listening to clopping hooves, rattling trace chains, and rough-looking men loudly conducting business, we felt we were right in the wild west.

Buck and I, incurable people-watchers, guessed the professions of both locals and transients that strolled plank walkways. The dapper fellows dressed in dark suits likely worked in banks. Trappers and buffalo hunters sported greasy buckskins. Gold prospectors, wearing suspendered baggy pants, led sleepy donkeys down the street. Cowboys were obvious—plank-popping, high-heeled boots, spurs jangling like pocket change, and weather-beaten, sweat-stained felt hats; almost all carried Sam Colt's equalizer.

Only a few women were on the streets, their long flower-print dresses looking uncomfortable in the heat. They sniffed with disdain at the crude streets, and you couldn't blame them. Garbage stacked near squat log houses and stores, along with horse manure littering the streets combined for an unpleasant odor.

Talk about flat country! I kept looking west, hoping to see the Rockies. Where were the trees? They must have squandered them to build the town. And all that sky, stretching from fingertip to fingertip! Everything was so different from eastern Minnesota; it seemed I'd entered a foreign country.

It was noon before Pa and Buck rode into town, looking hot, frazzled, and leading our four horses. Time for another feast at Mother Mabel's.

After apple pie and coffee, Uncle Roy became all business. He acted like the president of Northern Pacific about to propose a new rail spur.

Pa appeared as unconcerned as ever. I wondered if he'd fall asleep and slide under the table. He carelessly stirred his coffee, the teaspoon rattling ominously as he placed it on the saucer. Several days without alcohol were taking their toll. Did I tell you he caught a spent Minnie ball in the hip during the war? Army surgeons removed it, but he could still feel the wound at times. According to Roy, that's when he began drinking.

You know how easy we can recall some meaningful experience far in the past. It's how I best remember Pa on the manhunt—sitting in that restaurant after a hair-raising night and frustrating morning, gritting his teeth and...well, just bearing up and not complaining. I was mighty proud of him that day.

"Listen up men," Roy commanded. "Those killers will keep stealing horses if they have to." By now, I was used to his speeches, and didn't plan to take this one seriously. I figured the outlaws would probably be just ahead of us all the way to Missouri. Then we would limp home.

"We can't do that and our horses need rest," he continued. "My guess is, they're headed for Council Bluffs where they'll catch a Missouri River steamboat down to St. Louis—"

"Unless we can get ahead of them," Pa interrupted.

Roy scratched his bristly jaw. "Ya well...hopefully," he said, "but I doubt we can do that. We best leave our mounts at the Sioux Falls Stables and Grain and take a stagecoach south. We won't have to worry about feeding four horses, and meals will be included with the tickets. We need to stop them from getting on a fancy passenger steamboat! Then they'll have to bum a ride on a small freight-hauler. That way, they'll be easier to overtake."

"We have enough money for fares?" I asked doubtfully. I knew Buck's pockets were as empty as a haunted house, same as mine.

"I've brought plenty to cover us, so don't worry. Besides, Barkley at the bank won't mind paying our expenses later if we catch the killers of his bank clerk."

By six that evening, we rolled south in a red-and-yellow Wells Fargo Concord stage. A six-horse hitch pulled at break-neck speed. Minnesota had mudwagons, not near as fancy as that circus coach.

Other than our small blanket rolls, anything we couldn't carry in our pockets remained with the saddles and horses at the livery in Sioux Falls. I wondered if we'd live to see them again.

The trip started well and we were even able to sightsee. Besides the four of us, a pretty, young lady and a jovial machinery salesman for the Minneapolis Farm Implement Company also occupied the coach. Raife Windom loved to jaw; and with his stylish bowler hat cocked at a rakish angle, he explained a lot more than was healthy about harrows, rakes, plows, and corn-planters. I figured that if I talked, I wouldn't have to listen to him, so I asked the girl her name.

"Jas...Jasmine Bodecker. I'm from St. Cloud and going to Cheyenne for a teaching position."

A schoolmarm! Gosh, she wasn't schoolteacher-ish at all, not like Mrs. Hollins. She couldn't have been more than a year or two older than I was. Dark-brown curls peeped from under her brown hat, which matched her jacket perfectly. A golden tan set off a beautiful mouth of even white teeth. "Your folks must have liked flowers," I said, cleverly. She laughed like music.

"Mom did. She always said the one time she got her way was when it came to naming me."

I thought her as brave as Joan of Arc to be traveling alone.

"Which grades do you teach?" This was working; Raife wound down like a tired grandfather clock.

"One through sixth. I also teach dancing, but there isn't much call for that with young children." She paused a moment, looking at the four of us and our guns with understandable wonder. "Are you men hunting someone? I see you're wearing lawmen badges."

I could almost feel my chest puffing out. From the corner of my eye, I saw Roy give a slight shake of his head. I ignored it. "Yes, the James brothers—Frank and Jesse. They robbed the bank in our hometown of Northfield. We got into a shootout with them last night in the depot. If they'd boarded the train, they'd be half-way to Missouri by now."

"That was you shooting last night? Oh, I'm so glad none of you was hurt. People were in the street in front of my hotel, talking excitedly and wondering what was going on. Did they get away?"

Jerome A. Kuntz

I felt a little sheepish over that question, but we weren't exactly trying to capture them, just keep them off the train. "Ya, sneaked off in the dark, but we'll get them. Now they're running scared. We almost cornered them in the Speckled Loon Inn in Mankato a few nights ago, but the cowards slinked away in the rain and darkness."

Oh, me-o-mio. Mrs. Hollins repeated often, The fall cometh after pride. When girls are that pretty, lies are cheaper by the dozen. I suppose you considered me a better person. So sorry, but I'd soon be dining on chicken-fried crow.

As darkness closed in, the romance of coach travel evaporated. There were only two seats. Buck and I sat on either side of Uncle Roy, crushed against the outside walls. Pa, Jas, and Raife occupied the opposite bench seat. Raife was a bit portly, so Pa wasn't having the easiest time of it either. Jas was opposite me, so I had to be careful not to bang her knees. On top of that, we clutched our rifles the whole way. We'd learned to be ready for anything when pursuing the James brothers. Roy was lucky; he had dumped his two holstered pistols on the floor by his feet.

Imagine, six people squeezed in that tiny wood box, swaying and bouncing over rocks, listening to trace chains rattling, numerous hooves pounding packed earth, and so dark you can hardly see your fellow passengers. Then you'll have some idea of the boundless joy of stagecoach travel.

Some time in the night, the lack of motion woke us all. We'd stopped to change horses in a place called Canton before pushing on for Sioux City. A lantern hung outside the station house. Bleary-eyed, we all stumbled around the wagon yard for a few minutes, working out kinks. Jas went to "pick flowers" and the driver advised us to "hunt rabbits." With three hours to the next stop, we prudently lined up at the men's outhouse. The station house was a low, log building with a sod roof in which sprouted a joyful display of weeds and flowers. Inside, treats lay on a long wooden table in the dining room, and the stationmaster's wife fussily waited on us, especially Jas. Coffee cake and cookies along with strong black coffee persuaded us to live another day.

Northfield

The whiskery stationmaster stomped up the front steps after finishing the team swap. "Any strangers come through in the last couple of days?" Roy asked him.

"Strangers are our bread and butter, Sheriff," he said tiredly, without looking at us. Dealing with people daily, he'd probably heard it all. I didn't expect much help from him.

"I mean strangers on horseback—not riding the stage," Roy said patiently.

Stubbles finally eyed us closely, especially our badges. "Aren't you that posse chasing the James Gang?" he asked.

We all looked at him with mild surprise. How could he know us so far from Northfield? "Why do you ask that?" Roy said.

"Shoot, man, it's all in the papers." He reached behind and pulled a *Minneapolis Tribune* off the top of an unlit stove. There we were, our photograph on the front page. Pa and Uncle Roy looked professional, but Buck and I grinned like simpletons. COMPTON POSSE TACKLES THE JAMES BROTHERS, blared the headline in bold black letters.

Roy read the story aloud:

"The Compton posse, lead by Rice County sheriff, Roy Compton, his brother and two school-age nephews were thwarted in their clumsy attempt to capture Frank and Jesse James at the Speckled Loon Inn in Mankato, Tuesday night. Apparently, while the ever-alert posse soundly slept in an adjoining room after consuming a sumptuous repast skillfully prepared by the inn's chef, the killers casually strolled from the premises and mounted saddled horses tied in a nearby empty lot. They pounded away into darkness, leaving the hapless posse posing in the street in blazing-red longhandles."

Roy seemed to choke and stopped reading. I looked around. Raife and Jas stared open-mouthed at Uncle Roy. "There wasn't time to find our pants!" I protested. "Putting on boots in the dark was bad enough!"

Roy doggedly read on:

"Gunfire echoed down sleepy streets. One posse member, a 15-year-old sworn deputy sheriff no less, scattered a few wild shots and received in payment for his futile efforts a frightening bullethole in his cap. I ask you, is this the quality of taxpayer-funded law enforcement we must settle for in the glorious state of Minnesota? Personally, I see little to impede the James brothers' leisurely return to the an-an-anar-chis-tic, criminal infested state of Missouri."

Roy slapped the paper shut on the counter. "That does it!" he snapped. "From now on, no more pictures or interviews regardless of circumstances."

Pa seemed unperturbed, but Roy was steaming. Of course, it was all a matter of reputation in Northfield: Roy's re-election depended on his success as county sheriff. Pa attached little importance to neighbors' opinion.

Fame really was a double-edged sword: we'd spoon-fed make-believe bravery to that wily reporter. He appeared awed, but only mocked us to scoop a story. That's why, even though nationwide newspapers expended gallons of ink over the capture of the remaining James Gang in Minnesota two weeks after the robbery, few ever heard of the Compton posse chase of Frank and Jesse back to Missouri. We knew better than to go against Roy's orders.

Even Buck was furious, just not over something you'd expect. "That chair-polisher made us look foolish...and what was this sump-sump—"

"Sumptuous repast, son," Pa said, helpfully.

"Ya, that too. Hell, he could only cook half as well as Hennessey. My guess is, that reporter bummed a free meal off Billy Goat and figured he owed him something."

"Please watch your language, Buck," Pa cautioned. "There's a lady present."

Buck apologized, but I failed to see the necessity; that reporter smeared us, and I had a dozen choice names for him. It wasn't to be—Pa watched us closely.

We were in a foul mood as we grumped back aboard the coach. Talk about embarrassed! That line about "posing in longhandles" galled me the most.

Then something happened: Jas reached out and patted my arm.

"Don't take it serious, Custer," she said, smiling. "Everyone knows newspapers are written for entertainment so they can stay in business. No one I know believes half of what's published."

It was like turning off a lamp; my anger, actually all of our anger vanished and we spent several miles joking about it. Raife and Jas laughed ecstatically, wiping their eyes as we filled in more silly details.

It seemed a night for funny stories. Raife, a born salesman/storyteller, told of when he was living in Long Prairie and planned to marry. A hitch developed. A village of friendly Sioux kidnapped the preacher, who was traveling from a nearby town. The entire wedding party and guests armed themselves; and then, brave but drunk, swarmed into their saddles and flew to his rescue. When they found the frightened fellow, the Chief (Raife called him Chief Blowhard and it was a couple beats before I realized he was joking) wouldn't release him unless he performed the wedding ceremony in the village, followed by a great venison-and-turkey feast. There was one catch: the Chief claimed that if he couldn't "share a robe with the bride" the first night, he would scalp the gospeler the next day.

"I was willing to let it happen to save the poor man's hair," Raife said graciously, "but Marcie would have none of it and she stomped back to town with her friends. Then the Chief claimed he was only joking and just wanted to fish out the kind of wife I'd picked. Big laughs all around, backslapping and shoulder punching, you can imagine the scene. You should have heard those Indians carry on. We had the feast anyway, and Chief Blowhard generously pointed out a few choice maidens I might pick to replace my intended bride. Oh yes, tough call but I respectfully declined. You know, I never did marry Marcie. Right or wrong, she wasn't about to save the man's hair and maybe his life. Listen, whites claim Indians don't have much sense of humor. They should have been with us that day."

That was one of the funniest nights on the manhunt and I still laugh about it today. Jas begged us to stop; her sides were hurting her badly from all the laughing.

Maybe it's not as common an emotion as I think, but have you ever been *afraid* to know a prospective spouse better because you had so little hope of success? Silly maybe, but best described as fear of losing something you never had, and then feeling hopeless defeat. I felt that way about Jas, beginning with that hysterical night in the coach; later I thought the risk worthwhile and threw myself into the pit.

Oh yes, dear Jasmine. Little did I dream then what she would come to mean to the Compton family.

Chapter 9

When we finally rattled into Sioux City, I was convinced there wasn't a worse way to travel than a Wells Fargo stage (Smells Hardgo stage, Buck called it). Some of the teams we picked up were little more than wild mustangs, recently captured on the open prairie. The poor drivers would scream, curse, and condemn the panicked lot while hauling back on the reins, but they bolted down the track as if still free on open range. All we could do was hang on and hope we didn't flip on some curve.

The food got shabbier the farther south we rode. They certainly could have served something better than cold beans and biscuits. That along with warm drinking water, dust, and flies made for long days. Yeah, I know: whine and gripe. Still, if the stage-stop managers cared about passengers, they could have made small improvements with little added expense.

None of us was too disappointed to learn we'd have a layover in Sioux City; our coach was returning north and the transfer coming from Ft. Dodge wouldn't arrive for two days.

Jas was lucky. She had relatives who met her at the station. I missed her immediately, and my over-imaginative mind strayed to Cheyenne. I visualized it as a prairie paradise, overflowing with strolling, steely-nerved heroes who were taming the West.

We checked into the Iowa Hotel and then wandered around town asking about strangers who might resemble the James brothers. Like other places, locals generously treated us to a confusing hodgepodge of boasts, half-truths, exaggerations, rumors, and claptrap. People will invent anything to appear savvy. Curiously, the tallest tale came from a man folks looked up to. He gathered a crowd in the street and claimed to have met three strangers on the road late at night looking for the Missouri River. The two men, dressed in fine suits, drove a Stearling buggy pulled by matching black thoroughbreds. A lady rode between them, "sporting finery seldom seen beyond Omaha." He said they had to be the outlaws. Who else could afford such a rig? Humbug! Anyone could see he was an imposter: his eyes flickered

Jerome A. Kuntz

over the crowd, embellishing the story as necessary to hold everyone's attention.

Did you ever meet someone like that? I'll bet you did; it must have been his brother living in Northfield. Ten to one, we could've even swapped town drunks without people noticing.

We finally returned to our hotel late in the afternoon, no smarter for all our effort.

"Sheriff! Sheriff! Open up!" It was morning and someone was banging on our hotel door. Roy groggily lurched across the room, cussed under his breath, and yanked open the door. A tall, bald-headed man wearing a white apron stood in the hall. Roy warned, "This better be good, mister, this better be damn good!"

Baldy shouted, "I've been robbed and you gotta find who done it!"

"Furgodsake man, we're only passing through. Don't you have a lawman in town?"

"Ya, Sheriff Linus, but he's fishing on the Muddy. Won't be back till Saturday."

"We better check it out, Roy," Pa said dryly, swinging his long skinny legs over the side of the bed. "Might be the Jameses."

"Wait for us!" Roy barked and slammed the door in his face; early mornings generally put him in a bad mood. We dressed quickly, grabbed our weapons, and followed the distressed man to the street. The sun was just climbing the horizon. Roosters bragged they were up and doing. No one else appeared loony enough to be awake without good reason.

The stranger said he was Clem Robinson, and claimed he owned the Sioux City Mercantile. Roy quickly introduced us and asked, "What happened, Mr. Robinson?"

"Clem. Come in and I'll show you." Bristling with guns and ready for action, we followed him into the store. We naturally spread out, checking the store for whatever.

"See that?" Clem said, pointing at the open cash register. It was as empty as a farmer's pocketbook. "Someone broke in during the night, stole the money along with guns and tools."

"How'd they get in?" Pa asked, looking bored.

"That's just it," Clem said, scratching his polished dome, "the door's jimmied but still the lock is open."

I took a closer look. It appeared someone had tried to break the door lock and then lazily gave up and used a key. The bolt was open in the lock. Maybe the robber wanted Clem to think it was a regular burglary, not an inside job, so he grabbed guns and tools along with the cash. "Who else has a key to the door?" I piped up, surprising even myself. A master sleuth I'm not, but two plus two equals four, four plus four....

Clem wagged his head as if not believing his thoughts. "Well, my brother-in-law Max Conlin. He works for us. My wife's brother. Lives at the Missouri Hotel. Even so, I doubt even he would be dumb enough to pull a stunt like this." Clem looked around nervously as if making sure his wife was out of earshot.

"He might if he figures he can get out of town fast," Roy said. "Has he got a horse?"

"Has he got a horse! Ya, a damn wild racer at the livery."

Roy jabbed a finger at Clem while looking at Pa. "Harlen, go with Clem to check the livery. Custer, Buck and I will cover the Missouri Hotel." We scattered.

The Missouri stood a couple blocks from the mercantile. We ran to keep up with Roy. It looked slummy, not measuring up to the Iowa standards. "I'll talk to the morning clerk at the front desk," Roy said. "You two guys guard the back door."

"Ohfergodsake," I blurted out. It seemed like I'd read or heard that innocent order before: *You watch the back.*

"What?" The big fellow snapped.

"I didn't hear anything, Uncle Roy," I said. "We're going directly, we're going." Even through it was broad daylight, scurrying around behind the building gave me jitters. Call it a premonition. To this day, I tell myself I wasn't chickeny; I merely had a polished sense of self-preservation. Yeah right.

Our first hint of grief was seeing a fine horse with panniers tied in the alley. That racer easily stood eighteen hands and looked belly-full of oats. Someone was planning fast travel.

We barely had time to worry. There came a sound like a berserk hippo pounding down an inside stairway in the hotel. I guessed Max was leaving town.

As we ran up the back steps, the door slammed open, almost tearing off the hinges. "Hold it, mister!" I uselessly ordered. The big ugly brute never even slowed. Within seconds, Buck and I were on our backs and sliding down the steps. Our rifles clattered uselessly off to the side. All we could do was each grab a leg as he stomped us into the concrete. We had to stop him; if he reached that long-legged frog, he'd disappear like a Pony Express Rider. Still, our quick action was enough to send him grunting face-first into the gravel alley. He turned around and pounded both our heads. I hit him back hard as I could, but it was like slamming the side of a house. Now he *was* mad, and concentrated on flattening my face. That gave Buck a chance to scramble away. "Chunk him, Buck!" I screamed. I only had to hang on until Buck could bend a rifle barrel over his head. Blood squirted from my nose, covering both of us.

"Ow-w-w-w!" I screamed pitifully. Buck had swung his rifle, missed the brute's head, and slammed my arm. It went numb and now I only had one arm to fight back. Max tried to snag Buck, so I punched his face to give little brother another chance. It cost me: Max cuffed the side of my head, almost tearing my ear off. The bugger had fists like rocks.

"Sorry, Custer," Buck said amiably, seemingly unworried by his poor aim. I turned away so the gorilla couldn't smash my face again. Buck swung the rifle like a ball bat. I saw it coming and ducked until I heard a solid *klunk*. Fatso rolled on top of me.

"Get this pig off me!" I yelled. Did that big galoot stink! He made a skunk smell like it was heading for Sunday service. The combination of tobacco fumes, old leather, horse sweat, toast, fried eggs, and onions would have gagged our coonhounds. Why would anyone hire a lout like that to work in a mercantile?

Within minutes, Roy pounded down the back steps, knelt on the thief's back and slapped on handcuffs. I sat up, squeezing my bleeding nose.

Northfield

"Are you hurt, Custer?" Roy asked, glancing back over his shoulder.

"No—oh, no—I'm fine—" I said, spitting into the dirt. It sounded bubbly with blood draining into my mouth from cut lips.

Roy came over and placed a dirty rag over my face. "Lie on your back," he commanded, while pushing me backwards. "Buck, you all right?" He sounded worried.

"Okay for someone with a bashed face," Buck said, trying to keep the quiver out of his voice. Truthfully, I felt like bawling myself. Stinkpot had pounded us good, and black spots danced before my eyes. Max came to and complained how hard we'd hit him. I felt unhinged myself and didn't care doodly-squat about his problems.

"Let's take him to jail and get you guys cleaned up," Roy said.

"Better not," I cautioned. "If Pa sees us before we wash up, he's liable to beat Max to death."

"Ya…you're probably right. Go back to the Iowa while I throw this idiot in jail. And don't worry, deputies; I'll tell your dad you're fine." Roy walked off, roughly shoving the staggering prisoner ahead of him.

Deputies. He called us deputies. I already felt better. The bleeding stopped, but my shirt was a mess. Buck grabbed my arm and helped me up. Holding our faces, we staggered toward the Iowa. Little brother was rooster-mad. He had split the forestock on his Winchester.

"Now who's gonna pay for this, I ask you?" he groused. "I'll need a good rifle if we get into another shoot-out with those outlaws."

"Ah quit bitchin' about the damn rifle. I might have a broken nose, saying nothing about my arm." The comparison was lost on him. I could barely feel my fingers and kept looking down to check their location.

We washed in our room, and the damage soon became apparent. My cheeks were puffed up like a pocket gopher. At least my nose looked straight enough, so that was a relief. Buck had a nasty cut on the back of his head from going over backwards. He washed blood out of his hair, yelling and dancing like a wild Indian when cold water reached the wound. But still, the damaged rifle bothered him the most.

We caught up with Roy at the jail. Minutes later, Pa and Clem rushed in. Pa's face creased with worry. He pulled my hand off my face, grabbed my chin, and wagged my head like a boat paddle while looking me over. "Uh-oh, you're about to get a dilly of a shiner, two of them for that matter. What happened?"

I let Buck tell the story. He made me out a lot braver than I ever felt, but I didn't bother to dispute his version. What the heck—half those tales of Buffalo Bill were hot air and look what they did for his career. Pa kept shaking his head and repeating what a good job we did. I didn't care about the shiners and bruises after that. I sensed an opportunity and looked forward to seeing Jas.

Uncle Roy quickly told his part, "I just reached the clerk's desk when I heard someone galloping down a stairway. Max's room is on the balcony and he hadn't even bothered to close his door. Likely, he saw our badges as we came up the street and then heard me talking to the clerk. Say! What's the matter with your arm, Custer?"

I sheepishly glanced at Buck. Most likely I'd need a favor soon. Besides, he might have saved me from a worse fate. "Max must have stepped on it when he ran us down."

Roy looked at Clem, "I found your money in Max's pockets. The rest of the stuff is probably on his horse or in his room."

"Thanks, I'm tickled to get my money and merchandise back," Clem said, his face glowing, "and I want you men to stop by the mercantile before you leave and pick out some new clothes. Never would have hired him but he's my wife's brother and..." So that was it. He didn't bother to finish but we could guess the rest: her money bought the store. No one works harder for his money than the man who marries it, Pa liked to say.

"That's fine, Clem," Roy said. "We'll stop in this evening. In the meantime, you better notify the mayor and get someone to guard this hoosegow until your fishing-sheriff returns."

A white-shirted, suspendered gent rushed in carrying a notepad and one of those large box cameras, the kind on long legs and the viewer pulls a black cloth over his head. "Are you the sheriff who caught Max Conlin?" he asked, smiling at Roy in anticipation. Unbelievable how fast news travels! Can you guess what happened next? Ya, I figured you were paying attention.

"We're not giving interviews!" Roy bellowed, getting to his feet and backing the man toward the door.

"Now hold on, Sheriff. The taxpayers have a right—"

He never got to finish. "Hogwash! I've got two deputies beat up, and we're not even on the town's payroll." You ever notice nothing irks an officeholder faster that being told taxpayers' rights? They're right touchy on that point. Roy pushed the flustered man out and slammed the door. He turned around and glared at all of us with doubled fists. "I'm getting damn tired of people telling me what taxpayers want."

Buck and I carefully studied the alignment of the floorboards, saying nothing.

"Roy, we should be careful of our language around the young men," Pa found the nerve to say. No one paid him any attention. I think Roy figured we were about equal now. I felt it too. I'd learned more about life in the past few days than in months spent in Mrs. Hollins' sleepy classroom.

The stage wasn't leaving until morning. Roy told us to spread out and question the locals. Either the James brothers were still stealing horses or they were on the river. There was one other possibility, which we didn't care to dwell on: they might have worried a necktie party waited in Missouri and decided to head west.

My job was to check the docks. Everywhere I asked, I got the same answer: no strangers tried to hire a boat. People stared in disbelief. Both my eyes had blackened and I still wore my blood-splattered shirt.

I kept staring across the Missouri River. It was the gateway to the West. I had only to cross it, and I'd be where I dreamed of for years. I wanted to see it before the buffalo were history and Indians were breaking sod on reservations.

As planned, we met for supper at the Iowa Hotel. Being pounded certainly hadn't affected our appetite. It was hard not to notice the stares from other customers. Likely, the story of two teenage deputies capturing Max Conlin had made the rounds. Buck and I faked

Jerome A. Kuntz

indifference to the attention and enjoyed our meal. It was a nice place. Red-and-white checkered cloths covered the tables. There were even clear glass plates and cups, not the white crockery we normally found.

Clem met us at the door when we arrived at the mercantile. He was smiling and rubbing his hands. I doubt recovering the money was tops on his list; likely, seeing the last of his brother-in-law gave him the most pleasure. "Do you need new shirts or pants?" he asked, leading us to the men's clothing. "Just help yourself."

None of us had owned many store-bought clothes. Ma always had a clothing project in her Singer foot-treadle sewing machine. She made most of what we wore, so picking out something free was quite a thrill. Buck and I were wide-eyed as gypsies, staring at all those wonderful dyed shirts. Some of the trousers even had pleats.

I looked all around the store. It was a huge barn-like structure, and it carried about everything: plows, wagons, buggies and implements, canned food, whiskey, guns, notions, medicines, cast-iron frying pans, barrels of flour and sugar, burlap bags of potatoes, and shiny cans of syrup. Well, you get the picture. I could see Clem had oodles of money by the standards of the day, and I wondered if he'd bend on the choice of clothes. I knew going in what I really wanted: cowboy boots. The taller the better. No more heavy work boots with strings for me.

"How about cowboy boots?" I asked hopefully.

"Custer!" Pa exclaimed, "Clem didn't say anything about boots. Besides, your shirt's a mess."

"I can wash the shirt. It's not torn or anything."

Clem looked at me in surprise. With both hands, I tenderly explored my swollen cheeks and black eyes. Wouldn't most people have seen through the cheap theatrics? He was just a nice fellow. "I know how you feel," he said sympathetically, and then laughed. "It's a fine day when a boy gets his first boots. Go ahead and pick out a pair."

It was that easy. I'm sure he felt guilty about Max pummeling me.

Buck had ranted a few more times during the day about his split forestock, so what came next didn't surprise me. "I could use a new rifle," he said hopefully. All of us, including Clem, pretended to have

Northfield

gone deaf as posts. Lucky I raised the stakes first, or he might have pulled it off, and I could have kissed those boots goodbye.

Everyone except me looked spiffy in new shirts when we thanked Clem and left the store. Roy looked unusually pleased. It wasn't often he could find ready-made clothes to fit. There had to be some bulky fellows living in town or Clem would never have stocked shirts that large.

I couldn't stop looking at my shiny brown boots with pointy toes. You should have seen them. They even had four-inch "mule ears" for pulling on. Dark red stitching designs of interwoven leaves and branches decorated the tops. All I needed now were spurs.

Buck and I decided to walk the town. "What'd you want those fancy boots for?" he asked.

I could tell he was still peeved about not getting a new rifle. Now he'd have to wire the forestock like the Indians did. "I'll need them for working cattle over there," I said, while pointing toward the Rockies.

"Yeah, ah-huh. That'll be tricky telling Pa. Ma'll skin him alive if he comes home without you."

I wondered how much longer he would keep that to himself. Buck was bad for keeping secrets, leaky as an old bucket. I already regretted telling him anything.

So far, I'd managed to keep a lid on Cheyenne as my new goal—partly because of Jas. If they thought my only reason for going was a skirt, I'd not hear the end of it.

Chapter 10

The long-awaited stage from Fort Dodge rolled into Sioux City at dawn, and we groggily climbed aboard. When that coach was new it must have been quite the circus wagon. Now the red-and-yellow paint was chipped, faded, and mud-splattered. Manure graced the wheel spokes. Six sweating horses thickened the atmosphere considerably.

Jas and Raife continued south with us. Raife figured Omaha was a good home base for selling farm machinery. I didn't dispute it, not wanting to get him started. Jas planned to catch the train for Cheyenne in Omaha. We naturally assumed our original positions, with me sitting across from Jas. Riding with her in the coach, I knew the trip wouldn't be too bad.

Prudently, I'd washed my shirt the night before—a simple matter of borrowing the hotel's mop pail and dipping from a horse trough.

"My goodness, Custer," Jas said, "what happened to your face?" Cute worry-wrinkles creased her forehead. She must have been the only one in town not to hear the story. I pretended modesty, counterfeit of course. I had only begun my explanation when Roy took over. He must have felt guilty about sending us behind the Missouri Hotel because he layed it on thick.

Now, wouldn't you expect a normal person to have learned a lesson after that embarrassing newspaper article? Oh no, not me. Humpty Dumpty learned nothing from his great fall. I had about a nickel's worth of resistance to flattery anyway, so I let him carry on—even prompting him for clarity on important points that enhanced my reputation. I'd read way too many Beadle Westerns for someone capable of my soaring flights of fantasy. The poor girl said ou-u-u and ah-h-h in all the right places, even bringing both hands to her face to keep from fainting. It was too much for Buck; he giggled like a danged fool in the background.

Long before Roy finished, Jas likely figured I didn't have much of a future. Every time we met, there'd be another story of street brawls and gun battles with unsavory characters.

I was surprised to learn she was nineteen—just two years older than I was and already on her own. "Maybe we could look the town over, Jas, when we reach Council Bluffs," I said, completely forgetting why we were riding the coach in the first place. More giggles from Buck.

"Maybe we could," she said, giving me a smile I've yet to forget. "It would depend on when my train leaves. Family friends are meeting me at the Cheyenne station, and I wouldn't want to disappoint them."

Pa said dryly, "Son, I doubt we'll have time for idle sightseeing in Council Bluffs."

I felt my ears getting hot. That was Pa: treating me like a kid again now that we were out of danger. I wouldn't have to worry about that when I was on my own hook in Cheyenne. My mood soured, and I leaned over Roy's big belly and told Buck to stuff it quick. He laughed even louder until Roy gave him an elbow. Jas kindly pretended not to notice.

Lunch stop was at a secluded ranch house. We crowded around a long wooden table with no cloth. I assumed the cook was the rancher's wife. Her stringy hair and high-pitched voice were no reflection on her cooking: it was about the best sauerkraut-and-spare-ribs I've ever eaten. Mashed potatoes too. Wow, my kind of fare! And here I'd been complaining about the food.

Luckily, I was able to slip in next to the driver. We were not in the West yet, but he matched stage-drivers' pictures on covers of dime novels at home: shaggy red beard and hair flowing over his shoulders, a huge floppy hat that he wore to the table, and greasy buckskins. Smelled like a wet dog, but I didn't care. I soon had permission for Buck and me to join him on the driver's seat. That kid was going to owe me a passel of favors.

What a view from on top! Not far to the west, the tree-bordered Missouri River snaked its way toward Council Bluffs—steadily changing colors, blue, black, brown, and green as it loped along through shade and sunlight. It was late summer so the harvest was almost over. Ploughed oats and wheat fields, intersected by thick woods, rolled east to the horizon. Already I could see the trees

Jerome A. Kuntz

showing fall colors. Several acres of pale-yellow corn were still standing, fat ripe ears drooping. Six black horses trotted in rhythm far below our seat. A decent team for a change. Even though mid September, sunshine blared white-hot in a clear blue sky.

The biggest drawback was squeezing in next to the odorous driver. Jake was his name. Fortunately, I sat on his left. Poor Buck on his right had to duck whenever he snapped his bullwhip. Jake was so hemmed in he had to spit tobacco juice down to the doubletree, but he seemed pleased having company. I promised myself a ten-gallon hat like the driver wore when I reached Wyoming.

"This here's the best job in the world," he asserted. "No one to boss you around, good pay, and Wells Fargo buys all your meals." I thought it advisable under the circumstances to withhold my opinion of "Smells Hardgo."

"You ever been robbed?" I had to ask.

"Shucks yes"—SPUT-T-T!—"all the drivers have been robbed one time or another. Nothin' we can do about it."

"Who were they?" Buck asked with owl eyes. "Did they catch anyone?"

"Naw-w-w, it's just the price of doing business. My guess is it's the James Gang. Been operatin' on these roads since the war. Now I hear tell they robbed a bank up nort."

We'd heard this before: it seemed people blamed the James brothers for half the robberies from Texas to Minnesota. Even now, lawmen haven't sorted out the extent of their crimes. Boy, could we ever have put a bug in his ear. I remembered the newspaper article, which he probably read, and decided to change the subject. "Doesn't a job like this keep you away from home a lot?" I asked.

"Oh that." SPUT-T! Another gob of brown juice splattered onto the wheelers' hind legs. "Don't mind that a bit. Not with six squalling kids around the cabin. No, the place for a man is out working, not wipin' a bunch of snotty noses at home. See that left lead horse? He's doggin' it. They're clever that way if you don't watch um." Buck ducked and Jake popped the whip just behind the slacking horse's ear. "That's why you need a whip," he added. "Just a couple of soft touches and they soon change their mind 'bout not pulling."

He seemed a mite lonesome to me—never stopped talking the rest of the afternoon. Of course, later, we callously named him Rapunzel. Growing up in Northfield where winters were long, Grimm's Fairy Tales were our favorite until discovering Beadle Westerns.

I'll tell you, I felt powerful cocky sitting up there, pants stuffed into the tops of my shiny new cowboy boots. Tobacco-spitting Jake eyed them regretfully; likely, he hankered to break them in right.

It was dark when we pulled into Missouri Valley. I could barely see the horses' backs, but they seemed to know the way to the stage stop. As usual, we galloped into town, hooves pounding and Jake snapping his bullwhip like pistol shots over the team. When entering any settlement, a certain reckless tradition had to be displayed, no matter how tired the team, or however late the hour. It was good for business. The stationmaster stood by his front door holding a lantern. There would be a team change and a four-hour rest for the passengers. Bunks were available for napping, but it meant getting up in the middle of the night for the final long leg down to Council Bluffs. Evidently, the driver followed some vague schedule, but it made no sense to us.

After midnight, they rousted us out and we stumbled aboard. Buck and I were happy to ride again back in the coach. Jake had to be a tough bird to drive so many hours. I think we all promptly fell back to sleep—quickly becoming salty veterans of the gypsy life.

We reached Council Bluffs the following evening. It appeared a lively place with folks shopping and visiting on the streets, even at such a late hour. Buck and I were somewhat worse for wear when we left the coach but it was worth it. Our ribs and elbows ached from slamming against the seat rails of that lofty rocking bench the previous day.

There wasn't much point in poking around after dark in a strange town, looking for two killers. Besides, we were too tired to care. We trooped to the nearest hotel, toting rifles and our few belongings. Loud carousing floated into the streets from several busy saloons. We heard raucous laughter from soiled doves (you guessed it, Beadle Westerns again). No upstanding ladies would enter a saloon in those days.

Jerome A. Kuntz

It was my first chance to talk to Jas without my family listening in. Naturally, I carried her suitcase, which seemed full of rocks, but I pretended not to notice. For a change, Buck walked ahead with Pa and Uncle Roy. She seemed to treat me with more interest since we hog-wrestled Max Conlin into jail, so maybe Roy did me a favor after all. I didn't bother to remind her that Max was only a small-town, nickel-and-dime thief, thinking it would help no one. After all, we'd been hunting bear and only bagged a rabbit. Until then I doubt Jas even believed Buck and I were sworn sheriff deputies. She looked genuinely worried about my black eyes and puffy face. It was working. If given the choice, I would have repeated the experience just to get her attention. Scars and raccoon eyes were a badge of manhood to my way of thinking.

Jas rented her room from the sleepy clerk and Pa and Roy stepped up next. While they were busy, I steered her toward the almost-empty hotel restaurant. Both of us were too tired to eat but we ordered coffee. Dimly lit deer and elk heads lined the walls. The wallpaper was running with wild mustangs. A smooth waltz played on a Swiss wind-up music box near the back wall. On top of the box, a large revolving perforated copper disc reflected square-dancing spangles of light on the gold-painted, stamped-metal ceiling. It even made the mustangs appear to move. Romantic, I thought. This was before the wonderful invention of the phonograph. It seemed strange talking to her alone, and, now that my chance had come, I could think of precious few subjects.

"How long do you plan to stay in Cheyenne?" I asked. Tomorrow, she'd catch the train and I was worried she'd be lost to me forever. Maybe she had a boyfriend in St. Cloud and she'd want to see him again. I didn't have two nickels to rub together, but still fancied courting her some day. Truthfully, my longing for the cowboy life was as strong as ever; and I uselessly reminded myself, as every single man does, not to allow a skirt to derail my dream.

"Oh, it will be my new home," she said, while holding her hot coffee cup in both hands as if they were cold. "I'm in no hurry to return to Minnesota—not with a house full of younger brothers and sisters. No, it's best if I make it on my own. Besides, there are enough teachers in St. Cloud and the Cities. After working so hard to attain my Teaching Certificate, I want to be where I'm needed."

I figured I had nothing to lose. Put my neck in the loop, so to speak. "May I visit you in Cheyenne after this posse job ends?" Hopefully, I had used proper English.

She looked at me in total surprise. Smiling too. Maybe I had a chance after all. "Why yes, Custer. That would be nice, but I assumed you'd all be returning to Northfield."

I noticed that danged Buck peeping through the door window and listening in. A notorious tattletale, he'd report everything to Sadie. Those twins were as thick as Quixote and Sancho, sharing every scrap of information. Seems he was past due on a lesson in minding his own business.

"No, I won't return to Minnesota either. Not right away. I plan to find work on a cattle ranch in Wyoming." I gave her a few details on how I proposed to accomplish my goal, sounding much braver than I felt. Pretty girls will do that to you.

She was quiet for a time, staring down at the tablecloth. I wondered if I'd said the wrong thing. That'd be a surprise. Suddenly, she looked up at me, eyes dark from lack of sleep. "Custer, do you believe in women's intuition?"

I barely nodded my head, having just a vague idea from observing Sadie, but not really understanding it. Remember, I told you she seemed to know things that she couldn't have learned from Mrs. Hollins.

Unexpectedly, Jas reached out and clutched my wrist but she wasn't looking at me; she wasn't looking at anything at all, near as I could tell. She merely stared at the black windows of the restaurant's street front. Even her voice changed. "I have a bad feeling about your pursuit of the James brothers. All of you must turn back. Please, Custer, turn back before it's too late."

"Turn back?" I asked dumbly. Her hand was like a vise on my wrist. She spoke like someone who loved novels. It's not hard to tell.

"Yes, give up the chase."

"Well...we plan on doing that anyway. Roy said if they reach Missouri, it's hopeless." I was flustered by this sudden turn in the conversation.

"No, I mean go home *now.*" Then, just as quickly, she jerked her hand back in embarrassment, her face turning pink. "I-I didn't mean to intrude on your business," she said, looking around the restaurant in confusion.

What the heck was going on here? At seventeen, I had no more faith in women's intuition than reading tea leaves or pawing through chicken guts, and I quickly changed the subject to put her at ease. I don't recall that it made much of an impression on me at the time, and, without consciously deciding one way or the other, I didn't tell anyone what Jas said. Maybe that was a bad mistake.

We discussed her teaching job, which, surprisingly, didn't sound as certain as I first assumed. It struck me as risky for a girl to travel so far without guarantees. We couldn't visit long; she was falling asleep in her chair, and I wasn't much better off. We made hasty plans for meeting the next day, and I promised to help her to the train station.

When we reached her hotel door, I stayed long enough to make sure her key worked and then sleepily wandered off to find our room. Everyone was asleep and I had considerable trouble, stumbling in the darkness to find a place to lie down. Buck punched me in the gut for stepping on him. I hoped we'd sleep late the next morning. Something was bothering me but I didn't know what; I assumed it was the prospect of saying goodbye to Jas the next day when she caught the train.

Oh gosh, so many times in my long life I've wondered, was it another missed opportunity? Would Pa and Uncle Roy's response to Jasmine's somber warning have been different from mine?

Chapter 11

"Buck! Custer! Get up! They're on the river!" Roy shouted from the open door. It seemed I'd just turned in when he started bellowing. Who's on the river and who gives a damn, I thought. I looked around with one eye barely open. Buck sat up on the floor, sporting a cowlick like a mad snowdrift. Pa was gone; he must have got up early with Roy and poked around town. They're both crazy! "Don't you ever sleep, Uncle Roy?" I mumbled, crotchety as Scrooge.

"Get dressed!" he snapped. "And meet us down in the restaurant." He stomped into the hallway and slammed the door. Must have woke everyone on that hotel floor, but he didn't care. The game was on the move, and the big fellow had his dander up.

Pa had the pocket watch so I wasn't sure of the time. Out the window, it was barely first light. I sighed deeply, feeling sorry for myself. At home, chores began at seven, and even then we gracelessly did the work and complained of the early hour.

Within minutes, we were gobbling breakfast in the hotel restaurant. Roy had ordered for all of us to save time. The biscuit-shooters (a Western term for waitresses we'd learned from Jake) practically ran back and forth from kitchen to hungry customers. Gone was the whirling romantic light, the magic and soft music from the night before. All the rough edges of a busy working-man's restaurant showed clearly in harsh daylight. So much for moonlight madness, as they say.

My old worry was back. Roy was sure to have another plan, and we'd be off again chasing the James brothers. I wanted to say goodbye to Jas, but doubted she'd appreciate my waking her so early. The West suffered from a shortage of marriageable girls, and she wouldn't be single long. Not a pretty lass like her.

"We got lucky, men," Roy said, between mouthfuls of pancakes. "Criminals are generally lazy and will work as little as possible to get what they want. They're tired of riding and want to take life easy on the river. The hostler said they asked about boats heading downriver. Not too smart: that's how we learned their plans. He told them there's a hide hauler about to leave and will likely take passengers. It was good enough for those boys—they sold their horses and tack dirt-cheap.

"I hated telling the poor hostler the horses were likely stolen, and he would have to turn them over to the sheriff. 'Course, I doubt he'll bother—probably just keep them for renters and see if anyone comes asking. Besides, how would the law find the owners? Those outlaws came a far piece. Heaven knows how many times they swapped or stole horses on their way south. Anyway, near as I can figure, they sailed soon after we arrived. Probably decided not to wait for a river steamboat and to leave at once after spotting us."

"So, how'll we catch them if they already left?" Buck asked. He was still powerfully anxious to bag a couple of bad guys.

"I asked around," Roy answered. "We'll pay passage on a freighter too. They all have to make wood stops to feed the boiler. Woodhawks stack hundreds of cords of wood on the riverbanks to sell to steamboat operators. They won't expect us to be right behind, so surprise should be in our favor."

I think most lawmen would have skipped breakfast and tried to head the criminals off before they got too big a lead. Not Roy. There was a time to eat, and a time to chase outlaws, and the two shall never overlap as far as he was concerned.

Pa ate in depressing silence. His coffee cup shook and rattled like old bones when he set it back on the saucer. We pretended not to notice. Roy had tried for years to get Pa to stop drinking, all to no avail. I guessed now he enjoyed the rare time when his older brother had to stay off the 'shine. We all knew Roy was serious as a heart attack when he said, "no drinking on duty." Without that threat, I doubted anything would have kept Pa off the bottle for long. His advice had always been to finish everything you start, so maybe that strong belief kept him going.

Once while attending an estate auction in Northfield, I overheard a man telling his cronies, "Ya, that Harlan Compton ain't a bad fella. After all, he only drinks on days ending in Y." They all chuckled and I remember thinking, Flappermouth old boy, you probably only gossip on days ending in Y. I then moved off, not wanting to embarrass them. Now I wish I'd stopped to say hello. I was surprised that people knew about Pa's drinking, but, as I said earlier, he enjoyed the Exchange Saloon and word probably got around.

Back then, I considered Pa weak and thought a man should handle what life shows him. Not until heartache bows us low do we see the arrogance of that. Now, on this manhunt, I had a father who was easier to be proud of.

We checked docks on the riverfront and soon learned where two men bought passage on a hide hauler in the middle of the night. They had boarded the *Fair Weather* long before daylight, so we had to move fast.

Sorry to say, nothing was leaving that day except more freighters hauling buffalo hides to Kansas City and St. Louis. We had to go. Our boat carried the name *Pride of St. Louis*—a highfalutin title for a stinking, vibrating old tub run by a lousy crew that spoke little English. Luckily, the captain was as anxious to leave as we were; and, even though he looked with scorn at our badges, Roy didn't have to quibble long to get passage. We soon stored our gear aboard.

The crew was French, and a bunch of rougher men I've never met. Captain Charbonneau looked as bad as the rest, but spoke better English. He sported a bright red cloth knotted around his head, and his face was almost sunburned black, making him look like a pirate on the high seas. He proudly claimed as kin the shifty Toussaint Charbonneau, who had traveled with the Corps of Discovery seventy-five years earlier. It's true, Toussaint was an important interpreter for Captain Clark, but he doesn't come off well in history books. Yeah, I could believe our wild captain was related to that ruffian.

With appallingly foul language, a mixture of English and French, the captain and crew cast off and swung the heavily loaded freighter into the current. It seemed their major concession to the English language was learning our cuss words. Pa wagged his head in disgust. It wasn't his habit to allow adults to swear in our presence. Sadie could have taken notes.

What a thrill rolling on the coffee-colored current. Acrid coal smoke twisted from the boiler stack, and I could feel the power of the steam engine rumbling through the deck plates. The river was busy with two-way traffic: side- and back-wheel passenger steamers, freight barges, scows, fishing boats, and even Indian dugouts and canoes.

Tall, redbrick buildings of Omaha dotted the rolling hilltops west of the river, and beyond that stretched the vast prairie, populated by wild Indians and the countless buffalo that sustained them. Hilly farmland rolled east to the horizon.

Never had I breathed an atmosphere so vile. Buffalo hunters had not properly cured the hides. They would keep until reaching the tanning factories of St. Louis and that satisfied the buyer. Not only was the hold full, but huge bundles were also lashed on the squalid deck. Already, ugly black beetles wiggled out from those hides and crawled over the deck. Added to that was the stink of burning coal and a continuous rain of fly ash from the stack. When the coal was gone, we'd buy wood. Captain Charbonneau knew where woodhawks sold stacks along the riverbank.

Fortunately, the *Pride of St. Louis* carried a good cook. A small galley was on the top deck, but we ate while squatting on our heels—the original builders had forgotten the dining room.

Captain Charbonneau immediately assigned Buck and me to galley duty after the first meal. Not until then did we learn it was part payment for our passage. Perfect. Roy claimed he forgot to mention it earlier. I noticed he suppressed a sly grin.

Pa and Uncle Roy alternated on deck watching for the *Fair Weather*. When out of the captain's earshot, they debated whether to tell him what dangerous scoundrels we pursued, and that there could be gunplay before the trip ended.

Before long, Buck and I were up to our elbows in soapy water washing cooking pots. Supper had been good, but we could see that the cleanup would never end. The galley contained a regular home coal/wood cook stove. A large rusty sink stretched along one wall. We obtained hot water from a faucet in the boiler. Cold water came from the boat's large storage tank. Widely spaced steel hooks reached down from the ceiling to hold pots, pans, and utensils.

"Pee-yew! Squaw's work!" Buck sneered, holding his nose. "I didn't come on this manhunt to wash dishes on a smelly hide boat." At home, Ma almost had to tie him to the sink at dishwashing time.

He loved eating wild game, but hated the inevitable cleanup. I wasn't much better. Sadie and Ma usually handled it.

"Well, you know what Ma would say, 'If you don't work you don't eat,'" I said, trying to cheer him up. I wasn't happy about it either but we had few options. The rumbling steam engine drowned out most of his complaining.

My feet tingled from the deck vibration. Water puddles under our feet bubbled as if boiling hot. Oh yeah, we were having fun now.

Buck turned to me and shouted, "I noticed you've been into that novel again. How's the good knight and whathistoes getting on?"

"Say again?" I answered innocently, keeping a poker face. He couldn't seem to get it right.

"Cripes! You know who I mean! Don Co-yo-te. Did Ma drop you on your head when you were small?"

"Hah! Now I know who you mean: Don Co-yo-te and Sancho Pancakes." I let fly with a gob of soap bubbles in his general direction. Soon it was sailing both ways as we circled the galley, trying to duck and hide.

"You throw like a girl!" I taunted.

"Yeah? Well, I haven't lost every ball game *I* pitched," Buck yelled, wearing an ear-splitting grin.

That was a bit of a sore spot with me. I *accidentally* grabbed a huge sopping washrag and showed him my best pitch. It wrapped around his head, blocking his vision, and he bellowed in surprise and anger. Grabbing a small pot, he dipped it full of soap water and threw it. I ducked but his aim was good. Some splashed on the still-hot cook stove, and steam rolled toward the ceiling. Then I slipped and splattered face-first onto the soapy galley deck.

"Gol-damn you lazy bums!" someone screamed in a voice strangled with wrath. It was the cook, mad as a mud turtle and a lot more dangerous. He grabbed a vicious-looking spatula and I thought we were in deep dip, but he only used it to point to dirty pots while turning the air blue with a blistering stream of French. Then he stormed out with what I took to be promises to throw us overboard if he caught us horseplaying again. I knew he'd tattle to Captain

Charbonneau, who'd run to Pa and Uncle Roy. We didn't worry. They didn't like that ratty crew any better than we did.

I figured the galley was ours for a while, and we got busy as Bob Cratchit. First, we mopped the floor and straightened out the mess, then returned to washing pots. "Okay, Buck," I said, "I'll tell you what Don Co-yo-te's been up to. They went to visit Dulcinea, Big Don's supposed girlfriend who he's yet to meet but brags endlessly about to Sancho Pancakes." I slipped into my falsetto, which was pretty good. "'Oh what queenly beauty and so delicate, so clean, and such divine creamy complexion!' Get the picture? When the great knight finally points her out, Sancho sees a plain, coarse, shabbily-dressed peasant girl."

"Was she fat too?"

"A half-inch taller and she'd have been perfectly round."

Buck laughed so hard I thought he'd choke. "So, he sees a homely peasant girl as the Queen of Sheba?" he wheezed helplessly.

"You got it. I told you he was goofy as Kansas. He sees everything as he wants it to be, not as it really is."

"Holy mackerel! I wonder how he would see this boat. Maybe something used by the great pharaohs of Egypt instead of a stinking rusty tub."

"Ya," I said, getting into the drift. "It's probably Cleopatra's personal Nile River touring craft."

Buck pulled out the dishrag and let it drip into the tub. "This soapy slop-water would be Cleopatra's perfumed bath."

I held up a blackened pot. "And this, of course, is pure pounded silver—"

"Boys, come out here on deck a minute." It was Pa sticking his head in the doorway. "There's something you need to see." We skipped out the door—anything to get out of that stifling galley.

"See that?" he said, pointing to a distant hide boat much like ours. "That's the *Fair Weather*. Mark it well. We might be chasing it for days."

"I can hardly see it," I said. Pa handed me the captain's spyglass.

"It's them all right," Pa said, confidently. "The same two birds we last saw at the Speckled Loon in Mankato."

Two skinny men stared back from their fantail. It was obvious they knew we were right behind. Within minutes, they disappeared around another loop of the river. So much for our planned surprise at the first wood stop.

We ran on like that for a couple more days, occasionally catching a glimpse before they slipped out of sight. Frustrating as bunions! Sometimes we were unsure if it was the same boat or if they were even still on board. They could easily jump ship in the dark and we'd be on a wild goose chase to Grimm's fairyland.

Unpleasant as the boat was, the river was endlessly fascinating. I felt like Huck Finn, looking for that next adventure. Dangerous though because great tree snags would unexpectedly rear up as the current carried them south. It was rare to see out across the prairie due to the thick tree growth that choked the riverbanks, casting dark gloomy shadows on the swift-flowing current. Occasionally, great rambling V's of migrating Canadian and snow geese passed overhead, calling encouragement to their friends in the lead while following the river south to their accustomed winter home.

We came to several dingy river towns. People stood on the shores, waving until we again passed out of sight. Then it'd be hours before we'd see another town or boat. It felt like we were alone in the world, riding a watery conveyor to strange lands.

As we steamed south, heat and humidity reached unbearable levels, and danged mosquitoes tried to suck us dry. September was our favorite month in Minnesota and we longed for home. Dare I say it? Buck and I actually preferred the screened shaded galley to being on deck.

One afternoon while sprawling on the bow we gloomily discussed our slim chances of catching the James brothers. Uncle Roy had the most hope. Pa appeared listless and spoke little. Roy could see what he was going through and asked little of him.

Captain Charbonneau joined us. "We're running low on coal, men," he said. "Our first wood stop isn't far off now, so you'll have a chance to stretch your legs." He looked hard at Buck and me. "I hope you boys won't mind helping load wood." It sounded more like an order.

I dutifully nodded my head. Buck followed suit. After the soap fight, I thought it best to humor the testy captain. Of course, he'd complained earlier to Pa and Roy about our work habits but it did him little good. They thought it funny. Both decided we had paid too much for the trip anyway.

"How about that boat ahead of us, Captain?" Pa asked, appearing nonchalant as usual.

"Boat? What boat?"

"The hide boat, *Fair Weather.*"

Captain Charbonneau stood up and peered downriver. "All the hide boats are about the same. Reckon they'll need wood soon too."

Pa joined him at the railing. "Captain Charbonneau, we believe the two men we're after are on that boat. If they stop for wood, we intend to arrest them."

The captain snapped his head in Pa's direction, immediately suspicious. "What'd they do?" he growled. "I don't want any gunplay on my boat. That wasn't part of the deal."

"They robbed the Northfield, Minnesota, bank and killed two local residents."

"A Northern Yankee bank," he sneered (guess which side in the war he'd cheered for). He pronounced it "Nawthern Yankee" as if it was a disease. "It's no concern of mine. Anyway, you're wasting your time. They won't make the same wood stop we do. No woodhawk can cut enough for two boats. Your best bet will be St. Joseph, Missouri. We'll stop there one night and many of the other boats do the same. Besides, if you go after them at a wood stop, they'll likely flee on foot. There's plenty of settlements where they can get horses." One of the crew called for him and he stomped off.

Roy appeared miffed by this news, but Pa took it in his stride. Still, what the captain said sounded logical. There was even a chance they'd stop running in St Joseph and make a stand. They had to know how risky it was to keep showing the enemy their backside.

Within hours we stopped for fuel. It was the hardest I'd worked since leaving Northfield. Luckily, we were used to hard work; at harvest time, we'd go dawn-to-dusk to get the crops in before the weather changed in September. Still, I thought we'd never fill that sweltering hold. Even Pa and Uncle Roy helped when they saw the pile to take onboard. Not surprising, Captain Charbonneau, and even the mean cook found something elsewhere that needed tending.

We never saw the *Fair Weather* again. They must have loaded at night in one of the plentiful coves on that stretch of the river. We carefully checked the docks after pulling into St. Joseph. If the *Fair Weather* came in after us, the outlaws would likely bribe the crew to keep going. We asked the captain to pull up in some backwater to hide the boat, but that grump wasn't about to change plans for our sake.

First, we went to the sheriff's office. Lead would fly if we encountered the James Gang, and we didn't want to be mistaken for gang members.

Buck and I kept looking all around. Boy, this was history. St. Joseph, Missouri, was the eastern terminal of the 1860-61 Pony Express route. The trail stretched 1960 miles from St. Joseph to Sacramento, California, requiring eight to ten days to cover that distance. Relay stations were about 40 miles apart. Oh, how we wished we could have carried the US mail like 15-year-old Buffalo Bill.

There were people everywhere—it was so crowded we had to pass in single file along the boardwalks. The streets were just as bad. Why were there so many buckboards loaded with furniture, cooking utensils, dogs, and kids? At first we thought they were abandoning the town, but that wasn't the case at all. When we asked the problem, they brushed us aside with scared, impatient expressions. St. Joseph, Missouri, wasn't experiencing a merry social gathering or a celebration.

These people were frightened.

Chapter 12

"I'm afraid you've come at a bad time," Sheriff Baylor said. He sat with his boots propped on a scarred roll top desk, puffing a cigar. "We got an Indian scare on our hands. The Pottawatomie left their Reservation and are raiding north and south of town. People are pouring in from outlying settlements on both sides of the river. 'Course, it's hard to say how long the ferry will keep running. Only greed keeps old Buddy Tibbs on the job this long. You might say public service ain't in his character."

I had pictured lawmen on the edge of the frontier as wearing twin six-shooters and spiffy cowboy hats. This gent sported a black derby pulled low over one eye, a white shirt, and a flowery silk vest. Yellow daisies no less. I doubted his shiny pointy-toed boots ever crossed a corral. He looked more like a slick riverboat gambler than a sheriff. Either way, I guessed he had enough sand to hold his own in trouble. I was finding the world a different sight from the portrayal in schoolbooks or Beadle Westerns.

"Well, no wonder," Roy said. "We thought it strange all these people packing their belongings into town." We sat around the sheriff's tiny office clutching rifles as if war had broken out. In a way I guess it had. He eyeballed Buck and me suspiciously a few times and only addressed Pa and Roy.

"Ya, they been piling in here for two weeks. I hope you men can stay on a few days. We may need all the guns we can muster." He spewed a smoke ring over his head. Evidently, it would take more than an Indian scare to put this Missouri sheriff into a dither.

"What started it?" Pa asked.

"Oh, you've probably heard of this happening before. Indians butchered someone's damn cow and the ranchers tracked them down. Shot two Indians they say, but likely there was more. Supposedly, the Pots then attacked and scalped a couple of bachelor homesteaders but no one saw the bodies."

Northfield

"Well, we're right sorry about that, Sheriff, but our boat leaves tomorrow," Pa said. "If we're not aboard, we'll finish off walking to Kansas City."

Sheriff Baylor seemed unfazed. "We have armed guards surrounding St. Joseph, and they're badly in need of relief. Kids have gotten separated from parents, the grocery store's empty, the livery's out of fodder, and even Mother Maybelles, the local restaurant, is out of beef and coffee. She's now serving tea. Can you imagine? Tea!" He wagged his head in inconsolable grief—dead settlers evidently coming in a strong second to running out of coffee.

"As a matter of fact," Sheriff Baylor continued, "we need drovers to bring cattle into town from a nearby farm. The town's beef supply is kaput. 'Spose you could help us out there? If you left this afternoon, you'd be back tomorrow in time to catch your boat." He looked doubtfully at Buck and me. "The town would be mighty beholden."

Now he was starting to wheedle. Isn't that embarrassing to see in a grown man?

You guessed it, Roy caved. Big as a house but soft as a kitty-cat. Sheriff Baylor told us whom to see, and said they would provide saddle horses. Within an hour, we trotted out of town with clear directions from Abe Nelson for locating his deserted farmhouse and the cattle he had intended to butcher soon anyway.

I hated to think these people were more worried about their own skins than about four strangers arriving on a stinking hide boat, but that seemed to be the case. I couldn't explain it. Maybe they figured if you wore a badge, you had to accept the consequences. Evidently, our not being on the St. Joseph payroll made little difference.

Pa and Uncle Roy were well mounted, but Buck and I rode a couple of barrel-ribbed breeding mares. Oh boy, were they big too. Hooves like cast iron frying pans. I tried not to laugh, but you should have seen Buck mount up. He looked like he was climbing our huge oak tree on the farm. Falling would have been risky. We each should have carried a spare rope to rappel back to Earth. I figured the Indians would have a good laugh if we had to tuck tail and run.

Jerome A. Kuntz

We easily found the place about 20 miles east of town. First, we headed for the farmhouse. Roy's last meal was breakfast on the *Pride of St. Louis,* and I knew what the big boy had in mind. Before long, Pa had coffee and potatoes boiling. Bacon and wild onions snapped in hot grease on a nickel-trimmed cast-iron cook stove. Buck and I stood guard where we could spot Indians coming from any direction. I kept twisting my nose around, savoring those delicious cooking odors. Pa wasn't much of a hand for cooking at home, but watch out when he was living rough.

It looked like the Nelson family had piled out of there in a tizzy. Someone, maybe Paul Revere, must have warned them of Indians rampaging. Dishes and food remained on the table. Cupboard doors hung wide open. Likely, they'd pitched out canned food for the trip and neatness was their least worry. I was only three during the 1862 Minnesota Sioux uprising but heard plenty of horror stories first-hand. It wasn't hard to visualize the terror this family had probably felt.

The cattle were in the corral just as Abe described. We fed and watered them as they had a long walk ahead. A friendly team of coal-black workhorses was in an adjoining pasture. Abe had two work teams, which wasn't unusual for a farmer with large acreage. They would snort and bob their big heads when we stopped scratching their ears. More like dogs than working horses. Abe hadn't mentioned them, so we decided to leave them behind. They had it cushy with good grass and a full stock tank. All we had to do then was wait for darkness, figuring it safer to move the stock at night.

We made sure Indians weren't watching the place. Pa and Roy circled the buildings on horseback, looking for tracks of riders and checking if the coast was clear. Indian pony prints would be shoeless.

The day was hushed—the only sounds were preaching crows in nearby woods. It seemed even wild animals were waiting for something to happen. The idea that a band of screaming wild Indians could swoop down at any time seemed unreal, but we knew it could happen.

Before leaving, Pa made a hot supper and we filled our coat pockets with cheese sandwiches. It was bound to be a long night, and Sheriff Baylor had said the restaurant was out of food.

Northfield

We moved out at full dark. The two black workhorses in the corral whinnied pitifully when they realized we were leaving them behind. At first, the cattle milled, wanting to return home. After a couple miles, they seemed to forget where they lived—bovines fortunately not blessed with long memories.

Buck and I rode drag, pushing the herd from behind. That way Pa and Uncle Roy could keep to the trail and watch for an ambush.

Oh, it was dark! Stars sparkled but they offered precious little light compared to a laughing moon. Fireflies, like floating sparks in the humid black night, added to the strangeness. Only white marks on the cattle showed. We had to rely on Pa and Roy to retrace our path back to St. Joseph.

Buck and I came together frequently to keep from losing contact. "Custer," he whispered sometime after midnight, "I heard hoof beats behind us." Dark as it was, the whites of his eyes were huge.

I pointed at him. "Was it your own horse?"

He snatched at my finger as if to break it. "I'm serious, man! Something's back there!"

At first, I dismissed his worries but couldn't help remembering his cool head. He wasn't likely to imagine boogiemen.

I only heard coyotes complaining in the distance. "Did you discover Abe's 'shine?" I asked, trying to keep things light. Heat prickled the back of my neck.

"I tell you someone's following us," Buck hissed. "I stopped a couple of times and the hoof beats ended. Whoever's behind is close enough to know when we stop."

"Okay, okay, keep your shirt on. Let's keep the herd moving. Hell, man, if it's Indians, they'll leave soon. There's nothing to worry about. I think they'll go home when we get close to town. Don't you think they'll go home?"

"No, I don't."

No help there. "I don't either," I said.

They'd be more likely to attack before help was near. The mind will grasp for any thin straws of hope. It was just a habit of mine to put everything in a good light.

Jerome A. Kuntz

I hung back and made my own test. Sure enough, I heard the hoof beats too. I rode to Buck, grabbed his coat and motioned for him to stop. We waited. Silence. We tried it a couple times with the same results. Now we were both spooked. "You better ride ahead and tell Pa," I said, hoping my voice wasn't shaking too bad. "I'll keep them moving."

"Okey-dokey," he said, cool as pickles as he ghosted away to the front.

Did you ever notice when you're frightened, every scary story you ever heard pops into your skull, as welcome as measles? Easy to look back on now but as kids those local fears spooked us all.

Around Northfield in the late 1870s, there were vast tracts of dank, sun-blocked woods choked with giant ferns among ancient oak, birch, and box elders. Even Minneapolis had only 30,000 people, so for the size of Minnesota, it was still a far piece from settled. Strange, unexplainable stories about the woods were common then, but are now forgotten, or at the least given little credence. Too often, people who should have known better repeated them with added frightening twists. Many adults were as superstitious as Grimms' characters.

Deep in those melancholy woods were Indian mounds, long abandoned and over-grown with a tangle of trees, "stingweed," and ferns. Everyone assumed that's where Indians buried their dead, but since no one bothered to dig one up, it wasn't proven. People believed troubled spirits of those dead Indians lurked nearby, and it wasn't healthy to tarry there after dark. As usual, the supposedly gruesome danger they posed was left unstated, which only added to the mystery.

When the subject came up around our house, Pa used to say, "Don't put too much stock in dead people; there's enough live ones around to keep you wary." Easier said than done when neighbors were believers.

Another common belief was the existence of witches' nests. Coon hunters reported moving colored lanterns, and strange cries in the night not associated with wild animals. Still, they insisted the cries weren't quite human. They even claimed to have heard chanting, and witnessed wicked shenanigans in open spaces. Worse of all, these witches could supposedly inhabit your body and only you knew it. Possession. Now that'll curdle your blood. Horrible!

I always wondered if the witches lived in nests like hawks and eagles, or did they pig-pile at night to keep warm.

I know there were crazy nameless hermits living in those woods because they would come into town to trade. Endless speculation occurred as to their sources of income. They seldom answered when spoken to; a slight smile behind a haystack of whiskers would be their only response. They acted as if in possession of secret knowledge only they were privileged to possess. After living alone for decades with nature, what mysteries or riddles do you suppose they solved? Nobody was in a better position to settle the question of witches' nests, but they weren't talking. They seemed to disappear after a time and others took their place. Possibly, they carried their hard-won answers to the grave, provided anyone bothered to dig one.

Several stories circulated of unknown gibbering entities slowly rising and undulating above graveyards in the dark of night, most wearing white nightgowns. They floated effortlessly over the landscape, only to return to their graves before daylight, or so we hoped. That was enough to make me hotfoot away from cemeteries at night. Now that I think about it, have you ever heard of someone buried in a nightgown? I sure haven't. How about a corpse planted with a change of clothes? No one's coming to chat. People must have closely associated death with sleep and hence the bedclothes.

Religion played a part in some people's belief. They were convinced those were lost souls, condemned forever to night-walk the earth.

Indians, witches, and ghosts, these were hot topics for spicy conversation. There just wasn't a lot of entertainment back then, and I suspect people wanted more excitement in their lives.

Was I glad to see Buck return! My head was about to swivel off, trying to keep an eye on the cattle and watching behind for an Indian attack.

"Pa wants us to keep the cattle moving," Buck said. "One of us should keep looking behind. Keep your rifles handy. He said stopping wouldn't help and there's no place to hide."

Jerome A. Kuntz

"Ah...yeah, that's helpful. Did he even believe you?"

"How the hell would I know?"

That boy was getting testy. I was already leaving fingerprints in my rifle stock, so there wasn't much else we could do but hurry the cattle along.

We continued to make stops, and always with the same results. If it was Indians, why didn't they try to take the herd? Can you imagine what a long frightening night that was? We galumped along hour after hour, seeing little but the shifting white spots on the cattle.

To take my mind off the scary webs my brain was weaving, I decided to tell Buck more about the novel. "Don Co-yo-te and Sancho Pancakes," I began in a shaky voice, "stopped to rest and Co-yo-te's horse, Rozinante, ran off with a bunch of mares." Ever tried to tell stories with your heart in your throat? "The owners of the mares beat the stuffing out of Rozinante. That was too much for our heroes and they decided to avenge the shabby treatment of the horse by men they called Yan-que-sians. Only one problem: it was twenty to two. Not good odds. Hai-yaaaa! Move on there!" There wasn't much need of stealth; the cattle had been bellowing since we started.

"Why would two men without rifles take on twenty?" Buck asked, pretending interest.

"There were no rifles in those days."

"I know that. I just meant what if."

"Well, dadgummit young'un, if you knew that, why the devil did you ask? Anyway, they both got the hell beat out of them too. Sancho was so disgusted, he wanted to forget about being governor of his own country..."

And that's how we passed the endless hours. Pa or Roy dropped back to check on us a couple of times, and they heard the same hoof beats, so they had to believe.

"Halt! Who's out there?" Oh man, was I glad to hear that voice. It was Abe Nelson on the St. Joseph perimeter guard.

"It's the Comptons," Roy shouted. "Come and take charge of your cattle!" We waited right there; some of those men were bound to be trigger-happy. Several men rode out to circle behind the herd. Within minutes, our responsibilities ended. We replaced those same men on the perimeter and waited for daylight. After passing word down the line that we might come under attack, we strained to see if anything was out there. Buck and I were sure prepared to give someone a piece of our mind—or a dose of hot lead for that matter.

Foolishly, looking back now, Buck and I shakily told the townspeople that Indians had followed us the entire way, and we were lucky to make it through with our hair.

We waited. The eastern sky slowly turned from gray to a light blue. Finally, we saw two large black horses 200 yards away, grazing hungrily and staring blandly back at us. No riders. We thought it strange they had no saddles. If people meant harm, why would they pull off the saddles as if setting up camp? "Don't go out there," Pa cautioned. "Could be a trap."

Abe Nelson returned. Using his hand to shade his eyes from a blazing-orange sun crawling above the horizon, he peered out at the strange sight. "Well, I'll be hogtied," he said, a big grin stretching his face. "It's Popcorn and Barney. They must have followed you back to town."

Who the hell were Popcorn and Barney? By god, they were due for a good drubbing. It took a minute to realize he was talking about his other friendly work team from the corral next to the cattle. Evidently, they couldn't stand missing the fun and had broken down the fence.

Buck and I mounted up and galloped out to greet them, laughing all the way. We jumped off and patted their great shoulders. "Good boys, good boys," we told them. They snorted, stomped those pie-plate feet, and bucked us around like billy goats. Happy as puppies to see us again.

Imagine how clever those horses were: they wouldn't show themselves for fear of us sending them home.

Abe rode up and they were even more ecstatic to greet him. He must have treated his animals with special kindness. He didn't even need a rope—just clicked his tongue and they followed him quietly to camp in town.

The other men came back after driving the cattle to the butcher shop, and we left for town. All of us were dead on our feet and badly in need of a hot breakfast. Cleverly, we'd brought along all the coffee Abe had in the house. First we went to see Sheriff Baylor. It seemed he hadn't moved since we left—still sat with his feet on his desk. His job strain must have been terrific.

"Sorry to inform you men," he said. "Captain Charbonneau pulled out without you. I called him a dirty dog for leaving you behind, but he switched to French. Probably called me names in return because his filthy crew thought it funny."

"My god, man," Uncle Roy said with exasperation. "Couldn't you hold him?"

"How? At gunpoint? If I'd locked him up, his men along with other freight crews would have tried to break him out, forcing me to shoot a few. Those hide-hauling ruffians are tighter than bark on a tree. Besides, they spend a lot of money in town and that would come to a halt."

"Damn, we paid him passage to Kansas City," Roy said bitterly. "If we happen to catch up, we'll get our money back. I can promise you that."

There was no turning back for Uncle Roy. He had planned to chase the James brothers as far as Kansas City and wasn't about to change his mind. I figured it hopeless now, but kept my thoughts to myself.

Walking out of the sheriff's office, someone called, "Hey, Comptons, seen any Indians following you lately?" It was starting already. Buck, always the fighter, doubled his fists and started to say something, but Pa shushed him. A couple more wise guys snickered and didn't bother to hide it. Pa and Roy laughed good-naturedly—*they* didn't have hoof beats walking up their tail in the dark all night. I figured St. Joseph, Missouri, wasn't the place for us. We had to either find transportation to Kansas City or give up the chase.

Chapter 13

Pa liked to tell of pleasant days before the war when he and Roy, on horseback, chased two wolves close to one-hundred miles, from Northfield to St. Cloud in the dead of a Minnesota winter. At the time, few fences existed in the entire state. The predators had feasted on Grandpa Compton's cattle and several of the neighbors' stock. They were huge Canadian prairie wolves. Each winter, deadly Arctic blizzards drove starving packs south in search of food. "Manitoba raiders" is the name wary Minnesota residents gave to those cunning and vicious killers since way back in Territorial days.

Pa and Roy pushed their exhausted horses through deep snow until they could swap with another farmer, who was glad to see the wolves on the run. When those horses tired, they swapped again and pushed on. Far in advance, the gray-and-white ghosts loped on, saving their strength, instinctively knowing the lead required for safety. Even though out of range, Pa and Roy fired anyway to frighten them out of the country. When wolves find a meal, they'll always circle back for another.

The wily lobos followed in each other's tracks, making it appear that one wolf had escaped. They even swapped leads to save their strength in the deep snow. At times, they split up and pretended to circle back to Northfield—anything to throw off their pursuers.

The cold was merciless. During the day, snow reflected blinding sunlight. At night, a full moon showed a world of frigid poured silver. Pa was for turning back, but Roy wouldn't hear of it. It seemed nothing could stop him from getting those killers.

Late at night, the wolves entered the small settlement of St. Cloud. There the tracks disappeared in a profusion of dog prints. It was impossible to determine in which direction the lobos had left town. With their horses worn down and both men exhausted, Roy still hated to quit.

Finally, they turned for home and swapped back the horses on the brutal ride south to Northfield.

Now it was two-legged killer wolves. Roy hadn't changed. He stubbornly insisted there was a chance and the James brothers would get careless. He only got feeble arguments from us. Two dollars a day was still on our minds. After all, I was heading in the right direction and getting paid.

We rode back to Abe Nelson's camp to return the saddle horses. The kind man was a walking smile. There didn't seem to be anything he wouldn't do for us. Likely, he got top prices for his cattle and saved the expense of hiring drovers. Now, the townspeople could eat steaks until the military arrived from Fort Riley, Kansas.

We told Abe what happened. Would you believe he insisted we use his horses and tack, and leave everything at the livery on our return? Pa and Roy hated to be beholden. If anything happened to his property, it would take all our posse money to pay him back. We talked it over and figured we'd be back in two weeks. It was worth the risk.

Fortunately, Captain Charbonneau had dumped our gear and ammunition on the dock. We were now ready to resume the trail of the killers, cold as it was, but first we needed rest. We camped with Abe's family and left the following morning.

On the fifty miles to Kansas City, we stopped at every settlement and country mercantile. The brothers could easily have left the river. No one reported stolen horses, nor had they seen two men answering our description. We wore our badges openly and most people guessed who we were. By now, newspapers were loaded with news of the Northfield Raid, as the editors called it.

The first night, we camped alongside the road when it got dark. After a simple meal, Roy and Pa lit their pipes as we sat around the campfire. "They must have never left the river," Roy speculated. "Our only hope is that the *Fair Weather* will stop at Kansas City."

"What if they changed to another hide boat or maybe something faster?" I asked.

We waited for an answer as Uncle Roy stared off into the night. "I suppose then they'll get clean away," he said quietly. "They could even have gone southeast, back to Kearney, Missouri, their home town, but you'd think the Pinkertons would watch there. We know they killed two men in Minnesota. Who knows how many more died under their guns, and now they could go scot-free."

It appeared our chase was ending, and I planned my course after Kansas City. First the hard part: telling Pa I was going on to Cheyenne. Would Uncle Roy have enough money to pay me off? I badly needed cash until finding work in Wyoming.

Three days later, we rode into Kansas City. We checked for the *Fair Weather*. Several smelly hide boats were carelessly chained dockside, but not the one we sought. It was a drizzly day with stacked gray clouds hanging overhead. The weather matched our mood.

We found the sheriff walking the streets, and we dismounted to meet him. He appeared a hard thin man accustomed to getting his way. The stomped-over boots and greasy buckskin vest made him look like another buffalo hunter. Only the badge spoke of his authority. As he splashed toward us, he hawked something repulsive into the street, and then looked at us as if we'd slithered from under a rock. Not until later did we learn he was Sheriff Milo Culbertson.

"You boys are a little far from home, ain't cha?" he drawled.

Boys? Roy strained to be civil. "We're from Northfield and we're after—"

"I *know* who you are and what you think you're going to do. Those tin badges you're wearin' ain't legal down here."

"Oh, they're legal all right," Roy said, his face getting redder by the minute. "They robbed the Northfield bank in Rice County. I'm the elected sheriff there and these are my sworn deputies. If you like, we can contact your local magistrate and clarify that technicality."

"What I'd *like* is for you yankee doodle dandies to go back from where you came, or you might see jail before the James brothers. I don't cotton to bounty hunters."

Pa pulled up his Winchester and jacked a shell into the chamber. God, made my skin crawl. So-o-o, this was our first Johnny Reb. I thought we'd meet one sooner or later. Pa and Uncle Roy stood in front, Buck and I were winged off to the sides and a step behind.

My mind whirled. Roy had taught Buck and me plenty in the use of a Colt pistol and the rudiments of the fast drawn. I, of course, gravitated to the lunatic stage. Now was my chance. My hand

Jerome A. Kuntz

hovered over the imaginary notched walnut pistol grip. I knew I could take him. Buck was smooth as greased lightning; the Custer Kid, on the other hand, was faster'n blue blazes. I squinted my eyes and put on what I hoped was a confident sneer. Stealthily, I took a large step to my right...and bumped into Buck who'd stepped to his left. We glanced at each other in dismay, and quickly looked to the front. Now I was behind Pa, Buck barricaded behind Uncle Roy.

Roy said softly, oh so softly, "You sure have a right to try."

Sheriff Culbertson looked hard at each of us in turn. He knew the time for talk had ended. I scarcely breathed. Would he try to arrest us or run up the white flag? He sagged a little and the bluster left him. "Just watch your step in my town," he ordered, then spun on his heel and stumped toward his office.

There was a collective sigh as Pa uncocked his Winchester. We gathered reins and headed for the livery. His town? What malarkey! Ya, this was a swell start.

After dropping our horses off at the Kansas Livery, we found a room at the nearby Jackson Hotel. Lodging was pricey, so again Roy rented one room for the four of us. Anyway, it would be high living after all the camping out the last few nights.

The sheriff's bad humor was contagious: now we were grouchy and had little interest in looking for the James brothers. I knew Pa and Uncle Roy felt they were in hostile country. Do you remember before the Sioux Falls shootout when Roy was telling us about Missouri? They stayed in the Union, but thousands of its men had joined the Confederacy. Union soldiers hated a rebel who hadn't followed the lead of his own state. Twelve years earlier, some of these same locals might have tried to kill my father and uncle.

Buck and I decided to look the town over. First, we listened to strict orders to be back by six o'clock supper. Pa and Roy still planned to ask around in case the James brothers came into town. A long shot—why would they stop here, this close to their hangouts? Besides, we were in Clay County, the brothers' home ground, so it wasn't likely people would talk.

In a short time, it became plain that Buck and I had entirely different ideas as to what was worth seeing in a big city. Buck wanted

Northfield

to see the passenger steamboats. Not me. I'd seem enough of the Big Muddy. We agreed to meet at the Jackson at six.

The Farmers' Market near the docks was my favorite. Crops must have been good—overflowing vegetable stalls stretched an entire block. They auctioned cattle beyond that. Horses too. It was a busy place. People crowded the narrow walkways. Vendors bellowed rock-bottom prices whether anyone was listening or not. Several men stood before saddle horses and work teams, loudly praising the bored animals far beyond their obvious merits.

When I arrived back at the Jackson (late of course), Buck still hadn't showed. We quietly ate our meal in the hotel restaurant. The three of us, especially Pa, made repeated apprehensive glances out the front window at the fading daylight.

Finally, Pa broke the tension and said what we'd all been thinking. "We better start a search. Buck might have mixed up the location of the Jackson Hotel. Custer, you can check the streets and be sure to look in any stores that might be open this late. Roy and I will walk the waterfront. I know how that boy loves the river. Meet back here at ten o'clock."

I feared they'd blame me for not sticking with Buck, but no one mentioned it. They probably noticed how worried I was. I already felt something had happened to him. He was just too sharp; it wasn't likely he had lost his bearings.

Even though I knew it was hopeless, I searched the streets for my brother. When I arrived back at the hotel, Pa and Roy were waiting and looked as exhausted as I felt. "I hate to do it," Roy said, with a pained expression, "but we'll have to pay another visit to the law. Danged if that man doesn't grate on my nerves."

We found the hard-nosed sheriff at the Western Prairie restaurant. Pa took the lead. "We had planned to leave tomorrow, and got worried at dark when Buck didn't return to the Jackson."

Milo tut-tutted a few times before speaking. "You lost your deputy?" he said, as he started eating his steak and eggs. "I thought you were searching for Frank and Jesse."

Knowing Pa, he wasn't going to put up with that sarcasm for long. I didn't like the way Milo called those killers by their first names. What hope did we have of getting anyone to help us?

If Sheriff Culbertson had laughed, Pa would have been on him like white on snow. Then he would have thrown us all in the Kansas City jail. It turned out the Rebel lawman wasn't so bad after all. After asking several questions about Buck, he paid for his meal and we followed him to his office.

We stood quietly in the dark by the door as Milo fumbled with matches and a pokey lantern. While it brightened the room, he dragged chairs from the corners so we could rest.

The sheriff hung his felt hat on three-foot steer horns on the wall and dropped into a creaking chair. Handbills, curled and yellowed, decorated the walls. It didn't appear he had caught many of those desperate men. "Hopefully," he said, "Buck found something, or somebody for that matter, and completely forgot the time. Still, we've had some kidnappings here and may have to face that possibility."

"Kidnappings!" Pa exclaimed. "Who would kidnap a young boy and for what purpose?"

"Buffalo hunters. They've pulled men off the street before and dragged them to the slaughter fields. Likely, the ramrod tells them to skin buffalo or walk back to Kansas City. Of course, he promises them a share of the profits too. Three months later some of them have shown up in town, pockets stuffed with greenbacks and refusing to press charges. I'm sure the boss threatened them if they opened their mouths. More'n likely, they figure it was good luck and plan to go again with the same outfit. One thing for certain, it's the most money they've had in their entire lives."

"What if they refuse to work or try to run off?" Pa asked.

"Hard to say. I'm sure the bones of a few are bleaching on the prairie and people back home are asking, 'Why don't he write?'"

He even chuckled a bit over his own drab humor. I couldn't believe what I'd heard, considering the circumstances. I doubt he had any idea how callous he sounded.

"Are there buffalo crews in town, Sheriff? I haven't noticed any," Pa said.

Northfield

Sheriff Culbertson thought for a minute. "Only one comes to mind. Fritz Holtsinger has been here the last few days and was trying to hire skinners, but I wouldn't expect him to pull a stunt like this. He's a German immigrant and never made trouble before. Not like those other ruffians. Still, it's possible he's adopted the same nasty tactics as the rest.

"I don't like to paint people with too broad a brush, but those hide hunters are a dirty, unsavory lot; usually I'm glad to see them leave town. Greedy saloon owners like their money, but several had their places wrecked from brawling. When I throw their flea-bitten hides, no pun intended, in jail they soon pay damages and are back on the street. With more money than anyone in town, they think they can throw their weight around."

"This Holtsinger," Pa said impatiently, "Where can we find him?"

"That's simple. Check the Kansas Livery. Two blocks down on the left," he said, pointing. "You can't miss it. He's got a two-man crew. If their team and wagon's gone, they've left for the slaughter fields." He paused a minute, slowly wagging his head. "Tracking them across the prairie then would be a bugaboo. How would you know if it was the right wagon? Oh, and one piece of advice: don't try to overtake them in broad daylight. They'll be watching for pursuit an'll pick you off from a quarter mile with those Sharps 50s. Even the Indians learned the hard way and seldom attack buffalo hunters."

The sheriff was still talking when Pa ran out the door with us right on his tail. We knew where that livery was; our horses were there. There'd be hell to pay if we caught Fritz and his men holding Buck.

Now, I was more certain than ever that something bad had happened to my brother. If it wasn't Holtsinger, someone else must have dealt him off the bottom of the deck. So far we'd been lucky; now, like a bad dream, the things we could control were in short supply.

Chapter 14

Pa took the lead as we raced for the livery, boots drumming on the boardwalk. Uncle Roy puffed like a steam train, sweat popping from the big man's red face. All at once, Pa braked. I ran smack into Roy, but that stone blockhouse barely wobbled. The big man leaned forward with his hands on his knees. "Keep this up, Harlan, and the posse will be down to two," he gasped.

"Listen, men, we can't barge in there and flash badges," Pa said. "In fact, take them off, NOW! Likely, Holtsinger is a steady customer of the livery, and the hostler will clam up to protect his business. It always happens. I'll do the talking and pretend we're looking for work. That way, if he's gone, we'll have a better chance of learning his destination."

Fortunately, a different hostler was on duty from when we left our horses. We didn't care if he got wise later. He bought Pa's story as if it was a newly-discovered gold-map, especially when Pa looked at him in despair upon learning Holtsinger was gone. He'd pulled out hours ago and seemed in a hurry. Only one man was with him and they led another crewman's horse. Even so, the hostler wasn't much help as to where the German intended to hunt. The hide hunters followed the herds, and could be anywhere on the western Kansas prairie. He advised us to take the road to Lawrence and then pick the freshest trail west. "Listen for the big guns," he said. "Buffalo hunters gather where shooting is heaviest."

His advice wasn't heartening. At least we got a good description of them, their horses, and their wagon. Now we knew whom we were pursuing.

We thought it damning that one guy was absent. Could the missing crewmember be holding Buck? Maybe they planned to collect him on their way out of town. Probably a safe bet. Why else wouldn't the third man get his own horse?

Rescuing Buck was more important than trapping outlaws. We returned to Sheriff Culbertson's office and informed him we were pulling off the James brothers' trail. He promised to wire the

Pinkerton National Detective Agency that the outlaws were back in Missouri. Also, to include the fact a hangman's rope awaited the ex-rebels in Minnesota for murder and robbery. Milo couldn't have been more helpful. He even added more details of the hide hunters.

It was after midnight and too late to do anything until morning. Besides, no stores were open and we needed provisions. I would lead Buck's horse loaded with food and sleeping gear. When we found him, he would have a ride home.

The next morning, the rising sun warmed our backs as we crossed the wooden bridge over the Missouri, aiming for the slaughter fields. I took little pleasure in the prospect of seeing buffalo herds after all. Watching them being shot to subdue Indians wasn't the West I'd hoped to witness.

Heavy wagons carrying hides to Kansas City had cut deep ruts in the road. We passed several slow-moving freight wagons transporting goods west to settlements scattered across Kansas. Six-hitch oxen teams or mules pulled most at a snail's pace. The drivers shouted curses as they snapped cruel bullwhips over the straining animals' heads.

It depressed me that we'd failed to catch the James brothers. "What about Frank and Jesse, Roy?" I asked Roy, as we jogged along. "Are we giving up for good?"

"It's not so much that we're giving up. The trail's cold unless they steal horses or pull another robbery, but they're too smart for that. We'll leave it to the Pinkertons to smoke 'um out."

"Well...from what you told us about *their* chances, I'd say those boys are getting away with murder."

Roy slowly shook his head. "Only for a time, Custer. Only for a time. They were born to hang."

We could have reached Lawrence in two days, but it would have been pointless. Our horses were not toughened to such a long haul. Besides, the animals needed to stop and graze. We found a good camp on the Kansas River where grass was plentiful. It didn't take Pa long to fix a mulligan stew over a small fire, and it almost felt like another Minnesota hunting trip except no one talked much; we were too worried about Buck.

Jerome A. Kuntz

We were deep in Indian county—the Sioux, Cheyenne and Arapahoe. It was not a time to get careless. The least that could happen was to have our horses stolen. Being set afoot in that vast land could be a death sentence. At darkness, we stood two-hour watches, holding Winchesters. We were ready and they'd pay a heavy price if they tried for our mounts.

It was an agonizing night for dreams. I met Death in my sleep and he was real—real as the day of the holdup in Northfield: we rode the prairie and I saw what I thought was a pile of discarded clothing in the distance. Closer and closer we went, seemingly taking forever to reach it. Not until I dismounted did I realize it was a man's body lying face down. With sickening fear, I clutched the shoulder and rolled it over. It was Buck, staring sightlessly into a pure blue sky. I woke with a strangled throat, and I stared wildly about in the darkness. Roy was on guard, watching me. I must have cried out. I lay back down and tried to relax.

The nightmare seemed real; it felt like the voice of fortunes, certainly not good ones. Could dreams foretell the future? I consoled myself by recalling the words of Ebenezer Scrooge in Dickens' *A Christmas Carol:* "Are these the shadows of the things that *Will* be, or are they shadows of things that *may* be, only?"

The next day we stopped in Lawrence to look for Holtsinger's crew. There were no hide wagons parked in town or at the livery. *If* they came this way, and *if* they had Buck, they'd likely fear pursuit and move fast. That was a lot of ifs; I only wished we had more proof.

Knowing Buck, they had him tied in the bottom of the wagon and couldn't risk stopping in settlements. He would never throw in with a bunch of filthy hide hunters, no matter how much money they promised. That worried us. What would they do after realizing he wasn't about to work for them?

Occasionally, we passed homesteads—a few scruffy hens pecking in the front yard, a mule tied at the soddy door or working with the owner in the fields. We stopped at several to water our horses. It appeared they had little except dreams of better days to come.

Northfield

Did I tell you Dakota Territory was flat? I lied. It was right hilly compared to Kansas. Never had I seen so much sky, horizon to horizon at all points of the compass.

The second night, we again camped under the stars. We hoped Holtsinger wouldn't travel after dark. Dangerous country, we kept the cooking fire small and then quickly put it out. Two hours later, in total darkness, we moved a mile to a new campsite. No sense taking chances. Indians were bound to be angry over losing their buffalo, and they might have seen or smelled our smoke.

Pa and Roy had lived for years outdoors, and were able to identify dozens of stars and constellations. Many they had used to figure time and direction. Speaking softly, they pointed and drew with their fingers in the sky Aquarius, Cassiopeia (they called her "Cassie"), Leo the lion, Orion, Pegasus, Taurus the bull, Ursa Major and Minor—the two friendly bears, Southern Cross, Little Dipper and Big Dipper with their associated polar star, the mighty Polaris.

I doubted they were that interested in outer space. In their own way, they relived endless nights spent on Civil War battlefields from Gettysburg to Appomattox. I listened in awed silence; no, I couldn't break in on that. Could be those stars were an escape hatch from the horrors of combat.

Our bad luck held. The next morning, my horse came up lame. Likely it was a bad stone bruise. I couldn't detect any crack in the huge hoof. Those workhorses weren't used to such long travel. A few days rest might have cured it, but we couldn't stop. I switched the load and rode Buck's horse, leading the lame animal.

We continued to follow the deepest tracks, or, in some cases, where the grass was packed the flattest. Some wagons had cut off and a few joined from time to time, but we doggedly held on the main track. Our chances of missing Holtsinger increased the farther west we traveled.

The chiggers were bad—little red mites that burrowed under our skin, especially the ankles, and they itched horribly.

Two days west of Lawrence, we spotted a wagon with outriders, barely visible on the horizon. "Two men on horseback, just like Milo predicted," I said.

"Yeah, well, we'll have to get a lot closer," Pa cautioned. "Could be anyone out there."

"Pa! Look!" I had turned back and saw Indians racing towards us from the rear.

"Head for the wagon!" Pa ordered. We spurred our horses, doubling over on the saddle horns. The lame packhorse about pulled my arm off, but I couldn't let go of our supplies. We could use the strangers' wagon as a barricade. If we got close and those hide-hunters were friendly, they might even run the Indians off with their powerful buffalo guns. A weak hand to play, but it was all we had.

It wasn't to be. Another group from the south cut us off. We swung north, away from the wagon, frantically searching the flat prairie for a place to make a stand. Within minutes, another bunch came from the north. There was no place to run, and the workhorses had no speed, especially with one going lame. We could only swing in a large circle, desperately looking for a way out. Pa advised in his customary unemotional way, "Best not to shoot, men. Maybe they'll take our outfit and let us keep our hair."

It was hopeless so we stopped running, keeping our guns pointed down. They continued to circle, yelping and waving weapons. I noticed a few rifles, but most carried bows and quivers full of arrows. They had tomahawks and scalping knives in their belts. A few scalps swung from glistening lances. To their waists, they'd tied bull hide shields, brightly painted mostly in black with yellow snake designs. Long feathers and small animal bones bounced in their coal-black hair.

Could they ride! Scared as I was, I couldn't help admiring the primitive spectacle. There were few saddles, and those looked handmade—wooden affairs covered with buckskin. The majority rode barebacked.

Next, they raced their ponies toward us as if to strike, but wheeled at the last second with a piercing yell. Our horses shied and we fought for control; they were unfamiliar with the smell of Indians and their tough shaggy ponies. I had to release the lame packhorse.

Even to my unpracticed eyes, they didn't appear arrayed for war. No face paint was visible. Far behind this group walked their women, kids, and dogs. Some of the squaws' horses pulled travois, so it was likely they were moving teepees. Indians in those circumstances normally have little interest in battle, but they'll steal an outfit if the pickings look easy. I'm sure we looked weak to their large group.

Pa and Roy calmly sat on their rearing horses and I tried to copy them. I'd read enough dime novels to know never show fear when faced by threatening Indians. Easier said than done when your teeth are playing a march. Presumably, those rocking-chair Eastern authors had never enjoyed the playful antics of plains Indians.

Finally, they stopped and stared daggers at us. Two riders broke off and walked their horses our way. Both were naked above the waist. I assumed they were chiefs as they wore several head feathers. They stopped close by and used sign language. Roy, with signs and English, told them we weren't hide hunters and pointed to our guns to prove the point. One of them called over his shoulder and several braves rode closer, yanked our rifles from our hands, and then took Roy's pistols. They looked closely at the Winchesters, assuring themselves we didn't own buffalo guns. Likely, if we'd carried the Sharps 50s, it would have been over. How they must have hated those hiders!

They motioned us to get down. As soon as we were off the horses, they grabbed the reins and walked off, disdainfully looking back over their shoulders. Of course, they already had the lame supply horse in tow. I could only guess what they thought we were doing out there. Maybe they figured we were farmers because of the work team. That might have helped save us.

"Stand easy, men," Roy said. "We're still alive and that's the important thing."

"They were after the hide wagon until we came along," Pa said.

"Ya...that's the way I see it," Roy agreed. "They must have figured we were an easier mark. Like Milo said, they're scared of the buffalo hunters. If that's Holtsinger ahead, we probably saved Buck's life. I doubt *they* would have held their fire and surely would have been overrun."

The prairie was more uneven than it appeared. Within a short time, the Indians were out of sight. What a sick feeling, losing our entire outfit! Now we would have to pay Abe Nelson for the horses and tack. They took everything except the clothes we wore. Uncle Roy was sure glad he had left his saddle with the leg irons, chains, and padlocks back in Sioux Falls. He still lost two sets of handcuffs that remained in Abe Nelson's saddlebags.

The hide wagon was only a speck on the prairie. Pa looked ahead, using his hand to shield his eyes. "Way I see it, men," he said, "our only hope is to catch that wagon, and if Holtsinger's got Buck, we gotta take them."

"Without guns?" I said forlornly.

"Just hope they don't post a night guard," he growled, and started walking. We fell in behind.

This was bad. The same Indians could return, knowing we were on foot and unarmed. What if the wagon owner spotted the Indians and decided to push on until reaching the hunting grounds? We'd be exposed at least another day.

Not for the first time, you may recall, I longed for home. Better to be stomping clods on a Minnesota farm than in a lonesome grave on the Kansas Prairie.

Chapter 15

By six years of age, I had a gut-wrenching fear of Indians. Pioneers considered "benign neglect" a useful tool in child rearing—too much pampering definitely leading to rubber-kneed adults. Consequently, Indian and white atrocities were openly discussed before children. Who wouldn't be plagued with nightmares after hearing those blood-soaked stories?

Minnesota attained statehood in 1858, one year before I was born. Four years later, August 1862, the Dakota tribes revolted, left the Reservations on the upper Minnesota River and rampaged through the state, killing 500 settlers. It wasn't completely unexpected: we'd taken their world and they were trying to reclaim it.

The closest battle to Northfield was New Ulm, where Indians burned a large portion of the town before citizens finally evacuated.

Pa had been training troops at Fort Ripley for the Minnesota 1st Regiment Infantry, so we lived with Grandpa and "Grandmeny" Compton. Then, in early 1862, the 1st Regiment became attached to General George B. McClellan's Army of the Potomac. Pa and Uncle Roy left for years of fighting in Eastern Civil War battlefields.

My grandparents' farm was two miles from Northfield—too far to flee if we came under Indian attack. I remember some of those days and Ma has told us the rest. When Grandpa built his house, he installed plank shutters over the windows with space to shoot out. Drop two-by-fours locked them and the doors from the inside. They filled every water container they could find in case of fire, even the huge iron caldron used for pig butchering. Ma told of several knee-knockin'-scary nights when they fired out between the shutters at suspicious sounds. They wanted it known the residents were armed and ready to fight. Come and get it but you'll pay a price—that type of thinking. We had dogs and so did the neighbors; people wanted as much warning of attack as possible.

Even though only four years old, I still remember dogs barking in darkness, shadowy figures with rifles quietly walking the house in dim light, speaking in hushed tones. Back and forth, back and forth they paced, peering out the shutters.

Surprisingly, I don't recall any feeling of fear then. I suppose at that age, faith in adult care is unquestioned. Buck and Sadie slept through it all.

Our only news came from the *Minneapolis Tribune*, sometimes weeks old. The paper had brave reporters in the field, and even traveling with the military to cover the Sioux Uprising, as they termed it. Of course, there was no information as to which direction those bloody bands were heading. You can imagine the consternation adults felt, not knowing how far the Indians had ranged since their last battle.

It was over by December, lasting about four months. The army, along with banded settlers, drove the Indians deep into Dakota Territory and Canada. Minnesota hung thirty-eight Sioux before Christmas for rape and murder.

Even so, fear and rumors of more attacks circulated for decades. There was endless discussion and speculation about Indians in our 1870s school classroom. It seemed practically every student rejoiced in telling some bloody tale passed on by adult family members. Stories told and heard with childish mock terror in the innocent light of day took on new meaning in the dark of night. Little wonder I developed such fear of the Lakota Sioux.

It took many years before Minnesota felt safe again. Long after the time of the Compton posse, almost to the turn of the century, Pa stored Grandpa's old steamer trunk in the house, filled with hundreds of rounds of ammo for every gun we owned. Likely, neighbors did the same.

Now, here we were on foot on the Kansas prairie, unarmed and at the mercy of people I feared the most, knowing they were in the vicinity. Even our location was up for grabs. All we could do was doggedly follow the hide wagon, but in case it was Holtsinger, we moved with stealth. Only a fool would ignore Milo's advice: a Sharps 50 could reach out 600 yards. It was dark before we quickened our pace and closed the gap.

Walking in high temperatures without water was unbearable. Hard as I tried, I couldn't get my mind off the thousands of lakes and streams scattered over Minnesota. We had never carried water while hunting away from home; it was just a matter of scooping it up.

After midnight, we saw a large fire flickering in the distance. What *dummkopfs* would make a fire that big in Indian country? Not a lick of sense. It had to be the same wagon we spotted earlier. Even if it wasn't, we could at least obtain food and water.

I was learning Roy's tricks. "Suppose we pose as hide hunters, Roy?" I said. "We could claim Indians stole our wagon, team, and guns and ask to throw in with them."

He thought it over, or maybe he was just trying to humor me. "It might work," he said, "but we'd be relying on Buck not to give us away...if he's there, that is. Another consideration, you two look too much alike. No, I think that would be more risky than jumping them in the dark."

We crept closer, quiet as house cats and talking in whispers. It was spooky crawling in the tall grass after rattlesnakes had buzzed us twice earlier in the day. Sure enough, we watched a dark figure bring a food plate to someone under the wagon. It couldn't have been a sick or injured crewmember: there were three men walking around just as expected. Did they have a hostage tied between the wheels? I tried not to get my hopes up. The wagon was too far from the fire to see anything. Then we heard a thick German accent, just like plenty of newcomers in Northfield. It had to be Holtsinger.

We moved away from the campfire. When they fell asleep, we'd make our move. One of us stayed awake. I remember trying to locate constellations and then someone shaking my shoulder. "Time to go, son," Pa whispered. I sat up and rubbed my eyes, getting my bearings. Almost nothing was visible on that inky-black prairie, including the buffalo hunters' camp.

"How long has their fire been out, Pa?" I knew they hadn't pulled out or they would have called me.

"About two hours. They're either dumb as posts, or greenhorns, sleeping like that in Indian country."

We came together for a huddle. This time, Pa took charge. "Listen carefully, men. We'll only get one chance at this. Pick your man and get his gun. We don't wake anyone until we're all armed, and then I'll be the one to give the word. Everyone got that?"

We moved out slow as glaciers. They could have a night guard and we had to determine that first. None of them were moving. We could even hear faint snoring. What fools! We crept closer, stopping frequently to listen, our eyes straining to see in the darkness. When we got into Holtsinger's camp, we split up—each man moving toward a huddled form under a blanket. It was almost too easy. My man had a pistol lying next to his hip. I pointed it at his head, raised my other arm in the air according to our plan and silently waited.

Pa bellowed minutes later, "Get your hands out where we can see them! Now put them on your heads! No! Don't sit up!

"Buck! Is that you under the wagon?" Pa called immediately in case we were mistaken. No answer. My heart was in my throat. "Buck!" he yelled louder, "are you there?"

"Yeah...it's me. That you, Pa? Can you cut me loose?" He'd been sound asleep.

The one I watched sat up. Some people never listen. I swung the Colt, cracking him good in the head. He slumped back into his blanket. At that point, I didn't care if he was dead.

I hurried over with my knife and sliced Buck's wrist and ankle ropes, then ran back to cover my man.

"Hurry, Buck," Pa called. "Build up a small fire."

"Wait a minute," he cautioned. "They all carry skinning knives and Fritz has got a hide-out gun."

"Go get them," Pa commanded.

Buck was fast; he flipped the knives toward the fire pit and stuck Fritz's pistol in his pocket. "They're clean now," he declared professionally.

It was dangerous holding men in the dark. Buck soon had a small fire going. Within minutes, we had the prisoners tied across the wagon wheels. They were no longer a danger and we quickly doused the fire. None of them spoke, probably guessing we were family and prudently deciding to remain silent.

Daylight was coming fast. Buck handed us the water jug and then began rifling sacks and packing boxes for food in the wagon. There was even leftover stew and we ate it cold. O-o-oh, were we hungry!

It was scary watching Roy put away enough grub for three men. Keep in mind he was sneaking up on 300 pounds, and we'd walked all day and a good part of the night. That grizzly-bear stomach wasn't accustomed to churning on empty. At full light, we could make coffee.

Of course, we had to tell Buck about losing the horses, guns, and supplies. "Oh boy, you guys must have been scared," he said, wide-eyed.

"Scared? Naw-w-w-w! What are you talking about?" I said. "Still, it was lucky we all carried a change of underpants."

Everyone had a good laugh. Oh my, it was good to have Buck back. In the excitement, I forgot my dream; and, looking back, I'm glad I did. There was nothing to haunt me as our happy prairie days slowly wound down to a bitter-cold December.

It was our first chance to hear Buck's story. "There's not much to tell," he began. "I was on my way back to the Jackson—"

"What time was that?" I interrupted.

"Close to six. I was hungry and didn't want to miss supper—"

"Hey, Pa," I said, "we could have found Buck the easy way: just cooked a hot meal on the open prairie."

The kid ignored me and jerked his thumb in the direction of Holtsinger and his two crewman. "It was almost dark when those three dragged me into an alley and gagged me. I couldn't fight back much with three of them kneeling on me. Minutes later, they had me trussed up like a Christmas turkey and rolled in a buffalo hide. I heard the wagon pull up and knew I was going for a ride."

"Did they tell you why you were kidnapped?" Pa asked.

"Naw, not until days later. By then I could at least sit up and look over the side of the wagon. Only at meals were my hands untied. I had to hop around like a danged rabbit to take a leak. They kept promising me I'd be rich if I threw in and helped skin buffalo." He broke into a big grin. "I told them I was more likely to skin them than a mangy buffalo."

"Wha-a-a-t? You told them you'd skin them first?" I asked.

"Darn tootin' I did!"

We doubled with laughter. That boy had guts.

Pa didn't see the humor. I remember he was in a very dark mood. Soberly, he asked, "Did they say what they'd do if you didn't work?"

"Shoot me. I told them to go to hell…sorry, Pa. That's why they still had me tied. I figured there was nothing to stop them from killing me anyway after we had a load of hides."

Pa and Uncle Roy exchanged a look. Something passed between them—some understanding, and I got a cold feeling in my guts. I'd read in several Westerns that the only law west of the Missouri River was the gun and hang rope. Now I believed it. If those men had harmed Buck in any way, they would never have lived to see home and hearth. It was that simple. Pa and Roy had likely killed plenty during the war; three more wouldn't have weighed unduly heavy on their conscience. Never did any of us speak of it. There were things I could never discuss with Pa, but I think we all knew what would have taken place.

It was now daylight and Buck got the coffee going. Fritz and his boys had been gathering prairie chicken eggs during the day. Small buggers they were, but oh what nuggets of delight! We quickly fried up a few. Roy and Pa went over to check the prisoners. They looked plenty scared, especially Fritz. He was the boss and most responsible. "Where's your outfit?" he asked.

"Indians cleaned us out," Pa said simply.

"Maybe we can work a deal."

"If we let you live, the only deal you're getting is seeing the inside of Milo's jail. Likely, they'll hang the three of you."

"We didn't hurt the kid none," whined the one I'd cracked in the head. He'd been giving me evil looks since daylight. I guessed he was making sure he wouldn't forget my face.

"Shut up, Zeke! I'll do the talking," Holtsinger ordered, giving him mean looks. "We wouldn't have harmed the kid. If he refused to work, we'd have let him escape."

"Mister, he's my son, and his name's Buck, and how was he supposed to get back to Kansas City?"

Fritz was biting his unkempt moustache in fear. "There's full hide wagons leaving every day," he said. "He could have hitched a ride."

Northfield

Pa was getting madder by the minute, and I remember thinking this could go either way. "You see this pistol? If I hear one more lie out of you, I'll bend it over your head! You knew damn well he'd go to the sheriff with your names. Then how could you sell your hides with Milo waiting for you? If you had hurt Buck, you wouldn't be alive now to tell your filthy lies."

Their faces paled. Having an angry father with a pistol threatening your life isn't an easy listen. Fritz pleaded like a child caught with his hand in a cookie jar. "Take our outfit and let us go. All we need is our buffalo guns. We can throw in with other hunters. You can have the team, the wagon, and two saddle horses. There's plenty of food to get you four back to Kansas City. There are even three Colts and three Winchesters."

Pa and Roy were silent for a spell. Then Roy motioned us back to the fire.

"It's up to you, Harlen," Roy said quietly. "We'd have an outfit again without risking our lives guarding three prisoners back to KC. Buck's your son, and the call has to be yours."

I'd never seen a blacker look on Pa's face. I wonder even now if they would have killed the three of them if Buck and I weren't there. Pa looked off in the distance. "Get signed confessions from all three and a bill of sale for every item, or no deal."

"Don't worry, I will," Roy said. "I'll send the confessions to Sheriff Culbertson. They'll never be able to show their faces in KC again."

It didn't take long to make the deal. They were more than willing to do everything Pa demanded. They all carried identification, corny letters from girl friends or bills of sale, that type of thing; so we made sure they didn't use phony names. We threw their empty buffalo guns out on the prairie. Pa and Roy kept them covered while I untied the ropes.

Pa said, "If we ever see the three of you again, we'll figure self-defense and shoot you on sight. Agreed?"

They nodded their heads dumbly. "We sure could use our skinnin' knives," Fritz whined. He wasn't such a doofus after all. It was a safe bet those other outfits didn't need gunbangers. They'd want skinners.

Jerome A. Kuntz

Pa cocked his Winchester and set it square between his eyes. "Ten seconds. Move or I'll kill you where you stand," he said, ever so softly.

They moved. After snatching up their Sharps, they loped toward the slaughter fields and were soon out of sight.

That morning was the first time we heard the big guns booming like distant thunder. I was danged glad I didn't witness buffalo dying on those blood-soaked killing grounds.

It was time to go. Naturally, Buck and I each strapped on a six-gun, and Pa did the same. Roy just carried a lever-action Winchester, as the pistol belts would never have fit him. The two crewmembers had taken their spurs off to sleep, so Buck and I quickly made use of them. We loaded everything in the wagon and pulled out. Buck and I rode the saddle horses; Pa and Roy would swap driving the wagon.

Riding away, I had time to reflect. A miracle had taken place: how else could you explain finding Buck in that vast wilderness? Ya, I know, life is loaded with coincidences, but I couldn't believe this was one of them. Ma was religious…that much I knew, and she was praying for us. All my life, I believed we saw a miracle that day on the Kansas prairie.

Still, we faced a dangerous road ahead. How could we get back to the Missouri River without Indians robbing us a second time, or worse yet, taking our scalps?

Chapter 16

Neither Pa nor Uncle Roy had visited Kansas, but they heard plenty about it while freighting to Fort Laramie. They figured we were two days north of the Santa Fe Trail, and from there, a short distance east to Council Grove on the Neosho River.

Mrs. Hollins in Northfield had everyone's attention in school when she spoke of the famous western trails. Facts and figures. That's what she believed in. The more she could pour in our ears, the less time we had to get into trouble. I well remembered her telling of Captain William Becknell, "The father of the Santa Fe Trail." His entire party was dying of thirst on their first freight-caravan crossing. Some of the men stumbled away after seeing mirages—lakes in the sky, that type of thing. They never came back. Finally, the remaining men shot a buffalo, and while butchering it, found its belly full of water. It saved their lives. They followed that buffalo's tracks back to a water hole.

The teacher's lessons always prompted cowboy and Indian battles when I was in the lower grades. Later on, we settled for make-believe gunfights, a bystander declaring a winner. I can't ever remember a time in my youth when I didn't long for the Western life.

In 1825, the Osage Indians signed a treaty at Council Grove giving the United States government right of way across Kansas, and the Santa Fe Trail was born. It was probably a one-sided deal—19th century Indians not widely celebrated for shrewd land transactions. The road stretched close to 800 miles from Independence, Missouri to Santa Fe, New Mexico Territory.

If we reached Council Grove safely, we could join a freight caravan heading east. Indians seldom bothered a large force, especially traveling under treaty. It was reassuring to learn several military forts along the route protected traffic in both directions.

Oh, was it great to be on horseback again! Buck and I scouted all sides. If Indians were near, we wanted to know it long before they attacked. We were lucky the first time. Now, traveling with the wagon, they would consider us hide-hunters. No one needed to warn us to stay close to the wagon or risk being cut off. We quickly abandoned the black powder and pounds of lead that the hiders carried for their Sharps 50s, and even threw away the skinning knives.

Our new mounts suited us fine. After riding a sleepy work team from St. Joseph, we thoroughly enjoyed these trained saddle horses. They weren't afraid of new country and loved to run. We hadn't bothered to ask the surly previous owners the horses' names, so we gave them new ones. I finally settled on Monty for my palomino. Buck went with Cowboy for his big black.

Luckily, the water barrels contained enough until reaching the Neosho if we used it sparingly. Food was no problem either; there was plenty in the wagon to last a month.

Joking with Buck again felt good! Now I could enjoy traveling. Understandably, he was more wary than before—even waking at night to check with whoever was on guard. During the daytime, his eyes continuously swept the horizon for Indians. I figured he'd relax when we reached the Council Grove trading post.

"What happened to the Jameses?" Buck asked me as we plodded along that first afternoon. "Got them buggers hung yet?"

"Naw, we had to drop the chase and waste time looking for you. We did the next best thing though—sicced the Pinkertons on them, so I doubt they'll enjoy their usual haunts for a spell."

"Good...how about Don Co-yo-te and Sancho Pancakes? Still steppin' in cowpies?"

"Hard telling. Indians are reading the novel now. Dang it! If only I'd carried it in my pocket instead of on my rig. Anyway, I don't see why Old Don bothers with that young strumpet, Dulcinea. The boy's getting on in years—going to seed, as they say."

"Sap's dried up?"

"Ya, that too."

Now the devilish grin. "Getting a bit long in the tooth?"

"Will you stop! He still likes girls but not an actual relationship."

"No relationship, eh? Hmmm...not as half-baked as I thought."

"Buck, my boy, it's lucky not everyone feels that way or these saddles would be empty." I didn't miss many chances to play the wise older brother role.

Northfield

Other than the continuous fear of Indian attack, it was a glorious two days of travel over rolling brown-grass prairie, more interesting than the corn and oats fields of Minnesota. It was late September—nights were cool and the days comfortable for roaming. First frost was around the corner.

We paralleled dozens of buffalo trails, not unlike our cow paths back home. Almost all rambled north and south. The rivers generally flowed west to east and averaged 20 miles apart, so the buffalo could easily migrate with the changing weather and grass conditions and never be far from water.

Buffalo wallows were common, created by two bulls when a glitch developed over mating rights. With the vast herds, you'd expect plenty to go around, but who knows the appetites of bull buffaloes. Those wallows were handy natural basins, trapping water for our stock. Interesting too was finding a dead bull in a wallow. Evidently, the supposed loser ran off while the victor stayed behind, bleeding to death from his injuries.

"Hey, Buck," I called, "what do you suppose that buffalo was thinking before he died?"

"Oh, I don't know. *The girls are cute but are they worth dying for?*"

"Yeah, could be, but my guess is: *You figure I look bad? Bah! You should have seen the other guy.*"

It was the first time we saw mirages. We expected huge blue lakes in the sky, but certainly not massive animals with flagpole legs. How about several gigantic mountain men majestically riding horseback across the heavens? Believe it! Buck and I both saw them. We turned around to tell Roy and Pa, but the sky was empty when we looked back. I wondered if all history is recorded in the atmosphere, ready to view when the conditions are right. That experience brought to mind Sadie, Buck, and me lying on the grass at home, or on the low, long-sloping roof of the chicken coop pointing out cloud-animals.

By the end of the second day, we reached the Santa Fe Trail and turned northeast. Our four sighs of relief were likely heard in Kansas City. It wasn't a single track, but a mile-wide crisscross of deeply cut ruts. It had been in use for 70 years, and freight caravans strayed great distances to feed their livestock.

We rode for hours in darkness, following the ruts, and hoping Council Grove was east of where we met the trail. Finally, yellow squares of light appeared in the distance. Talk about a welcome sight! Soon we were at the trading post, but we didn't go in. The horses were tired and needed feed and water, so we settled on an open place near the river and set up camp. Oh, did they roll when we removed their saddles and harness.

There was a mule train in town (we heard their raucous celebrating in the saloon), but we decided to wait until morning to meet the wagon boss.

Pauley Higgons was the train leader, and lived in Independence, Missouri—a short Mexican shaded by the biggest straw hat I'd ever seen. He looked like a tree trunk wearing a straw umbrella. Heaven knows where he got the name. Coming up with a nickname would have been too easy so we didn't bother.

The round-trip had taken them four months and Pauley was anxious to get home. After a long night of boozing, the other skinners resembled buzzard bait and didn't appear in a hurry, but Pauley didn't care how they felt—he was ready and goaded them on. Most of them looked like Northfield's town drunk as they harnessed the mules.

Pa asked Pauley for permission for us to join the train. "Yeah, you can travel with us," he growled, rolling a massive after-breakfast quid to the opposite jaw. "Even better," he added, pointing to Buck and myself, "those two men can scout ahead." Then he took a closer look and spewed a slough of brown juice into the street. "Jumpin' Jehoshaphat," he muttered, turning on his heel. We soon learned that he used that expression a lot.

That was fine with us. We were already puffed up with our scouting duties coming south. Buffalo Bill couldn't have done better.

While the skinners hitched mules, Buck and I sat on the same oak stump where the US government and the Osage Indians had signed the treaty. They intended to preserve that landmark for future generations to mark the historic event.

Northfield

"How far ahead you want us, Mr. Higgons?" I asked, just before the train inched out of Council Grove.

"Never let us out of your sight. If you see an *Indio,* high-tail it back, *amigos,* so they don't get your hair."

We both yelled as we touched the spurs and slapped the horses' rumps. "Wa-a-a-a-ah-hoo-o-o!" Great rooster tails of dust swirled off to the side. Yeah, Brother Buck and The Custer Kid were on the job. Everyone could relax. About a mile out, we stopped to let the horses blow. It was all for show. There wasn't much to see, just the Santa Fe wagon tracks winding generally northeast over the flat prairie stretching to the horizon, wavering in the early fall heat. An hour later we rode back to fill our canteens. Take it from me; scouting is thirsty work.

Later that afternoon, my brother and I rode side by side not far from our own wagon. I thought I'd better caution the young kid. "Buck," I said. "Stay close to me. I've heard stories about what Plains Indians do to prisoners."

He was ready and looked at me blankly. "Really now, what do they do? You don't have to sugarcoat it."

"Bury you in an anthill up to your neck in the boiling sun."

"No, I'm serious, Custer. Just tell me the truth. I can handle it."

"Tie you to a post standing up and strip all your skin off, one slice at a time."

"Listen, fella, I'm almost your age. If these people are rude, I think I have a right to know. I might get cap—"

"You boys tend to business out there, and keep your eyes peeled!" Pa yelled. He must have overheard us.

Twelve massive wagons made up the caravan, each pulled by eight mules or the same number of oxen if Pauley had used them, but he considered them too slow. The loads were much heavier traveling from Independence to Santa Fe than the opposite way, so we were actually moving quite fast compared to the outward trip. Sometimes, if the loads reached close to 5000 pounds, they hitched up as many as twelve mules. The freight wagons had to be constructed heavier duty than the prairie schooners used by early settlers on the Oregon Trail.

Jerome A. Kuntz

    We continued to ride completely around the train, keeping a sharp lookout for Indians. Travel still seemed mighty slow to me; I couldn't imagine going the other way. How hard could scouting be, moving at that pace? It would take years to reach Missouri. Now I really missed my *Don Quixote*.

    The country was greening up as we moved east. In the distance were groves of cottonwoods hugging nameless creek banks. Sloughs became plentiful, loaded with cattails, red willow, and squabbling redwing blackbirds. Prairie birds were everywhere. I spotted several not commonly seen in Minnesota: red-tail hawks, sage hens, blue grouse, and prairie chickens. Still, back home we had a few they probably never heard of either, like the loon, coot, and lordly blue crane, which the locals called "sloughpumpers." It was pleasant watching for wildlife and not having to worry much about hostile Indians.

    Those Muleskinners were a hairy, smelly, seasoned bunch; and it took an iron hand to control them. Pauley fit the bill. When he said how far they would travel in a day, he meant it, not caring what they thought. I heard later, one or two had challenged his authority and came out a little worse for wear.

    Occasionally, there were breakdowns with the heavily loaded wagons, requiring a stop for repairs. Most of the skinners were veterans of several crossings and came prepared to handle any emergency. They carried screw jacks, spare canvas, brake-blocks, iron wheel rims, wood spokes, felloes, linch pins, tar buckets for greasing axles, extra wagon tongues, and singletrees. A couple of wagons even carried small logs in case someone had to fashion a new axle-tree.

    They even brought live chickens for meat and eggs. I felt right at home listening to those cock-a-doodle-doos from morning to night from the many confused roosters.

    There were no free rides out west. Everyone had more work than he could handle. We stood night guard along with the rest. It seemed, ever since we left home, someone was shaking me and growling, "Guard duty, Custer" or "Time to roll, Custer."

    I counted twenty-four men on the train, including another scout about my age. He rode everywhere: off to the sides, to the rear, and several times he cut between us and the train. One evening Buck and I met him outside the circle of wagons. "Name's Johnnie Ketchum," he said, bored and jabbing a hand in my direction. "Santa Fe." He had coal black hair, sunburned face and hands, and his clothing was so faded, he seemed part of the landscape. I felt green talking to this veteran of several crossings.

"Custer Compton…Northfield, Minnesota," I said, trying to copy his nonchalant style.

He suddenly looked interested. "Jesse James robbed a bank there," he said.

"Yup, I saw him do it. Uncle Roy is the sheriff of Rice County and we're his posse."

"You're *those* Comptons?" he exclaimed with a grin. "Hey man, I guess Jesse got clean away."

Perfect. The newspaper article again. Would we ever live it down? Amazing how news traveled in a vast land with so few people. People didn't throw newspapers away like today. They carried them around the country, passing them hand to hand until they fell to pieces. Everyone was keenly interested in events back in the States.

"The Pinkertons are tracking him in Missouri now," I said grimly, and let it go at that.

"Oh, okay then…we can all feel safe. By the way, who taught you guys to use a Colt?" he asked, looking bored again.

"Sheriff Roy."

"Yeah, well, lawmen aren't noted for being fast."

"Hell you say. Hickok was lightning," I protested.

"True, true, but most lawmen aren't that good; they got the law on their side and their specialty is funerals, not fightin' fair. That aside, both of you are carrying your guns too low."

"How so?"

"Look here…notice where my pistol grip is,"—he stood natural, arm hanging down relaxed—"it should be halfway between your elbow and hand. That way, you won't have to lift so far before you fire. Watch."

He was so fast I couldn't see how he did it. Buck and I unloaded our guns, hitched them higher, and gave it a go. It made it easier but we weren't close to his speed.

"Oh, horsepucky!" he said, shaking his head hard. "Don't pull, cock, and fire. Do it all at the same damn time. Pull the trigger first and let the hammer drop when you're on target." He emptied his Colt first and then demonstrated.

"What about aiming?" I asked. "You're not high enough to use the sights."

He looked at me like I'd gone simple. "Stop to aim and your toes will be straight up," he said, smiling without joy or humor as if remembering something. "Just point the gun like you're pointing your finger."

So that was the beginning of our friendship. We spent the evenings swapping stories while he continued to give Buck and me lessons. Of course, he never tired of hearing of the Northfield Raid, appearing overly impressed by that snake, Jesse James.

Johnnie had that cool dry look of the pool and card sharpies that drifted through Northfield. They wouldn't stay long; likely, they soon noticed a shortage of pigeons in such a small town and drifted north to Minneapolis where the "pickings" were bound to improve.

When I told Johnnie my plans for working Wyoming cattle ranches, he was all for going along. It seemed he didn't really belong anywhere, and simply drifted about the country, looking for new opportunities. We made plans to travel together after reaching the Missouri River. The train out of Omaha was the fastest way west so we decided to meet at the depot.

I couldn't help noticing Johnnie never came near our wagon, and especially avoided contact with Uncle Roy. He seemed a loner anyway, preferring his own company except to play poker. I wondered if he was a wanted man somewhere, something I never would have questioned before becoming a lawman. Surprising how a bitty piece of tin makes one suspicious of human nature. People out west didn't ask much about anyone's past. Most accepted who you said you were and judged you by your actions. I figured if Johnny had a troubled past, he'd spill the beans sooner or later.

Now Buck was talking about going too. Wow! Did I do my best to squelch his plans! Ma was already going to take it hard when I didn't return. I promised to find him work in Wyoming when he finished school, but he didn't say yea or nay. He always was hard to figure. I was only two years older than Buck, and maybe that was the problem. He hated taking my advice. If the span had been greater, maybe I could have exerted some influence in the end.

Twenty miles a day was tops for the mules pulling those heavy loads. I already decided hauling freight wasn't my cup of tea. Luckily, it was early fall and nice for traveling.

The evenings were the best part of the day. First, the skinners allowed the mules to graze. Then, before dark of course, they brought them inside the circled wagons. That's when the men relaxed, told stories, and even dug out battered guitars and harmonicas. Along with "When Johnny Comes Marching Home Again" and "Oh! Susanna," they sang a song clearly of their own making called "The Santa Fe Trail" to some vaguely-Irish melody.

Been on the Santa Fe Trail all my life,
Never had time to find me a wife.
Bacon is apoppin' on a red-hot griddle,
Listen to the man playin' that fiddle.

Gonna ride to heaven in my old wagon,
Singin' and smilin' but I ain't braggin.'
One wrong turn and I could end up in hell,
But at least I could stay in one place for a spell.

Cookin' hot by day and freezin' at night,
The way the crew smells is a holy fright.
Flapjacks in the mornin' and beans at dark,
Haulin' freight all your life is sure no lark.

They added verses all the way to the Missouri River, and I wish I'd written them down.

The poker games were endless. At home, we played draw poker with pennies or buttons, depending on our rise and fall in fortunes. The muleskinners preferred a variation called Jacks Back, a form of lowball where the lowest ranking hand won the pot.

Days passed in monotonous repetition. We were tired of the pokey train and looked forward to striking north for Council Bluffs when we crossed the Missouri. That's where I decided I would leave the posse.

Only one incident marred the usual pleasant days and added to my worry about throwing in with Johnnie. We were relaxing around our fire one evening when shouting erupted down the line. Grabbing our Winchesters, we hurried over to learn the cause of the commotion. A small crowd had gathered. Johnnie and a Mexican mule driver, called Julio, faced each other across an overturned card table, the pot carelessly spilled in the dirt. I watched in fascination, fists locked and loaded. Yeah! This was right out of our Western novels.

"You dealt off the bottom of the deck, *Señor.* I seen you plain," Julio said, an evil grin on his scarred stubbly face.

"That's a lie," Johnnie protested with little emotion. "If ya can't afford to lose, best not to play."

"Not a matter of losing, more a matter of how a man loses." He whipped a gleaming knife from his belt. "Maybe if I take your ears, *muchacho*, you'll learn not to cheat."

Pauley barged his way to the front of the circle. "Jumpin' Jehoshaphat! You *bastardos* know the rules against fighting on my train!"

They ignored him. It was obvious things had gone too far. Pauley was smart enough not to get between them.

I never took my eyes off Johnnie and still missed what happened. He stood calmly, campfire flickering red-and-yellow shadows on his sunburned face, his pistol pointing at the Mexican's belly. Johnnie didn't bother to answer—he just waited with the cocked pistol to see what the Mexican would do next. Each man held a trump card, but who would throw in his hand first?

"Oh, a gun slick, eh, *perrito?"* sneered Julio. "That's what I expect from your kind." Julio was a fool; I could see Johnnie's thumb holding back the hammer. The mule driver didn't seem half as threatening as a moment earlier. He prudently slipped his knife back in his belt and stalked off.

Johnnie looked sad as he scooped up the cash, appearing to have little interest in it. Anyone could see it wasn't the first time he'd pulled a gun on someone. Even so, it was to his credit that he hadn't shot in self-defense.

For some reason, I didn't feel like talking to him, instead I walked back to the fire with my family. I turned back once to see Pauley lecturing Johnnie while shaking his finger in his face. I doubted he was listening.

Chapter 17

Was it great to see the Missouri River again—the famous waterway of the Corps of Discovery only seventy-five years earlier!

How incredibly fast the country had changed. Yellowstone National Park was already four years old. President Grant, Civil War hero, signed the bill creating the park in 1872, four years before the Northfield Raid and Custer's Last Stand. On the Fourth of July, we celebrated the Centennial of the United States and it was the biggest parade ever put on in Northfield.

I never expected such rapid development in my lifetime. Each generation must find the vast changes in living surprising. In the 19th century, we assumed people would use horses indefinitely.

Seeing that old river was like finding your best friend. The sun was dying in the west, spreading sheets of red and gold over the swift-flowing current as it aimed for the Mississippi at St. Louis, Missouri.

We said goodbye to Pauley and a few friends on the east side of the river. I sure didn't envy those muleskinners. As soon as they unloaded in Independence, they'd pack for another four-month round trip. The shine of the road would tarnish quickly after endless days of slow, hot travel. Pauley may have made out fine, but his drivers would never get ahead. They talked of starting their own train, but liquor, women, and gambling appeared to eat up most of their pay. Those men led a hard life, but were still a good-hearted bunch.

It seemed strange to be finally turning for home—everyone but me, that is. I had asked Johnnie to ride with us, but he shrugged it off, saying Pauley could only pay him in Independence. True or not, he still avoided Uncle Roy, and that worried me.

Days later, we again stopped in St. Joseph. Fortunately, the Indian scare had evaporated and people had gone back to their farms. Wouldn't you know it; the soldiers from Fort Riley never arrived. I wasn't surprised. It had been the same in Minnesota: hundreds of pioneers died in the 1862 Sioux Uprising before the army bothered to take a stand. Likely, the Pottawatomie got bored and went home, finding the St. Joseph area even duller than the Reservation.

Northfield

Abe Nelson, generous as always, refused payment for his lost horses and tack until we reached home. That was fine with Pa and Uncle Roy. Now they had transportation back to Sioux Falls. They planned to sell the wagon and team there after reclaiming our horses from the Sioux Falls Stables and Grain for the final leg home.

We knew several people in town and their inquiries were endless: Did we catch Frank and Jesse? Where were they now? How could we let riffraff buffalo hunters kidnap Buck? Why didn't we bring the kidnappers back to face justice? Worst of all were the questions about why we didn't fight the Indians to keep our stock. I say, when faced with those impossible odds, most people would have acted the same. We were still alive so Pa must have made the right decision. If it's a choice of dying instantly or gamble on losing your outfit, what would you have done? I was there and saw our chances. What did those villagers know? You weren't there either. After General Custer's defeat, you'd expect people to remember the results of overpowering odds. It wasn't long before the questions sounded like accusations.

Remember how we mistakenly assumed Abe's sleepy work team was bloodthirsty Pottawatomie Indians? Townspeople hadn't forgotten either and the friendly ribbing continued. Likely, St. Joseph idlers, warming the boardwalk loafer benches, are still joking about it.

Pa now seemed anxious to get home; maybe he was worried about Ma and the farm work. We left St. Joseph next morning before daylight. The days melted together and passed quickly as we plodded north. South of Council Bluffs, I knew the time had come to tell Pa. If I went home, within days the West would be pulling me again. Even if Wyoming didn't pan out, well…Northfield was still a nice place to live. I rode forward to come alongside Pa and Uncle Roy on the wagon seat.

"Pa, I won't be going back to Minnesota," I said, trying to sound determined as possible. "I'm crossing the river into Omaha. Johnnie and I are catching the train for Cheyenne." Just like that. I knew if I asked permission, it'd be a no-go.

He didn't answer right away, just pulled his old cloth cap off and scratched his head, something he always did when faced with a problem. Roy was silent too, staring at the two of us in surprise.

"Where do you plan to meet him?"

"Omaha train depot. We can be in Wyoming in three days."

He finally turned to look at me, and he didn't look happy. "It'd be best if you came home first. Then you can think it over and decide if it's really what you want. Your ma will kick up a row if you don't come back with us."

"Sorry, Pa, but my mind's made up. You know I've been talking about it for years." I glanced at Roy. "I only hope Uncle Roy has enough to pay me off for posse duty."

Roy didn't respond, not wanting to take sides. We traveled a ways in silence. I looked back at Buck but he turned away. Nobody wanted to look at me.

"Is it Jasmine, son?" Pa finally asked. "Is she the reason you're going?"

I hadn't really settled that in my own mind. I just didn't know. If I hadn't met her, I might have waited another year. "Maybe, Pa. That might be part of it, but now that I've come this far, I want more than ever to see the West before it's gone. You saw those hide boats. What will disappear after the buffalo are gone?"

He didn't respond. Everyone knew the answer. "She's a nice girl, Custer. I know Jenny would like to meet her." We traveled a spell in silence. Then he added, "You better go and ride with Buck. I want to talk with Roy."

Buck stared at me when I dropped back beside him. "Jeepers, you really *are* leaving," he said, as if finally realizing it.

"Darn tootin' I am." I don't think he believed me until then.

I thought Pa might call me forward again but he didn't. He and Roy were in earnest discussion.

We made a subdued camp that evening near the river. No discussion of job duties was necessary; we all knew the routine. Nights were getting colder the farther north we traveled. I could easily visualize the frequent hints of winter in Minnesota by now. After watering the four horses, we staked them to graze. Pa didn't say any more about my leaving—no one did. When daylight drained away, we placed our duffel rolls under the wagon, not even bothering to build a fire. Hardly anyone spoke. Occasionally, a team and wagon passed by, or even a single rider, but it was generally quiet except for a few frogs honking along the riverbank. I could even hear Pa's pocket watch ticking away the short time I had left with the Compton posse.

For the first time in my life, I felt like an outsider in my own family. They would gladly return to Northfield, content with their lives, but figuring it wasn't good enough for Custer; he wanted something better.

We reached Council Bluffs at noon the next day. Pa pulled to a halt in a wagon yard next to the old wood bridge connecting Council Bluffs to Omaha. Redbrick commercial buildings were scattered over several hills across the river, the painted advertisements on the walls clearly visible. I wondered now if Pa might refuse permission to go. No matter what happened, that bridge was my gate to the West and I was going through.

Buck and I tied our mounts to the back of the wagon. I waited until Pa waved me to the front. My knees felt like water. Understand, I'd never been more than a mile from at least one family member and here I was, aiming at the unknown, with or without Pa's permission.

Pa spoke first. "Custer, are you sure you want to do this? We want to make Missouri Valley tonight and Sioux City in a few days, so we can't stop long."

"Yes, Pa," I said, staring at the dirt. "My mind's made up and Johnnie's waiting." Empty words now without a nickel's worth of conviction. All the excitement and anticipation I'd felt so long seemed to have melted into apprehension.

He looked at me a spell and then turned back. "Buck, pack him enough food for several days and tie it behind his saddle," he commanded. I stood open-mouthed. I had planned to start west on foot, as far as the train station anyway.

"We want you to take Monty," Pa added.

"But you'll need him to pay Abe Nelson."

Pa flapped his hand in my direction. "Naw, take him. With this swell team and heavy-duty wagon, there'll be plenty to pay him off. If need be, I can even sell your horse in Great Falls. Oh, and Roy has enough to pay your posse wages."

Uncle Roy reached over with a roll of bills. Then he shook my hand and turned away. I guessed it to be more than I was due, and it was; Pa and Roy had both added their own cash.

"One piece of advice," Pa said.

"Yes, Pa?" I said, expecting something fathers always say when their sons leave home.

"Watch out for Johnnie. If you find he's not a square shooter, get shuck of him fast."

"Aw, he's all right. Just stubborn and a little quick-tempered."

Pa's forehead creased with worry. "Maybe," he said, "but there might be more to him than you figure. Promise me, Son."

"I will. You don't have to worry about that." We shook hands and I walked back to pick up Monty's reins. Buck was there and I punched his shoulder. He pushed me back hard—too hard I thought. He mounted Cowboy and walked ahead. I had no idea at the time what he was planning.

I climbed on Monty and rode off. "Custer!" Uncle Roy called. I looked back and he was waving me over. "I'll have to ask for your badge, Deputy," he said. I solemnly handed it over; and it felt like the final break with my old life, my family, and everything I held familiar.

Monty's pounding steel shoes echoed down that lonesome river as I raced over the wood bridge. I knew I'd have to stop and look back—dreading what I'd see. Sure enough, they all waved wildly, like Ma and Sadie had back in Northfield so long ago.

The Custer Kid raised his hand high, touched Monty's ribs, and galloped into Nebraska. His great Western adventure began.

Chapter 18

You probably noticed I began by telling Pa we were taking the train to Wyoming. After our Kansas Indian encounter, I figured he'd have a conniption if we traveled some other way. He took it pretty calm, don't you think? Pa had left home quite young too, so I doubt it surprised him greatly. Keep in mind, this was 1876; youngsters grew up fast and got on with their lives. In Northfield, I had friends married by seventeen and that wasn't unusual. It was odd when they continued school together, same as before they tied the knot. If Mrs. Hollins thought it strange, she didn't let on. She appreciated anyone trying to learn, no matter his or her circumstances.

Johnnie was waiting at the depot. He sat on the station platform, swinging his legs over the edge and wearing the same lop-sided grin, not a care in the world. He didn't act surprised I showed, or that he cared one way or the other. I guess I felt the same about seeing him after Pa's warning.

The Union Pacific wasn't pulling out until the next morning, but we bought tickets to Cheyenne and paid freight on two horses. The ticket agent gave us the numbered car to load Monty and Feathers. Even though the railroad provided hay and water, we had to do the feeding. That was all right with us; they had to be unloaded and exercised anyway, and this way we knew they were well cared for. It wouldn't do to reach Wyoming with a lame horse.

We didn't bother with a hotel for that night; instead, we just camped along the Missouri River. Johnnie even had with him a hook and line and a frying pan. He fashioned his own pole and we had catfish for supper. After eating he dug out a white bag of Bull Durham and rolled cigarettes for us. Like an old salt, he poured the tobacco and pulled the drawstring tight with his teeth. We sat on the riverbank, smoking and watching the Big Muddy race for Kansas City. It was the first time I told him about Jas.

"Custer, you old dog, are you going to marry up with her?"

I felt uneasy telling him anything personal, but he had a down-home grin that would encourage anyone to blab. "I might, but hard to say if she'll have me." Actually, I hadn't spent a lot of time thinking about it. I was too young to start wearing the lead bell. I just wanted to know her better. "How about you, Johnnie? You ever come close?"

"Naw. There ain't hardly any women out West anyway. About the onlyest ones I've seen are either married or saloon gals."

"There's always mail order," I said. "White from the States or Chinese from California." It was just something Raife Windom, the traveling salesman had told me.

"Yeah, reckon so if you got the scratch."

"Anyway, Jas has a high school education and a teaching diploma from a correspondence college in St. Paul," I said. "Maybe she'd like someone better educated."

"Au-u-u-uk, take it from me, girls don't care none 'bout that," he said, waving me off. "Most just want to see if you got enough sand to raise a family. Pansies need not apply."

"Well, I'm not afraid of work—been doing it all my life," I said defensively.

"Work is for suckers," he said, lying back on the grass with his fingers laced behind his head. "When I get a stake, I'll try saloon gambling. Lots of guys make a living at it."

That declaration didn't impress me. I was old enough to know gamblers were broke at least half the time. Pa's warning continued to niggle me. Cowboying was hard work. Smooth hands and easy talk wouldn't hold a job, provided you got one in the first place. I knew Johnnie was a slippery card player; now he was a lazy bones to boot. I wondered if he could "cut the mustard" after all.

Whom do you suppose was at the train depot the next morning? Buck! Sitting there and holding Cowboy's reins as if we were expecting him. Actually, I was glad to see the rascal, but my first thought was he had run off and I'd be caught in the middle.

"Looking for someone, kid?" I asked. "I doubt Frank and Jesse are heading west on the Union Pacific—not unless they're planning to rob it."

"If you don't own this train, I'm going west too."

"How'd you keep Cowboy?"

Northfield

"Same way you got Monty. Pa said I could go as long as I took the train. Which car you got the horses?"

"Not so fast, buddy. How do I know you got Pa's okay?" He handed me a scrap of brown butcher paper. I didn't look at it too close, but I could see it was Pa's scratching, and hard to cipher as usual:

Custer
I'm only letting Buck go west knowin I can count on you
To watch him Make sure he contacts Jasmene to continue his schoolin help him to find work write Ma and me when you reach Cheyene.

Pa

I looked up at Buck. "You won't find Ma's biscuits and gravy in Wyoming. In fact, nothing's gravy about the West."

The boy grinned from ear to ear. "Ah-huh…and this from a guy who gets the willies if he doesn't see pancakes six mornings a week."

"Nice shot, John Wilkes Booth, but have you read this?" He hated school and I couldn't see him going back to classes on my say-so.

"Yeah, I read it," he said, sulky like. "What of it?"

"Then you're still in school like Pa says."

"Oh, you're funny. What comes next? How much would a woodchuck chuck if a woodchuck would chuck wood?"

"Now listen. We'll look for Jas at her school after we get you settled in." I was already sounding like Pa. Sure, I was glad to see Buck, but now, besides finding work I was supposed to keep him in school.

"Get me settled in? What about you?"

"Cattle are right scarce in Cheyenne. Hard telling how far I may have to go for work." He had no response to that. As always, when he didn't like what he heard, he just didn't answer. I doubted he would stay in school if I left town. Still, I would try, just as Pa requested.

"You got money for the fare?" I asked.

"Ach, no. Pa said you had enough for both of us."

Jerome A. Kuntz

"Oh boy, is he whistlin' Dixie! Rich as Solomon, I suppose. And how are we supposed to live when we get off the train?"

Buck shrugged his shoulders and looked off. He never worried about something until he bumped against it.

"C'mon, Buck," I said, exasperated. "Let's get you a ticket." What else could I do? I wondered why Pa let him ride off broke after being so generous with me. I hesitated to ask Buck, thinking it would sound like I was bragging about my special treatment.

We waited on the platform as the train screeched to a halt, steam whistling from its belly, black smoke pumping. The horses were already loaded on a sidetracked rail car. The wind had wound up and we squinted against the dust, caps jammed down on our heads. Johnnie ignored the blow, even with his large felt hat. Later, I learned cowboys bought their hats tight as tree bark so they would stick on in a tornado.

The first hours were exciting, but after we reached the open prairie and an end to shabby homestead soddies, it seemed we could get off and run faster. I didn't look forward to three full days and nights of that. Still, it was classy compared to riding a swaying, bouncing, dusty Smells Hardgo coach.

Everything went peachy until Gothenburg: we made our scheduled stops; fed and exercised the horses; bought food along the way at family groceries near the train depots, and had a high old time. It was too pricy to eat in the dining car, but that was all right—by now we were used to the hobo life. Even my initial homesickness had withered. Buck coming along had something to do with that. At least I was no longer in danger of becoming the prodigal son. That story always bothered me some, and I didn't want to end up like that. Finally, I was living my dream: going cowboying and riding the range with my swaggering heroes who had "tamed the West."

I started singing. "Ein pro-o-o-sit, ein pro-o-sit...!" Buck joined in. Most folks in Northfield were of German descent, like the Comptons. Both my grandparents had grown up in Germany, so we understood some of the language. On happy, rare occasions when a polka band played at the town hall, that was the most requested song. Sadie, Buck, and I had the lyrics memorized. "Du Leigst Mir In

Herzen" ran a strong second. Oh, we loved our polka music! Square dances were popular too, but infrequent—not enough fiddle players and callers. Those dances were so funny; the callers would bellow "allemande left!" or "do-si-do right!" and we'd always turn the wrong way.

Johnnie screwed up his face and covered his ears. We sang all the louder. The other train passengers shook their heads and laughed. The world seemed in good spirits.

The train slowly screeched to a stop in Gothenburg. Several folks stood with boxes and shabby suitcases, anxious to get off. "Say guys," Johnnie said, "check on Feathers, will ya? I got a friend in town I'd like to see."

That surprised me; we didn't have time for visiting. "Hey, we're only stopping for a half-hour," I objected. "That's cutting it mighty fine to roust someone who doesn't know you're coming. Why not go with Buck and me to see the Pony Express Station?"

"I've *seen* Pony Express Stations," he said, sarcastically. "Besides, I know where he lives."

He jumped off when the train stopped so we couldn't argue. Buck and I checked the horses and threw in a little more hay.

We soon learned the Pony Express Station was too far out of town for us to see in such a short stop. That was a disappointment, but we could still visualize riders passing through right where we were standing. How often had I read stories of Buffalo Bill riding with the Pony Express! Imagine, he was Buck's age at the time. Surely he had come through this very station. Pa said people who used the Express wrote one way on a page, turned it 180 degrees and wrote again to save weight, and, of course, postage. At five dollars per half ounce, you couldn't blame them.

Old Bill was our hero for sure: buffalo hunter for the Union Pacific railroad crews, scout and guide for the U.S. Fifth Cavalry, and winner of the Congressional Medal of Honor in 1872. Just the previous July, he fought his most famous Indian battle, killing and scalping the Cheyenne warrior chief, Yellow Hand.

We made it back to the train and waited anxiously for Johnnie. This was Sunday and we were both in fine spirits.

Jerome A. Kuntz

Oh, how we admired Sundays in Northfield. The other six days were much alike: farm work or school, bustle, and chores. Sundays were quiet as high-noon owls, and we'd relax the way Bubbles and Mr. Moses did every day. Ma fried chicken after morning church, and then we had a long afternoon to play games, visit friends, swim and fish in warm Minnesota lakes, or explore. Sometimes, Pa would harness Prince and Jack and we'd pile in the buckboard for a visit to Northfield's penny-candy and ice cream store. Of course, in winter we hitched to the sled, pulled blankets over our legs, and were on our way. The special treat excited even Ma and Pa. Sadie was a notorious sweettoother, and always the first through the front door. No one worked; it was just something you didn't do. The Lord rested on the seventh day and we respected his lead.

Within minutes, the conductor bellowed "board!" and picked up the little wood step, pulling the door shut behind him. Johnnie was nowhere in sight. We hurried from window to window trying to spot him. Several passengers wagged their heads in disbelief. Danged fool! I'd told him there wasn't time. We were moving! Then I spotted him, running pell-mell for the train. "He's coming, Conductor!" I shouted. The conductor frowned disgustedly, but he opened the door so Johnnie could swing aboard.

"Boy, that was close," I said. "Did you find him...or her?"

"Sure did and pretty as ever," he said, grinning like he was simple.

"Oh, he was eh? Did you hug him goodbye?"

"Shut-t-t-t up," he said, taking a playful swing at me.

"Okay, okay, where did you meet *her*?" I said, emphasizing the last word.

"Ah...Santa Fe. She was an army brat, passing through town with her father."

I noticed the hesitation. He didn't offer any details and I didn't much care anyway.

In a few hours, we reached North Platte. This stop was longer and it would be a good place to exercise the horses. We decided to unload them and put the saddles on. As soon as we stopped, I spotted two lawmen wearing stars and watching carefully as we got off the train. Johnnie hurried out the door with his big hat jammed down over his forehead. We quickly saddled and rode from the train. Johnnie kept looking back as if expecting someone to join us.

"What's the matter, Johnnie? Those lawmen looking for you?" Buck asked, never being one to mince words.

"Shut your mouth, kid!" he snapped. I thought Buck had only been kidding and didn't deserve that treatment. My temper perked up.

"Let's ride to Cheyenne, Custer," Johnnie blurted. "We can make better time than this danged slow train."

"Are you nuts?" I said in dismay. "We already paid through to Cheyenne. Why ride the horses into the ground for nothing?"

He kept looking back at the depot as if worried about something. "I think it's best to leave the train, that's all."

"Why?" I asked. He was lying about something. "Are you in trouble?"

He patted my shoulder, as if trying to reassure me. "It's nothing, really. I needed money so I borrowed a few dollars from the Gothenburg General Store."

Slapping his hand away, I shouted, "You dirty thief! You robbed someone!"

His face went cold, anger flaring in his dark eyes. Guess he didn't like me accusing him of something so stupid. We dismounted and met behind the horses. "So what if I did, you dumb hick!" he said. "I'm not wastin' any more time on you." He pushed me off balance.

"I'm dumb? You're the one those lawmen are after."

It was just as Pa warned. He must have seen through Johnnie right off, but not me—oh no, I had to find out the hard way. I was so mad, I tore into him without thinking. Within minutes, we were rolling in the dirt, pounding each other's face. It seemed whoever was on top got in the most licks. We jumped to our feet and I swung at his head, but he ducked under. I tried to kick him in the stomach. Johnnie was fast and used the old trick of grabbing my boot and flipping me on my back.

Evidently, fisticuffs wasn't his style. Before I could get up, he clawed for his six-shooter. I'd made a dumb mistake: fighting a man still wearing a sidearm.

I heard the click of a cocking gun behind me. "LEAVE IT BE!" Buck commanded—his gun already leveled at Johnnie. Roy had taught us when you pull a gun on someone, you'll do well to look anxious to use it.

Buck looked anxious.

Johnnie slowly folded his arms over his chest, his face paling. It might have been his first experience on the sour end of a gun barrel. I continued to stare at my brother—shocked at what he looked eager to do. "Buck?" I said. I turned back to Johnnie. "You better ride out …now!"

Johnnie backed toward Feathers, leaving his hat on the ground and never taking his eyes off Buck. Then he climbed on and slowly walked off, pretending he wasn't scared. He rode east, likely giving Gothenburg a wide berth. He'd be back on Pauley Higgons' crew within a week. Bet on that.

"Good riddance of that buttinsky," Buck said, dropping his six-gun back in the holster. "Some day that worm's gonna finish on the end of a vertical rope."

We stood quiet for a spell, making sure he didn't double back. I turned slowly to Buck, "I just want to know one thing kid," I said. "Did you outdraw Johnnie or were you ready for that?"

"I drew when he touched his gun."

I let out a long low whistle. "Woo-whee! That was close," I said. Remember my telling you about Buck's natural ability with guns?

"I've been practicing," he said, matter of factly. Not bragging.

"Well, we can't go back to the train."

"No…no, we can't do that," he agreed mournfully.

I thought it kind of Buck not to raze me for traveling with a thief. I was dumb not to see through that ne'er-do-well. Still, it was spooky how ready Buck had been to use his gun. To this day, I believe he came within a whisker of shooting Johnnie. By the look on Johnnie's face, I think he believed it too.

Like Pa, I didn't have the stomach for that kind of violence. During a rare moment, he had once told me, while slowly wagging his head, "I hated the war, the daily killing. Politicians could easily have prevented it. Slavery couldn't last in America and would have ended soon anyway. Six hundred thousand dead and the South destroyed forever." It was a long time before he mentioned the war again.

I can't say I agreed with him. I didn't believe those Southern states would ever give up their slaves, but I understood his bitterness.

We rode off a ways into a grove of trees. If someone on the train implicated Johnnie, the law could rope us in too. It wouldn't be long before they questioned the conductor; he had seen Johnnie coming from town on the run. Now there might be lawmen at every train stop, and it was too risky to go on.

Finally, the train pulled out, tophat-stack pumping smoke as it strained for speed. We watched until the red-and-yellow caboose shrank to a dot on the hot, empty prairie.

"Well...ain't this a fine kettle of fish." Buck drawled, sleeving sweat off his forehead.

I tenderly explored my bruised face. "Yah-h-h, but keep in mind that things might be worse. We could have been pulled off the train with Johnnie, and be on our way to jail." It was a habit in our family: if things fall apart, invent an even worse scenario. Come to think of it, my classmates were the same, so maybe it's a Minnesota thing. Just a way of playing the cards you're dealt.

"Still, it makes a body feel guilty, hogin' all the bad luck in this ol' whirl," Buck said. He had Hennessey down perfectly.

I had to chuckle a bit even though that was the lowest I felt since Buck's kidnapping. Here we were, close to a town we couldn't visit, a couple hundred miles from our destination, and possibly, hostile Indians roamed the plains watching for favorable odds. On top of that, we'd be broke by the time we made Cheyenne. All because I wanted company on my journey west.

There was nothing for it except to ride the remaining distance. We couldn't get lost; just follow the Union Pacific tracks into downtown Cheyenne. We'd get supplies at the next settlement.

Hours later, we reached a country trading post. This was the old Oregon Trail, but there wasn't much traffic since the US government completed the Transcontinental Railroad in 1869. We thought it strange to find such an isolated business until we found Indians hanging about, eying the trader's supplies with amazement. Several furs hung on the walls: coyote and wolf pelts, and some prime beaver plews. You ought to have seen the fine elk skin! It would come in handy in Wyoming winter. I guessed that's how the owner made his living—trading supplies for pelts. The trader, who looked at least part Indian, sat wrapped in a shabby blanket and paid us scant attention. That was fine with me. Those lawmen in North Platte might decide to track us, knowing we were aiming for Cheyenne.

We bought two army plates, two army forks, and two army spoons, a frying pan, Lucifer matches, and a small coffee pot. Along with canned tomatoes, we laid in a good supply of jerky and dried apples. Of course, we needed a scoop of Arbuckle's coffee beans. Hopefully, we could hunt along the way. Prairie chickens were plentiful. I wished we could afford a couple of Hudson Bay trading blankets, but they were far beyond our means. I did find a good second-hand rain slicker. Buck was lucky; his came with the horse. My last item was a black flat-crowned cowboy hat, much like the travelers wore on the train. The hat along with my boots and spurs made me feel like a salty hand of the West, even though it was a long road from the truth.

Someone had tacked a crude map of the Oregon Trail to the trading post wall. By rough measurement, it was 225 miles to Cheyenne. Figuring 25 miles a day, we expected to be in Wyoming by the middle of October.

Johnnie had really thrown a monkey wrench into our plans. Now it was even more important to find work. With these added expenses, we wouldn't last long in Cheyenne. Imagine, our train fares thrown away. We had to reach Wyoming before winter and the ranchers quit hiring. Any more danged flub-ups and we'd be dining on grasshopper soup and chicken-fried prairie dogs.

Chapter 19

We camped on the side of the trail that first night and pushed on early the next morning. Long sloping hills rolled to the far horizons. Very dry too—just sagebrush interrupted by battered cottonwood trees desperately clinging to life near the stream banks. The country appeared to have seen precious little moisture, and more than its share of sun and wind. Dust devils spun mindlessly over an empty prairie.

At noon we slowly overtook a family in a covered wagon. Since the opening of the Transcontinental Railroad in 1869, most people moving west loaded their belongings and traveled by train, so I figured these folks were poor.

Robbie Bradford and his wife, Judy, weren't having an easy time of it. Plenty of ribs showed on the four mules pulling the wagon, and no one in the family had to worry about getting fat. Their two youngsters, Phoebe and Elliot, ten-year-old twins, had their mother's red hair and freckles. They stared like owls at us, especially our low-slung six-guns.

We stopped and had a little picnic with them, sharing each other's food. Buck and I gobbled Judy's crusty baking-powder biscuits while the Bradfords especially enjoyed our jerky. Hard to say what kind of meat it was when still roaming free, but it wasn't a concern. One thing we all soon learned on the prairie: eat anything that doesn't move. If it does move, shoot it, then eat it.

Their wagon wasn't in much better shape than the passengers. The canvas bonnet sagged through a couple of broken hickory hoops, the wheels squeaked, and the steel rims looked loose enough to fall off. If those wheels weren't soaked in water soon, they'd be rolling on wood. Even that was a temporary solution: once the felloes have shrunk from the dry climate, it's best to pull the steel rim, heat it in large fire, and tack iron barrel hoops around the outside of the felloes to make the wheel larger. Then install the hot rim. It will contract when it cools, pressing on the felloes, driving the loose spokes back into the hub. Then it's like a new wheel. That's how we did our wagons at home. I doubted we could find enough firewood here for that.

Jerome A. Kuntz

They had traveled with a group who decided to homestead in western Nebraska, so they'd only been alone for two days. "We planned to live off the land more than we did," Robbie said. "Now we're running low on supplies." His high-pitched voice wavered with worry. With his weak chin and rounded shoulders, he looked like a person who expected few breaks in life. They came from West Virginia, and things must have been bleak for them to go west with so few reserves.

"We have a homestead waiting in Wyoming that my brother filed on," he continued. "The longer we take getting there, the more chance someone could take it over. We're already past due on meeting the residency requirements."

"Couldn't your brother hold it for you?" I asked him.

"Naw, he has his own to worry about. Besides, you're supposed to build some kind of house on the property and break the land. With his own family to care for, he hasn't time to hold two 160-acre homesteads."

There didn't seem to be anymore I could say, and he looked so depressed that I decided not to mention it again. Evidently, Wyoming homestead laws were stricter than Minnesota.

Buck and I were anxious to reach Cheyenne. We hung back a ways trying to decide what to do. I clearly remember the prickly heat on that particular morning and the unnerving stillness. No birds sang. Not a breath of wind. We were edgy, standing in our stirrups, looking around and wondering what was coming. Have you ever had that feeling of trouble and later kicked yourself for not acting?

"What do you think, Buck?" I asked. "Travel with these folks or go on ahead?"

He hesitated a moment, watching the covered wagon rattling on ahead. "They seem house-mouse poor," he said. "Maybe we ought to stay close...at least for a day or two."

"I figured you'd say that. There's something else too: this weather's spooky. Humidity's a killer! I tell you, something isn't right. Remember our bad storms in Northfield, especially the one that took the roof off the school's bell tower? It was just like this before it slammed us."

Northfield

The northwest horizon kept drawing my attention. If something hit, we'd see it there first. Buck was doing the same—looking all around. I knew he was searching for shelter. Storms had caught us out before, but Pa and Uncle Roy felt them coming, giving us time to prepare. Those guys knew weather. Usually, it was during late-fall hunting. At least in Minnesota there were plenty of trees acting as windbreaks and places to stretch a canvas shelter of some kind.

It started with a dark pencil line on the horizon, just above the short-grass prairie. Slowly, it climbed straight up, not appearing to come closer. Higher and higher it raised, black as coal. No wind—just a blocking of the sun and gathering darkness. You wouldn't believe how vulnerable you feel on an open prairie with a noon sky turning to night. I thought of digging a hidey-hole. "Buck, we got to find a place," was all I said. He knew the danger as well as I did.

"Already looking," he said, standing in his stirrups.

I automatically checked his saddle. He still carried his lariat, so we had two. Most Western men owned them whether they worked cattle or not.

We needed high ground in case of flooding and trees to tie down the wagon and picket the stock. Horses and mules aren't nearly as bad as cattle, but they too can panic. Lightning at night, terrible thunder, and bad hail can make them run before a storm. We heard plenty of runaway stories back home. If we didn't hitch the team to something solid, it could happen here. That could shatter the wagon and cripple the team in the bargain.

Finally, we spotted cottonwoods a half-mile off. Likely that meant a stream of some size—a chance of flooding, but what choice did we have? Those rolling hills were bald. Now the wind gradually started to walk, and it was turning cold. Hail was on its way! Could we make it on time?

"Robbie!" I shouted, pointing south. "We gotta make those trees before the storm hits." He nodded his head hard, stood up, and slapped the reins. The twins squirreled off the driver's seat and into the wagon. Judy tied down her poke bonnet and turned back to keep dust out of her eyes. Even at a dead run I knew it'd be close.

Buck and I spurred ahead, loosening our lariats as we went. Upon reaching the trees, we tied them off to stout trunks. Robbie pulled up and we waved him between us. We quickly cinched the wagon box down on both sides. Those ropes were strong enough to throw 1000-pound cows from a galloping horse; they'd hold. "Hurry, Buck, tie it tight. We gotta help Robbie," I shouted.

He grinned back at me, seemingly not bothered by the danger. "Okay, hotshot, but I'm not standing here counting my money. Hey, don't forget our rifles on the saddles."

"You get them and remember to throw our blankets in the wagon. I'm about done and I'll help Robbie. It's almost on us."

I soon finished and ran to Robbie. He had already unharnessed three of the mules, dropping the harness on the ground, not even bothering to disconnect the trace chains.

"Robbie, what are we tying them with?" I asked.

"There are more ropes in the wagon. Get Judy to hand them out."

He had several short, stout ropes, so he was well prepared. We roped the mules, along with Cowboy and Monty, to the lee side of the largest trees. We didn't bother with halters, just knotted the ropes around their necks. Leather halters will never hold a panicked animal. Saddles were left on to protect from hail, but with loose girths same as we did at home in storms.

Just as I had feared, a small stream passed through the trees, but we had to chance it. Flooding wouldn't compare to having the wagon tumbled across the prairie.

Oh, that wind was cold. Judy elected to stay in the wagon with the twins. She snapped tight the "puckering strings" at both ends of the canvas top and knotted them securely. The cottonwood trees were already bowing and creaked with the pushing wind. The three of us dived under the wagon for protection, pulling a heavy canvas over our heads.

As soon as the rain hit, the sky switched from black to a dirty gray. The horses and mules were hot after their run and steam rose from their backs before the wind pulled it southeast. Next came hail—large as eggs and rattling through the branches, pounding everything, including the animals. They yanked back, testing the ropes. When they saw little chance of getting free, they instinctively bunched together as much as their short ropes would allow.

The roar of hail through the trees was like nothing I had heard before, even in the damaging windstorms in Minnesota. Our visibility was no farther than the stock. Branches cracked along the creek, snapping off and sailing downwind.

That wagon rocked with the wind. Even though the ropes were tight, a little play was bound to develop. It had to be scary for Judy and the kids. Still, it wasn't a picnic underneath either. Hail bounced into our backs, and the canvas wasn't much of a block.

The animals looked miserable with their heads down and water pouring off exposed backs. The mules got the worst of it. Monty and Cowboy had saddles to protect them. Some of the stock had bloody eyes from the wind-pushed hail.

After a spell, the hail and wind slowed but the drenching downpour continued. Buck's coat was wet and his cloth cap hung like a rag on his head. He gazed mournfully over a prairie of white ice. "Well men, aren't we living now?" he said.

I tipped my head forward to let water and hail drain off my hat brim. That rain felt as cold as melt from our icebox back home. "I swear, Buck," I said, "if you were served your last meal before hanging, you'd bitch if the steak was well-done instead of rare. Maybe you're missing that classroom after all."

"Sure, miss it like a toothache."

Oh yes, the boy needed a little cheerer upper. "Hey guys, know why the farmer's pig had a peg leg?" I asked.

"I know," Robbie claimed. "Three legged pigs are cheaper than pigs with four legs."

"Damn sure I wouldn't pay as much, but that's not the answer."

"I got it," Buck said. "The pig was too much to eat all at once, and the farmer couldn't afford ice."

"Close but no cigar, and if you got it, don't give it to me. No, the farmer claimed only a fool would eat a hog all at once that tasted that good."

"Good one, Custer," Buck said. "Makes you wonder how many body parts a good-tasting hog can spare. Now listen to mine. You

Jerome A. Kuntz

remember those huge meals served after funerals at home, at least six different kinds of hotdish?"

"Don't I though! Washed away a lot of regret for the loss."

"One farmer says while rubbing his big belly, 'Oh, what a swell feed *that* was! Just too bad Uncle Amos wasn't here to enjoy it.' Another old-timer answers, 'Yeah...and to think the poor guy only missed it by three days.'"

Much later, the rain finally stopped. We duck-walked from under the wagon and then stumbled around trying to work out kinks from being cramped so long. As far as we could see, it was white with hail—at least four inches on the ground.

To our dismay, the canvas wagon bonnet was flat. Not even the roof hoops were intact. We went to the back and lifted the canvas. Three scared faces stared back at us. Judy and the twins were okay; the linseed-oiled canvas kept out most of the rain, and they'd crawled under the beds when the hail began. I didn't blame them for being frightened. That wagon had pitched hard against our tie-down ropes. Luckily, they held fast.

Robbie quickly peeled back the canvas so they could get out. They were okay but shivering. Elliot had a snap-down cap like Buck's and Phoebe wore a thick red scarf, but their coats looked small and threadbare. Farming in West Virginia must have been even costlier than Minnesota.

The youngsters smiled with relief. Judy had tears running down her cheeks. She came over and gave us both a big hug, saying, "Thank God for your showing up. I know He sent you to save us."

I wasn't sure how to take that. I couldn't quite grasp the idea that Buck and I were instruments of the Lord, but anyway, the hug was nice. It was the first since Northfield. Why not make the most of it? Then Robbie shyly shook both our hands and thanked us too. It was turning into quite a day, and I was glad we had decided to hold back. Some people would have puffed up and needed a new hat, but not the writer of this book. Now I wondered if we were seeing the last of the bad luck or was this only a start.

There were plenty of chores before it got dark. The Bradfords had a small stove in the wagon, so we mended the roof hoops and pulled the canvas back over the top. Judy soon had a fire going to dry out bedding and cook supper. Prudently, they'd carried firewood and buffalo chips under the wagon, so at least she had dry fuel.

With the fire crackling, we all crowded into the wagon and sat on steamer trunks. That gave us a chance to warm up and dry out a bit before going to work. It was dark in there and our faces glowed red from the reflected flames. Everyone chattered like sparrows about our narrow escape. Then we all went back outside; Judy needed room to cook supper.

After giving each of the horses and mules time to drink in the creek, we staked them out along the bank to graze on the tall grass poking through the hail. We hadn't even had time to cover the harnesses before the storm; so now, after wiping off mud and water, we hung them in the trees to dry. The last job of the night was filling the water barrels from the stream.

Before the storm, I had told the twins about Ma and Pa, Sadie, and our two bloodhounds. Probably my fault but something got lost in translation. Now, back in the wagon again, confusion sprouted like winter-stored potatoes.

"Does Sadie sleep outside?" Phoebe shyly asked me.

"No, not often. She has her own room." I thought she meant does Sadie like to camp out?

"Does she run around at night?"

Sadie? "Not that I know of, but it wouldn't surprise me. Naw, just kidding. Pa wouldn't let her do that anyway."

"Ours did and Daddy tied him up. But where does she eat?"

Tied who up? I wondered. "Ah-h…at the kitchen table."

"At the *table*?" Elliot exclaimed. "Where does she go to the toilet?"

Why not the table? Was someone here speaking Chinese? "Same as the rest of us—the outhouse."

They exchanged looks and then both stared at me with the strangest expressions. I waited. Sweet Phoebe's little mouth was working, but nothing came out. Finally, she said in a small voice, "Our Bennie had his own supper bowl."

"*Wa-a-a-ait!* Is Bennie a dog?" I asked. Two freckled red heads bobbed swiftly. "No, no—Sadie isn't our dog. She's Buck's twin sister." Big smiles on both faces. You could see they liked that. I thought the parents would fall on the floor, they laughed so hard.

Judy had put together a fine stew and then set a well-blackened coffee pot on the stove. It was our first hot meal since leaving the train. We pitched in like Manitoba raiders. Judy baked what she called "johnnycake." At home, we simply called it corn bread. The twins laughed when they saw Buck and me dunk it in coffee. I thought everyone did.

We never again discussed riding on ahead. As always, we were sticking to something once started, so there was no question of striking off on our own. We turned our whole kit and caboodle of food, plates, and stuff over to Judy. Now, the six of us were like a little family, and everyone seemed happy with the arrangement.

It'd been a busy day and we were ready for sleep soon after dark. Of course, there wasn't room inside; so Buck and I cleaned ice from under the wagon, spread a spare canvas, and rolled out our blankets.

Stars glared from the heavens. At least the storm had moved on. No one could travel under those conditions, so we didn't bother with a night guard. I fell asleep to the sound of yipping coyotes, wondering what tomorrow would bring. With the condition of those mules, I wondered how we could climb the muddy hills.

Chapter 20

There was no hurry the next morning. We woke a bit stiff and sore and were grateful for morning sunshine. The hail melted fast, but then we had the mud to contend with. If we went on, it would be slow going at best.

Judy made a fine breakfast of bacon, fried potatoes, and fresh-baked bread. Unbelievably, she'd set the dough to rise near the stove the night before. Funny, isn't it? I forgot several things about our trip, but not the cooking. The wagon was too small, so she and Phoebe handed out plates of hot food. Never have I enjoyed a breakfast more.

We borrowed soap and towels from Judy, and even though the stream was icy, it felt good to wash up.

Another advantage came with the storm: Robbie had plenty of wood wedges he'd brought from home. First, we pounded them between the steel rims and the felloes and sawed off the ends. Then we carried bucket after bucket of water from the stream and dumped it on the dry wood wheels and spokes. Before long, those steel rims were tree-bark tight. Next, we decided to stop that squealing. Every wagon owner carried a tar-bucket, a mixture of tar and lard for greasing wheel hubs. Using a screw jack, we raised the axles, and then pulled the linchpins and wheels. The squealing stopped after we filled the hubs with grease.

Now that Phoebe and Elliot knew Buck had a twin sister, they followed him like puppies, acting as if they'd been acquainted for years. I'd seen it happen before. Not that there were many twins in Northfield, but the ones there, regardless of age, seemed to bond. When I tried to talk more to them, they acted shy and clammed up, so I didn't press it. I think they figured I was a practical joker, and were not about to get caught again in one of my tricks. I hoped they'd warm to me later when we knew each other better.

I told the Bradfords about Jasmine Bodecker, "Some teacher we met on the coach." I pretended the only reason I'd look her up was to enroll Buck. Romance wasn't mentioned and I avoided Buck's eye. I knew he'd be grinning and enjoying my careful description of how Jas and I met, and the plans I had made to see her in Wyoming. Judy kept looking back and forth at both of us, eyes dancing. She likely suspected more to the story but politely refrained from asking questions.

It dried a little by noon, and we decided to hitch up and try our luck. Water barrels strapped to the outside of the wagon were full and we replenished the firewood. Finding more was bound to be chancy.

Oh, it was a hard go even though the mules were well fed and rested. At times, those thin ironbound wheels cut six inches into the mud. There was added weight from the iron moldboard walking plow Robbie had bolted on the wagon side opposite the water barrels.

When going uphill, Buck and I tied our ropes into the pole-cap ring and pulled some of the load. Monty and Cowboy took it in their stride. Those were fine horses and well trained. They wall-eyed back a few times at the four large mules, but then decided it was a common enough job. It reminded me of the time we pulled "Adam's Apple" out of the mud southwest of Northfield. How long ago that seemed!

We made it a few miles before the stock tired and we camped again in late afternoon. In the following days, the prairie dried completely and we made good headway.

The best times were around the fire before turning in at night. Robbie, Judy, and the twins never tired of hearing of the Northfield Raid and our subsequent chase of the James Gang. Hard work and little excitement seemed to have made up their past lives in West Virginia. They were flabbergasted that we were ex-lawmen and wondered how anyone as young as Buck could become a sheriff's deputy. Well, they just didn't know Pa and Uncle Roy.

I'm afraid we couldn't overcome the Compton habit of embellishing stories: there seemed to be more bullets flying than I actually remembered. Conspicuously absent, of course, was how scared we were at times. Buck had to show his cap again so everyone could poke their fingers through the bullet hole. No wonder he didn't switch to a cowboy hat. It was too good a conversation piece.

The twins enjoyed hearing of our soap fight on board the *Pride of St. Louis*. Buck was a natural at imitating the mad cook's French and broken English. Hennessey's pet duck, Lester, flying over the supper table got them to laughing too. They loved the story of the frolicking work team, Popcorn and Barney, terrorizing us in the darkness. Of course, we couldn't leave out how we woke everyone in the middle of the night at the Speckled Loon Inn and chased the James Gang in our red underwear. Each retelling triggered another spasm of giggles. My confession of flipping head-over-teakettle and cracking my head on the hallway of the Speckled Loon even caused Buck to break up. Until then, I'd prudently kept that stunt to myself, so it was the first time he heard it. We included a few scary events too, but toned it down so we wouldn't frighten the youngsters: the gunfight in the Sioux Falls train depot; our ambush of the rum-dumb buffalo hunters; and the showdown with rambling gunfighter, Johnnie Ketchum.

Even though few settlers used the Oregon Trail since completion of the Transcontinental Railroad, ample evidence existed of people still traveling the historic route. Bones of horses and cattle lined the way.

As the pioneers' teams played out, they had to lighten the loads. Discarded furniture, farm machinery, and abandoned wagons were left to rot and rust. We even passed a once-beautiful stained oak hutch beside the trail. Hand-painted dishes were carefully stacked and displayed as if in someone's parlor. Can you imagine a family unloading that and placing the dishes as if proud of what they owned? Amazing it wasn't disturbed after setting there for months. We enjoyed it and left it undisturbed for later travelers to marvel over.

Several days later, we split from the Oregon Trail leading to Fort Laramie and followed a lesser track in a westerly direction for Cheyenne in southern Wyoming Territory. The nights were cooler and the air thinner, so we knew we were climbing in elevation. We appreciated the cozy evening cook stove fire as much as Judy's cooking.

A job Buck and I shared was operating the back wheel brake down hills and gullies. The iron brake lever protruded from under the wagon rear, so it was necessary to walk behind to apply the proper amount of brake. The steeper the hill, the harder we pushed on that doohickey.

It took another week to reach Cheyenne. I was glad the Bradfords planned to spend a couple days near town. Robbie's brother, Dirk, and his family lived on a homestead a few miles south of Hat Creek Station, a stage stop on the new 300-mile Cheyenne to Deadwood stage route. Robbie and Judy planned to winter with them until they could build a cabin on their own homestead. Robbie first wanted to buy tools and supplies so they wouldn't be beholden to his brother.

The Bradfords even wanted us to join them and help build a cabin and break sod in the spring. Buck seemed willing, but I had my heart set on cowboying. My guess was he didn't want to go back to school. Actually, I had trouble thinking about anything beyond finding Jasmine. Besides, can you imagine the six of us squeezing in with Dirk's brood? Talk about cozy cousins!

We camped on some high ground above town, not overly concerned with who owned the land. The view wasn't impressive. The buildings of Cheyenne were scattered haphazardly over the dried brown hills as if fired from a shotgun. The Bradfords looked ready to return home. Judy said, "Look Robbie! There are no trees."

"Well, there used to be a few," he said. "Look at all the stumps along that creek."

She held both hands to her face. "Oh, I can't see how we can live in a place with no trees."

I didn't blame her. If there was one thing we loved about Minnesota, it was trees. This was going to take some getting used to.

The Bradfords decided to wait until the following day to shop. It was only noon and I was anxious to find Jasmine. Buck and I washed up, and after promising to bring groceries and be home for supper, we galloped away. This time, we agreed to stay together.

As we neared town we saw the American flag proudly waving over Fort D. A. Russell on the west side of Cheyenne, and I heard a calling bugle. It was another reminder that only four months earlier, General George Armstrong Custer had led the Seventh Cavalry, including over 200 men that were to die with him on the Little Big Horn, from Fort Abraham Lincoln, Dakota Territory. As they marched out the front gate, his Regimental Band had played "Garry Owen," battle hymn of the Seventh Cavalry. The *Minneapolis Tribune* carried the shocking news. Danged Custer, getting himself killed like that. Teasing hasn't stopped since. Going to whip the entire Indian nation, he was.

"How do you plan to find a ranch job?" Buck asked. "Wearing a cowboy hat and boots doesn't exactly make you a cowboy. Neither does riding plug horses in Minnesota."

I thought that a little harsh. After all, what did he know about that kind of life? "Ach, how hard can it be?" I said shortly. The question rankled. He was closer to the truth than I cared to admit. "First we do as Pa ordered. If Jas is teaching, we need to get you signed up." I figured a little return goading wouldn't hurt him. Pa gave me this chance so I wanted to follow his wishes. I would make sure Buck had the opportunity to study, but the rest was up to him. You can lead a horse to water...

Cheyenne wasn't exactly the diamond of the prairie I had in mind: building locations appeared haphazard, without even regard for straight streets. Dried up ruts zigzagged through the streets and horse manure was building near hitch rails. The homes were low-roofed affairs of either logs or adobe. Only the train depot looked permanent—a beautiful red sandstone building with a round turret. A few horses stood hipshot in front of the downtown false-fronted businesses and saloons. Sleepy dogs dozed beneath loafer-benches under roofed boardwalks. If Judy didn't like this town from the hilltop, she sure wouldn't be impressed close up.

Bawdyhouses stretched down the street next to the tracks. I was particularly interested in the saloons. From my reading of the West, I knew people called saloon girls soiled doves, strumpets, harlots, and Jezebels. With such exotic names, they had to be something to see.

"Where is everyone?" Buck asked, looking all around as we lazily slogged horseback along empty streets.

"Hard to say, Little Feather," I answered, slipping into my old-salt-cowboy persona. "Probably out hanging danged rustlers."

"Y'know, Custer, one of these days they'll come to string *you* up...for bad acting."

"Aye, aye me lad,"—Irish now—"mon the towers, governa, an' look sharp. Whir 'bout ta meet the King's foe. We kin lick um, a'll be bound."

The poor boy rolled his eyes and spit off to the side. There's no accounting for taste.

Jerome A. Kuntz

"Why hell, Buck," I said. "If a medicine show comes to Cheyenne, I'll be a shoo-in."

We headed directly for the school. It wasn't hard to spot with the bell tower on the roof. Class was in progress so we waited outside, kicking stones around. Finally, someone rang a hand-bell and kids piled out the door. A rather severe-looking woman followed that I foolishly took for Mrs. Hollins, our teacher in Northfield. Well, anyway, she wore the same dark dress and hair fixed into a tight bun on the back of her head. Instinctively, I expected to get dressed down for something.

"Jasmine Bodecker, you say?" She cupped her ear as if hard of hearing. I thought that peculiar for a teacher. All the schoolmarms I'd known had ears sharp as foxes. We dumbly nodded our heads.

She looked us over closely before answering, especially Buck. I doubted she approved of anyone that young carrying a pistol. "She isn't a teacher, young man. She works at the Plains Hotel Saloon."

"Doing what?" I asked innocently. "She said she was a teacher."

Her nose went up like a pump handle, and she answered primly, "Yes, aren't they all." After checking the kids, she hurried back inside without so much as a fare-thee-well.

It sounded like a party as we entered the Plains Hotel lobby. A registration clerk with a thick black pompadour stood behind a heavy oak counter—he was a pompous-looking fellow appearing to suffer from indigestion. To one side were doors into the saloon. They were large shinny-black batwings with some kind of yellow design—maybe flowers but I'm not sure now. A piano player and fiddler played a lively version of "Oh! Susanna" accompanied by the sharp clicking of heels on a wood floor. A girl counted cadence as if a dance rehearsal was taking place. We walked over to see the fun.

"Hey, sonny, you can't go in there," someone growled. The columns must have hid him when we came in. He was a beanpole-man in a black suit, string tie, and a flat-crowned black felt hat. His hatband was a string of shinny dimes. He looked every bit like the Western professional gamblers I'd seen in Ned Buntline novels back home.

"I'm nineteen," I lied. Sorry to say, I'd learned another bad habit from Johnnie.

"Uh-huh, and how old's he?" he said, pointing at Buck. "Twenty-five?"

I ignored that. He likely figured we were a couple of hayseeds. "We don't want a drink, mister. We're just looking for a friend."

"Yeah, well...aren't we all. What's her name? I know about everyone in these parts."

I wondered how he knew it was a girl. "Jasmine Bodecker," Buck piped up. Gosh, he did sound awful young.

"Jasmine? Now what do you young sprouts want with her?"

"We don't appreciate being called sprouts, shidepoke," Buck said acidly.

The man's face flamed. "Whadaya mean shidepoke?" he snarled. "What's a shidepoke?"

"You!" Buck snapped back.

Damn! Couldn't that kid ever keep his mouth shut?

"Never mind him, mister." I said, waving Buck off before this got out of hand. "She's a teacher and I plan to enroll Buck here in her class." If I had half a brain, I'd have realized by now she wasn't teaching school while working at the Plains Hotel Saloon.

"A teacher?" He cackled like an excited chicken. "Yeah, I reckon she could teach him plenty."

"Oh! Susanna," ended abruptly, and a man and woman began shouting at each other.

Just then, the saloon batwings banged open and into the lobby stormed a young lady wearing a gold evening gown and makeup. We jumped back to get out of the way. A corn-fed fellow wearing a gray bankers' suit and a gold watch chain belly-slung below his vest followed her. He grabbed her arm. "Keep your filthy hands off me," she screamed, pulling from his grip. He tried to slap her face. She expertly ducked under the swing as if this wasn't the first time.

"That's enough of that," I growled without thinking. Before I could react, he punched me in the face and I staggered back to the clerk's counter, trying to keep my feet. Thinking I was alone was his mistake, and he would have plenty of time to regret it. Like a striking snake, Buck pulled his Colt and clobbered him over the head. He sank to the floor.

"Custer! Buck! What are you doing here?" the lady cried out. She stared at us with both hands on her face. I heard running feet, as if more people were coming to defend fancy-suit. Oh God, we were whistlin' Dixie now.

"Jas?" I managed to croak. I looked at her with double vision, but neither of the two girls resembled the one I'd met on the stagecoach. Both had a pile of brown curls on top of their heads, wore heavy makeup, and looked mighty worried about me. I stared at their low-cut tight dresses. You couldn't buy dresses like that in Northfield.

More people burst through the door and everyone seemed eager to join the fight. The men were employees of the Plains Hotel. All the showgirls were friends of Jasmine and intent on protecting her. They carried fancy umbrellas, props used in their dance act. Everyone shouted at once.

"What happened, Jas?" one of the girls asked.

"Marty tried to slap me," she said, pointing with glee at the chubby guy just sitting up.

"Auk-k-k, *you* are no-o-o-o gentlemen!" The girl cracked him on the head with her umbrella. Another girl joined her in the fun. I guess it wasn't Marty's day.

A male employee came to his rescue. "Hold on there, sisters," he said, trying to sound tough while reaching for one girl's umbrella. Not a good move—they weren't about to be disarmed. Both girls turned on him with umbrellas and his face paled.

Buck desperately called from across the room. "Custer! Get this bum off me!"

A big bruiser wearing a brown bowler hat was pummeling him in a corner. Buck was trying to protect his face. I ran to help the hot-tempered kid before he pulled his gun again, but another guy tripped and fell into my legs. Down I went. A girl ran over and began whacking him on the head.

Another fellow slapped a dancer and her friend, with blood in her eye, came in swinging. "Let her alone, you bully!" she ordered. He slugged her and she slid to the floor. In rage, the other girls screamed oaths and chased him back into the saloon.

Beanpole's fancy hat of dimes was gone, and he stood braced against the wall as if afraid to fall. "You girls will pay for this!" he threatened.

"I'm leaving and you can cram your damn job where the sun doesn't shine," Jas yelled in his face. Actually, she used a few other choice words, but she wouldn't want them repeated here. Oh gosh, Sadie would have appreciated the show.

"You can't leave. We have a contract!"

"So sue me, you drooling ape! See how much you get!"

I ran toward Buck. His attacker looked too big so I shouldered him hard and spun him off to the side. "C'mon, Buck! Let's get out of here!" I yelled, grabbing his arm.

"I'm going with you," Jas called.

Some people tried to stop us, but we pushed them out of the way. Kicking and gouging, we fought our way to the door. Just before leaving, I looked back and saw the hotel clerk running toward us, black pompadour toupee swinging off the side of his bald head. I regretted not having a chance to pop him, but we had to make tracks before the law showed.

Jasmine looked wildly up and down the street. "Gee willikers, you got horses?" she asked, desperately.

Buck and I each grabbed one of her hands and ran down the boardwalk, all of us laughing like crazy people. That long dress looked impossible to run in but she kept up.

Monty and Cowboy reared back as we approached. Chances are they'd never seen the likes of Jasmine Bodecker. It took a moment to mount with both horses shying sideways. Then, leaving an empty stirrup, I reached for Jas. She pulled her long dress way above her knees and stepped up. Until then, that was the most I'd seen of a lady's legs. Within minutes, we pounded down the street, dust clouds rolling out behind.

Shots came from the Plains Hotel and inflamed hornets whined overhead. I doubt they meant to hit us but we rode bent over leather. Buck was in the lead and I followed. He turned at the first intersection and raced Cowboy flat out. "Hang on, Jas!" I shouted. "The kid's hair's on fire!" At every intersection, Buck changed direction—first left, then right, left again. He figured to lose anyone tailing us. People on the boardwalks stopped and gaped. I kept looking back but saw no one.

There was nothing for it but return to the Bradfords' wagon. Even though it was a hair-raising turn of events, I enjoyed Jas hugging me around the waist.

With Cheyenne behind and no sign of pursuit, we slowed to a walk. Now Jas and I led.

She looked around with concern. "Are you all right, Buck?" she asked. "That was Rollie, the house bouncer you were fighting and I've never seen him beat." Buck's shirt was blood-flecked and more dripped from his nose onto his saddle.

"Yeah—I'm all right—he was just too big. I couldn't get close enough to do any damage." He clamped a dirty rag over his nose.

Jas had a million questions. Buck and I both talked at once, relating how hide hunters kidnapped him, the loss of our outfit to the Indians, our travel with the mule train, and the fight with Johnnie Ketchum. Then we finished by telling her about the Bradfords and the bad storm. "Oh, you guys are like storybook heroes—like King Arthur and the Knights of the Round Table," Jas exclaimed, girlishly. I didn't argue—figuring if she was impressed, it was worth it.

"What happened to your teaching job," I asked, pretending to change the subject out of modesty.

"The school board gave the job to an older woman, claiming she was more qualified."

"Oh yeah...her we've met," I said.

"They got a piece of my mind. I can tell you that. I told them they promised the job to me and I traveled a thousand miles to take it on. They looked guilty but refused to change their decision. What a bunch of nincompoops! I needed a job and there were no other openings. A new restaurant, called The Tender T-bone, is opening soon; and the owner said he could take me on in a few weeks. I couldn't wait so I took the dance instructor's job at the Plains Saloon. The girls were great and we put together several different shows, so the crowd could keep coming and not tire of the performance. I did enjoy it until recently. Do you remember my telling you I taught dancing in St. Cloud?"

"In a saloon?" I asked. I actually meant it, but she thought I was kidding.

"No, not in a saloon, silly" she laughed and punched me in the back.

"So, what was the problem? Why was fat boy grabbing you?" Buck asked.

"You mean Marty? He's the owner of the saloon. He's also in cahoots with, Slade, that tall thin man in black, in other businesses. They'd been after us girls for weeks to wear skimpy costumes. Until today, I'd been able to put them off, but then Marty got rough. He claimed he couldn't make our payroll. The crowds liked our shows, but there weren't many cowboys in town during the week. They're all working and I told him that."

I felt guilty about returning to the wagon without groceries, but hanging around Cheyenne was out of the question. Hopefully, our hunting luck would improve.

It was great to see Jas, but now my face was hot and swelling again. It had just begun to look normal after the fight with Johnnie. Buck was worse off. His head seemed to be growing into the shape of a squash with ears.

Many times I've thought back on that ruckus, trying to figure how everything went wrong. I didn't even know it was Jas when I told that gent to back off and that's how it all started. Eyew, how could a fight break out by simply visiting my girl? After all, I had my fair share of common sense; but in my youth, it was untrustworthy and prone to wander off and amuse itself, leaving me to swing.

Have you noticed this too? In almost every Western saloon gunfight story I've read, the bartender (fool!) whips out his stubby, double-barreled shotgun and is killed even though he doesn't have a dog in the fight. Why doesn't he (dope!) simply scooch down under the bar and ride it out? I vowed never to act like those silly bartenders, and in the future, stay out of other people's squabbles. Life might be a lot healthier.

Chapter 21

I looked forward to telling Pa and Uncle Roy of our fleeing Cheyenne with bullets whistling overhead. They experienced a similar incident during the war. We heard it from Uncle Roy. It just wasn't in Pa to reveal much of his past, especially the war. We listened to Roy tell the story to various people, and for some reason, they thought it funny. I never quite saw it that way.

It happened in Harpers Ferry, Virginia. Technically, it was enemy territory but located just across the Potomac from Maryland, so the town changed hands dozens of times during the four years of war. No matter whether the North or South held control, enemy sympathizers infested the place, attempting to nose out information on one side or the other. In some cases, informants merely sold intelligence to the current occupying force.

Pa and Roy often spied for the Minnesota 1st Regiment Infantry, so they carried civilian clothes in addition to their uniform. One night, the 1st Regiment camped outside of Harpers Ferry, preparing for a raid deep into Virginia. Without permission, Pa and Roy decided to go into town and smoke out the latest news. They changed into civilian clothes and casually rode down the main street. Roy always said right here, "Cold beer is really what we had in mind." Then we'd hear that great laugh of his. Imagine, risking your neck at night in enemy territory for a cold one. Both the North and South shot as spies any soldiers captured in civilian clothes.

They bellied up to a dimly lit bar, the place almost empty. Only the bartender moved around, washing glasses and casting ghostly shadows on the walls from a single lantern. Very soon, several riders rode up, dismounted, and stomped through the front door. It was obvious this wasn't their first liquor stop that night.

Within minutes, men with whiskery, greasy faces and stinking from moonshine surrounded Pa and Roy. They asked casual questions about where they were from and what business they had in town. Both men had been in tight spots before, and they played it for what it was worth, namely their lives. Finally, Roy claimed they were from

Charles Town just down the road. He kicked himself later for picking a town so close to Harpers Ferry. A guy with crooked yellow teeth wanted to know Roy's name so he could check with his brother, who was mayor of Charles Town. As soon as Roy hesitated, they tried to grab his arms, and the bull was in the china shop. It was Pa and Roy against a half dozen and they had to get out fast. Back-to-back, they made their way to the door, slugging and pushing with all their strength every inch of the way.

They raced out the door and bellowed in the faces of several horses tied out front. The horses reared back and ripped out the hitch rail, dragging it into the dark street. The poor animals panicked and galloped away, with several men in hot pursuit. In the confusion, Pa and Roy ran pell-mell until reaching their own mounts tied on the edge of town.

By now, bullets whizzed overhead as they headed directly into the heavy woods along the Potomac. They quickly lost their pursuers in the blackness, but spent several hours searching for a way through the steep mountains surrounding Harpers Ferry and back to their unit.

It had been a long and terrible night. The company guard they expected on duty had gone to his blankets, and a different one stood watch. Bad luck! The new one was a conniving fellow and forever on the lookout for advantage. In return for keeping his mouth shut, he cleaned Pa and Roy out of their week's supply of coffee beans and coiled-rope tobacco.

It had been close: the next day, Roy dug a minie ball out of the back of his saddle cantle. Never again did they go on a spy mission without written orders—orders, of course, that remained in Roy's haversack in camp. That way, they could always prove they were on official business.

While our escape wasn't nearly as exciting or dangerous, I figured Pa and Roy would get a laugh hearing about us picking up Jas and racing out of Cheyenne with bullets flying.

The Bradfords' wagon was unusually quiet when we returned from Cheyenne. Only Robbie sat out front, looking like he had lost his favorite coon dog. "Where's Judy and the twins?" I asked.

Robbie jerked his head toward the wagon. "In there," he said dismally. "We got buzzed by a rattler and now they won't come out."

A snake? I froze, my hand dangerously close to my six-shooter. Steady, Custer. Easy big fellow. Jas was right behind. No one moved.

"Robbie…where's the snake now?" Buck asked evenly.

"Ah heck, I threw rocks at him until he wiggled away."

I remembered to breathe. "Hey Judy," I called bravely, "see …it's safe to come out. Phoebe, Elliot, come on down and meet Jas."

Three tear-stained but smiling faces poked out. They stared all around at the ground before stepping down.

If Judy thought Jasmine's dress was a bit revealing, she didn't let on. We told the Bradfords what happened, and explained why Jas worked as a dance instructor at the Plains Hotel instead of teaching. Calling it the Plains Saloon wouldn't help anyone, so I never let on it was a rough-and-tumble drinking establishment.

Jas quickly made friends with Judy and the kids and she seemed to feel right at home. Judy loaned her a flowered-calico housedress, and they both had ideas on how to remodel the fancy show dress. Now Jas looked like the girl I'd met weeks ago on the stage: the same china-white teeth, strawberry lips, and peaches-and-cream complexion. Yeah, you guessed it. By then I was crazy about her.

I was all right but Buck's face was bloody and swelling. The girls carefully washed his cuts and applied healing salve to the bad ones. Frankly, I think he enjoyed all the attention. He should have hit the deck and protected himself instead of fighting with someone who evidently enjoyed inflicting punishment. I wished I could have pulled him out sooner; even a few minutes would have made a difference.

After supper, Jas tensed with fear when we described our Kansas Indian encounter. "Custer," she said with her hands on her cheeks and eyes wide, "you just have to write your adventures down. People in Northfield will love to hear everything that happened." It was the first time I'd considered that, and I didn't forget what she said. Several weeks later, I began writing this story. Funny thing though, I didn't finish it until I was an old man.

Before the evening ended, Judy talked Jas into staying with them on the homestead and tutoring Phoebe, Elliot, Dirk's youngsters, and any other pioneer children in the area. Dirk had written them the Hat Creek area was settling up, and the "town" even expected a post office the following year. Along with being a Cheyenne/Deadwood stage stop, it was a telegraph station on the Fort Laramie military post to Black Hills Line. That was a load off my mind, knowing she wouldn't have to return to saloon work.

Judy had books and before turning in, Jas read *Robinson Crusoe* to the twins. She changed her voice for the different characters. We enjoyed it as much as the kids did.

The next morning, Robbie and Judy went into town for supplies; and they had a written message for Jasmine's roommate to turn over to the Bradfords her valise and a small steamer trunk containing books and school supplies that Jas had expected to use. The twins stayed with us. As soon as they left, Buck and I set up a little canvas shelter for the five of us.

They returned in the best of spirits in early afternoon, laughing when they told us how our rhubarb at the Plains was the talk of Cheyenne. Jasmine's roommate was one of the dancers, and she said the cowboys in town gave Marty and Slade a nasty time for getting rough with the dancehall girls.

We spent the next few days reaching Dirk Bradford's homestead. It was an enjoyable trip on the well-traveled stage route. Nearby, telegraph poles marched north to Fort Laramie and on to the Black Hills. Buck even bagged his first antelope, so we ate high-on-the-hog. Things were easier for Judy too, having another woman to help cook and care for the twins.

I thought I could get used to that life real quick. It being flat country, we didn't have to work the wagon brake. Our main duty was to help Robbie care for the mules.

We did keep our rifles handy. Residents in Cheyenne had told Robbie that robbers plagued the Deadwood stage route, and to keep a sharp eye out. Indians weren't a big worry because of the troops stationed at Fort Laramie and Fort Hat Creek.

Jerome A. Kuntz

At times, Buck gave up Cowboy so Jas could ride with me, following the wagon. He owed me favors anyway and I thought it time to collect. It was the first time I learned of Jasmine's brothers, sisters, parents, and how they lived in St. Cloud. Knowing them, I came to know her and felt a closer bond.

I was pleased to learn that Jas sang as well as danced. Judy, Phoebe, Elliot, and Buck all crowded to the back of the wagon to listen. It was so quiet out there. There was only the creak of the wagon, jangle of trace chains, and the squeak of saddle leather as she sang "Our Minnesota Soddy Home," an old favorite going back to our state's Territory days.

"Drifting snow coats our plowed fields of black prairie loam.
There's no money for fancy clothes so we have to make our own,
But we eat like wealthy English kings from the garden we had sown.
We're snug and warm in our Minnesota soddy home.

We're poor as our bashful little mice, we never long for more.
Wolf packs call to ask us can they slumber on our floor,
But there's only room for you and me behind the heavy door.
We're snug and warm in our Minnesota soddy home.

To visit dear friends and family our horses pull the sleigh.
In swirling snow and darkness we fear we'll lose our way,
But the team prances straight for home like any summer day.
We're snug and warm in our Minnesota soddy home.

We are happy as a clown on the land that we have found.
There's no way to see what scary fate may come around,
But you and I forever will stare those troubles down.
We'll be snug and warm in our Minnesota soddy home."

Oh my, there came only silence. Those sentiments were so sweet; no one dared break the spell. None of us would admit how homesick we really were.

Northfield

I'd never seen so many antelopes before. In every direction, prairie grass gently waved in the breeze to the far distant horizon.

We skirted Fort Laramie, the halfway point for the wagon trains on the Oregon Trail. Of course, those days were long gone by 1876. It had also been another important Pony Express station. Now it was just a military post to keep the peace among settlers, Indians, and ranchers. I was sure glad to see the blue-coated soldiers riding purposely about the area.

We filled our water barrels at widely spaced homesteads and ranches. It seemed those pioneers wanted to live as far from neighbors as possible. Still, they were always glad to see strangers and appeared hungry for any news at all.

Dirk had built a large comfortable home for his wife, Libby, and three children. They couldn't have been happier to see us. Added to their joy was our bringing a schoolteacher. None of the children had attended classes.

Dirk appeared much different from his brother. While Robbie seemed indecisive and needful of other people's opinion before acting, Dirk knew what he wanted and how to get it. This was his third year of raising crops, and each summer he had increased his harvest by breaking more sod. Under the Homestead Act of 1862, the government allotted 160 acres to each claim. In five years, Dirk expected to have his entire farm under cultivation.

One day, I was walking with Dirk while he pointed out the progress he'd made. "Why not stay here and file on your own claim?" he asked. "In a few years, you can prove up and it will be yours clear. Of course, you're required to live on it the entire time."

I was looking for excuses. "But I can't file under age twenty-one."

He waved me off. "Ah, that's nothing. Your folks can make the claim and then put it in your name after they have clear title. It's done all the time. Besides, if you're head of the family, that age requirement doesn't apply."

Damned if he didn't wink at me. Much later, Jas said Dirk assumed I planned to marry her. "Nah, Dirk, but thanks," I said. "Farming in Wyoming isn't my cup of tea. I didn't come this far to do the same thing I was doing in Northfield. I want to work on a cattle ranch."

He seemed disappointed, as if he couldn't believe how anyone could pass this up. "I hear Frank Pierce is hiring for fall roundup," he said reluctantly. "They're behind in the job as they couldn't find enough cowboys to do the work. They're even branding large stock, cattle that should have been branded last spring."

I saddled up the next morning. The Rocking Bar P was 20 miles north of Hat Creek Station. I hated leaving Jas, Buck, and our new family behind, but now was my chance. If it didn't work out, I could still return and work alongside Robbie and Buck. Robbie had no money, but at least I'd have a roof and Judy's good cooking.

Just before leaving, everyone except Jas hurried away and pretended to be busy with other things. I silently thanked them.

"When are you coming back, Custer?" she asked, her arms crossed and cupping her elbows. Wyoming's endless wind billowed out her long calico housedress and white flower-sack apron.

"I guess it depends on the weather. If winter holds off, we could work cattle almost to Christmas. Will you still be here?" Even while I said it, I knew I didn't have a row to hoe and no right to ask for a commitment.

"I can't say. If the teaching jobs are filled, I may have to return to Cheyenne."

That's not what I wanted to hear, but what choice did she have? Dirk hadn't built his house for two families and a live-in schoolteacher.

Just before climbing on Monty, I kissed her lips for the first time. I knew it surprised her, but I could feel her arms around my neck, kissing me back. My face flamed with lack of experience. Then, just before I turned away, I saw something in her eyes. The memory of that moment carried me through the lonely weeks as 1876 finally spiraled down to a cold and tragic end.

As I rode away, I felt a loss I couldn't explain. Have you planned something, talked about something so long that you couldn't change your mind no matter how bleak or silly it appeared? You'd be admitting weakness and defeat. My plan was supposed to be exciting, but now it only looked stupid. Still, I had to do it!

The Custer Kid sat straight in the saddle as he aimed in some vague direction for the Pierce ranch. He stopped, turned Monty halfway around, and waved. Yeah, you know me by now; it was all for show. Not my fault: blame those danged Western novels. There she stood, blue dress billowing out, curly brown hair lifting in the breeze. Whenever I looked back, she waved again until I went out of sight.

That scene was in my mind's eye for the rest of my life.

Chapter 22

Dirk had given me detailed directions with assurances that I couldn't miss Frank Pierce's ranch. Ever heard that before? Miss the place is exactly what I did. As far as Hat Creek, I was fine; I only had to follow the telegraph poles. Beyond that, Dirk's easy-as-falling-off-a-log landmarks melted together. The West's Second Greatest Scout seemed to have taken a wrong turn. (Even with my vast experience, I graciously continued to concede first place to Buffalo Bill.) Lucky no one I knew was around to see me. Isn't that common in life? My only hope was to stop at lonely homesteads and ask for directions.

Things got a bit silly at the first place I visited. I came upon a lonely shack set in a vast open prairie, and it looked so slapdashed together that I wondered how it could survive the Wyoming winds—winter or summer. The morning had been nice, but the wind was kicking up again.

The owner came out shirtless, wearing bib overalls, and he had a "pig-shave" haircut. He hungrily chewed an apple. God only knows where he got it. Couldn't have been a tree within a hundred miles. He looked as weather-beaten as his house. I dismounted and told him I came from Hat Creek and was looking for the Pierce ranch, but now I was lost.

"Remember where you left the main trail north out of Hat Creek?" he asked.

"No."

He appeared to study me for a moment as if suspecting I was pulling his leg. "It was just south of the lake," he said, looking again at me hopefully.

"No," I said again, still not feeling any better about it. "Never saw no lake."

"How could you not see the lake?"

"It dried up?" Sometimes humor helps to break the ice when a small travel glitch develops.

He turned around and stalked off a ways, spit, and kicked up some dust. I waited. Finally, he turned again and came back, one hand clutching his apple and the other balled into a fist on his hip. "How the devil do you expect me to tell you where to go if you don't know where you been?"

"I don't," I said soothingly. "If, as you say, it's impossible to get where I'm going unless I know where I've been, then I'm hoping you can tell me *both* where I been and how to reach where I'm going. I warned you I was lost. Then again, I wonder if a person can actually get there from right here without having to backtrack."

I'm afraid things went downhill from there. I could have yakked with Crabby until the cows came home and been no closer to my destination. He ended up pointing in the direction of the ranch without mentioning any particular track to follow, and said I couldn't miss the place. There was definitely something peculiar about him: while giving me these simple directions, he ate his apple, core and all. Probably the stem too if it had one. I guessed he had a nervous disorder, so I quickly mounted up and left before the troubled man had a breakdown or something.

When I finally rode into the Rocking Bar P, only a few hands shambled about, none acting too friendly. They barely grunted while jerking their thumbs in the direction of a shabby log cabin. I assumed it was the owner's home. All the buildings were sun-warped, and barely enjoyed a hand-shaking acquaintance with paint. Corrals of pealed, wind-wobbled poles appeared to search for a soft resting place. It appeared Wyoming ranching paid as well as Minnesota farming. Later, I learned Frank Pierce was rich as Solomon by 1876 standards, and owned cattle scattered over two territories and one state. He just didn't believe in wasting money on the comforts of home.

The front door was open but I knocked anyway. Four men played poker on a rickety table. More money than I'd seen in a spell lay scattered carelessly about. The dumpy room reeked of tobacco smoke, old leather, horses, and whiskey. No sign of a woman's touch (big surprise). After a quick glance at me, they returned to their game. "Excuse me," I said, trying to sound as old as possible. "I'm looking for Frank Pierce."

"That would be me," the oldest guy said, without taking his eyes off the cards. He was the smallest of the bunch. In fact, I wondered

Jerome A. Kuntz

how a scrawny runt like that could be hiring anyone. He must have quit growing in the sixth grade. Even his voice sounded like a kid. I could tell he had a high opinion of his card playing: each time he dealt a card, he whanged it down with his fist, making the table tremble. I won't play with people like that.

"Dirk Bradford said you might be hiring."

"Dirk? That nester?" He pronounced nester like it was a contagious disease.

"Ya...well, he's homesteading south of Hat Creek."

Finally, he turned to look at me. "I said nester!" Spit flew from his mouth. His little red face was twisted in a sneer.

At least I had the sense to humor him. "Yes, sir. Damn nester he is. I'm looking for a job."

"What kind of a job? Your deal, Bill."

"A cowboy." What the hell other kind of work was there on a cattle ranch?

"A cowboy? You look more like a sodbuster packin' a six-gun. You ever work cows before?"

Now we were in familiar territory. "Yes, sir," I said, confidently. "I did the milking at home in Northfield."

All four of those idiots leaned back in their chairs, laughing and choking. I just assumed I'd said something stupid. Later, I learned ranchers called everything cows: bulls, heifers, calves, steers, yearlings—you name it. My face flamed and I didn't even realize what I'd said. All I could do was stand there until those jackasses either laughed themselves out or choked to death. It made little difference to me.

Frank stood and slouched against the doorframe. "You came to the right place, cowboy," he said. "I got 10,000 cows that need milkin' twice a day." That started them off again. I'd heard enough. I turned on my heel and headed for Monty.

"Hey, what's your name, boy?" Frank called after me.

I looked back. "Custer Compton...from Northfield, Minnesota," I said. This time he stayed serious, but I heard those smartasses inside burst out laughing again. Danged General Custer getting himself killed! Someday, I'd have to drop that name.

"All right, *Custer*," he said, in a mocking tone. "You'll get your chance. Pick an empty cot in the bunkhouse. The crew will be back soon. See Tad Polson. He's the foreman."

I thanked him, not even remembering to ask about wages. I fairly floated back to my horse. My first job as a cowboy! Now I'd finally live the life I dreamed of for years.

I pulled the saddle off Monty and gave him a good rubdown. After turning him into the corral, I tossed in the best hay I could find and then headed for the bunkhouse.

A kitchen with a dining table surrounded by hard benches took up one end of the building. Bunks filled the remaining space. Each bed had a rickety chair next to it. The owners had piled gear and dirty laundry next to their bunks. Wow, smelled as bad as a bucket of dead walleyes. A potbellied stove with a black stack running through the rafter-exposed ceiling had been plopped in the center aisle. Not exactly homey.

The cook was hard at work on the evening meal. Something sure smelled good. I tossed my bedroll and a small flour sack of clothes on an empty bunk and went to investigate. Fresh-baked baking-powder biscuits covered an entire tabletop. A five-gallon stewpot bubbled happily next to a huge coffeepot on a snapping wood stove. Hot as it was in there, even with all the doors and windows open, the cook seemed right at home.

Has anyone sagely advised you not to put your trust in a skinny cook? Life was rocking-chair-safe with this fellow in the kitchen. He was as pot-bellied as the bunkhouse stove. I figured to look the other way when I ate though: his sweat-streaked brown derby hat and chewing-tobacco stained beard were bound to shade my appetite.

Deciding I was part of the crew now, I washed up at an outside basin, introduced myself, and offered to help. Big mistake. He said his name was Coosie, and then set me to washing pots and pans. There were so many, it appeared they'd been piling up for days. Later, I learned coosie was Spanish slang for *cosinara*, and it meant "cook."

Before long, hands filed in for supper. "Hey, Coosie," they called, "you got yourself a Mary Ann?" I grinned good-naturedly at the men, having no idea what they meant by "Mary Ann."

"What's a Mary Ann, Coosie?" I finally had a chance to ask.

He pointed in my direction. "Cook's helper. That's you. There's still more pots coming when you get those done."

"Sure, boss, but when do we eat?"

"Cooks eat last."

He talked as if he only had a pocket full of words and didn't want to waste any. Not good news: Libby had made a fine breakfast twelve hours ago, but I'd covered a lot of ground since then. "That right?" I asked. "And why is that?" (I know: too many questions only irritate people.)

He scratched his face and considered for a moment. "Hard to say. Always been that way."

"Oh...I once read Roman rulers had food tasters. If they lived, then the king ate."

He popped a stubby index finger to his lips. "Ssshhh! That's *my* secret."

"Ah-h-h-huh, now I get it; take a head count before you eat."

I was relieved to learn he at least had a funny bone. Another hour dragged by and I wondered how long I could last. "Let's eat," Coosie finally said, wiping his hands on a greasy apron stretched over his big belly. Luckily, there was still some beef stew left; I was surprised because the crew had shoveled it in like hogs. Those new biscuits were now cold. I loaded two plates and wandered into the sleeping area. Some clown had thrown my stuff on the floor, so I moved down to the next empty bunk. Nice fellows. Not everyone appreciates close neighbors.

Oh, did that bunkhouse stink! A released canary wouldn't have survived the night.

No sooner had I sat down when someone bawled, "Are you Custer?" I looked up to find a burly cowboy with a sandy mustache and a dirty black felt hat. I didn't answer—just nodded my head and began stuffing food in my mouth.

"Name's Tad Polson, foreman on the Bar P. You can help Coosie for a few days. We're running a bigger crew for the fall roundup and he needs a Mary Ann."

"I planned to work with cattle."

Northfield

He had already turned on his heel and was heading for the door. "Yeah, I heard you was good with cows," he said dryly, without looking back. Some of the guys snickered. Word must have got around about the blunder I made earlier.

So, my first day as a cowboy and I'd already stepped in cowpies. Pa always said, "Don't be afraid to start a new job at the bottom." He probably guessed that's exactly where I was likely to start. Like most teenagers I suppose, I wondered if my parents thought I'd ever amount to a hill of beans.

The routine varied little over the next two weeks: roll out at four in the morning; stumble around a dark, cold kitchen lighting lanterns; fill the coffeepot from the outside pump; then set out crockery and silverware—eatin' tools, the crew called them. The clean up after meals was endless.

It was no wonder Frank paid Coosie as much as the foreman—he worked harder than anyone on the crew. Sometimes the men were too far from the ranch to come in for dinner. Even then, we had sandwiches ready for them to pack along after breakfast. They were good. Thick slabs of roast beef between fat slices of Coosie's homemade bread. It was common knowledge: if the cooking lagged, crewmembers would draw their pay and look for work elsewhere.

With breakfast over, the men entered the corral to rope their mount for the morning. Only a few were properly broke for saddle. As soon as the cowboys climbed on, they buckjumped and fishtailed as if cockleburs were under the saddle blanket. Seldom was a rider thrown. Those boys could ride! After a bit, the horses settled down and were ready to work. I thought it nuts that the men preferred a horse that bucked, especially on frosty mornings. All along I'd taken pride in the way Monty behaved, and I wasn't about to change my mind.

I soon noticed the men treated Coosie with exaggerated respect. No one wanted to get on his bad side. Luckily, some of that spilled over to me, even though they continued to call me Mary Ann.

Several of the guys answered to a nickname. There was Slim—in fact, two of them—Tall Slim and Short Slim, Stubs, High Pockets, Churchy, Smiley, and Banjo. Two went by the states they hailed from: Texas, and the brand new state of Colorado. They called one, Lover

Boy, because he had braided a pocket watchstrap from his sweetheart's hair. It's possible a couple were on the dodge, so that could partly explain the fake names.

Silly, I know, but I hankered for my own nickname, and definitely not Mary Ann. It got stale listening to those jokers chuckling over "Custer." I told them, Sure, General Custer had a bad day on the Little Big Horn, but he was still a great Civil War hero. They just laughed. I knew there was little hope of a change as long as I worked for Coosie.

At the end of the two weeks, it was time to join the crew on the prairie. The roundup and branding had moved too far from the home ranch, so Coosie and I loaded the chuck wagon. He would drive that while I followed with the "hoodlum" wagon. They each had a two-horse hitch. When trailing cattle to market, four-horse teams pulled both, but we didn't have far to go and would stay put after setting up our first wagon-camp.

The hoodlum wagon carried the men's hotrolls—dirty-white canvas sacks containing a quilt, called a soogan, which they slept in. Fortunately, the Rocking Bar P owned spares for po' folks like me. The men also rolled in guns, ammo, whiskey bottles, and tobacco—both the smoking and chawing kinds, along with a few luxury items like soap, toothbrush, comb, and change of clothes.

I was glad to get out with the cattle. That danged bunkhouse was a cushy bedbug hotel. They likely hiked miles to relax there.

Of course, now I had the added chore of caring for the teams. Coosie had even tied his mare, Sugar Babe, to the rear of the chuck wagon. I tied Monty to the hoodlum. If I worked cattle, I wasn't about to start the day with one of Frank Pierce's wild broncs.

By the way, was that Sugar Babe ever ugly! A hammerhead, I think they called them. Jeepers, have you ever seen a horse growing horns? Yeah, first one for me too. Swaybacked too, a little like the Speckled Loon Inn's stable. Well, you know Coosie by now: a fine cook, but he didn't appear likely to cross the street to impress his own ma.

It was beautiful country. Rolling prairie as far as the eye could see. Antelope and deer roamed at will. Prairie chickens flew up ahead of the team. Cloud shadows swept the timeless land along with that of the hawk and eagle. The scent of wildflowers and sage rode sweet on the breeze.

Boy, was Coosie tough in the field! No one rode his horse near the chuck wagon—you got off, tied your horse, and walked over to eat or pick up your hotroll. I was the only one allowed under the canvas fly stretched off the back of the wagon. Woe to anyone who walked under that tarp without an invite from Coosie. It was simple wagon-camp etiquette, and not even Frank Pierce was exempt. Those traditions were common on all ranches, and are still in effect today.

Frank was gone most of the time, and that was peachy with me. He had other crews out close to the home ranch, so he covered a lot of ground.

As before, my main job was dishwashing. They had a wooden rack that held two tubs of heated dishwater, and that's where I spent a good part of my time. Actually, I enjoyed one of my jobs. Someone had fastened a hand-cranked coffee grinder to the side of the wagon, and I used it to grind the daily requirement of Arbuckle's beans. Each one-pound bag contained a stick of peppermint! You'll be relieved to know Mary Ann generously shared the candy with the wiseacre crew.

Coosie cooked almost everything in Dutch ovens. We also carried several cans of tomatoes and peaches, called "airtights."

Everyone's favorite desert was chocolate apple dumpcake. First, Coosie dumped dried apples into a hot Dutch oven and added water. After they were cooked, he dumped in dry chocolate cake mixings and stirred. Oh, what a great gooey cake that made! As a kid, did you lick the mixing bowls when your mom baked? That's what I did before washing that Dutch oven: spoon out every tasty leftover morsel of chocolate apple dumpcake.

I enjoyed turning in at dark, my work done for the day. Stars shone like signal lanterns placed on a stormy coast. By then, the cattle had gone to roost, and no one spoke loudly or made unusual noises for fear of causing a stampede. The men had already discarded jangling things attached to bridles and saddles, and noisy ornaments on spurs, such as tiny chain loops hanging from strap buttons or bell-like pieces of metal, called jinglebobs, which dangled near the spur rowels. I could clearly hear cowboys sing as they circled the herd, keeping them calm. My favorite song was "The Cowboy's Woes."

> I'm warmin' the saddle afore first light,
> And I follow the herd until stars shine bright.
> For forty a month and beans all the way,
> I sleep on the ground and ride the long day.
> It's so cold in the mornin' my teeth are a-chatter,
> The boss hates complainers and growls, "What's the matter?"
> I tell him, "I'm draggin' and want to draw my pay."
> He laughs cuz he knows we're all here to stay.

I'm afraid that's all I can remember. Like the muleskinners, they added new verses anyway, but you get the idea. Some guys sang it to a slightly twisted version of "Oh! Susanna." It always reminded me of our fracas at the Plains Hotel in Cheyenne. Another song heard nightly was "Sweet Betsy From Pike." One Texas boy didn't sing at all: he softly played his harmonica. If I cherished any memory of Wyoming, it was listening to cowboys sing in silent darkness on the bed-ground—maybe a coyote or even a far-away woof calling in the distance.

One day, life suddenly got tougher. Tad Polson, the foreman, ambled over. I knew it wasn't good: he only spoke to me if there was more work waiting. "The nighthawk quit. You can take his job tonight," he said. The nighthawk grazed the horses the cowboys used the following day.

"Why'd he quit?" I asked suspiciously. Seemed a logical question.

"Crazy fool. Said he's going to Cheyenne to join the army."

I wondered if fighting Indians beat nighthawking. "No more kitchen duty?" I asked with fool's hope.

"You won't get off that easy, Custer. You'll bring the horses in at first light, sleep until noon, and then help Coosie until time to take the herd out again. Look me up after supper and I'll ride out with you."

Oh, swell. Now I had two jobs. Why didn't I just give up sleep and work around the clock?

Northfield

Knowing better, I asked Coosie how tough nighthawking was, but he only grunted. Finding a hot bath on the prairie was easier then getting him to talk about anything except cooking. I figured I'd just have to keep the horses from rambling too far, and get them back on time for the men to go to work. How difficult could that be? It appeared I was gradually inching my way up from the bottom.

During spare moments, I slipped sandwiches into my saddlebags and tied on my trusty yellow slicker. A little fuel around midnight would hit the spot. I didn't wear my Colt while cooking, but made sure it was with my saddle. Who knew the evil that slinked through dark prairie nights?

Just before dark, I saddled Monty and rode to the cavvy of saddle horses. Amazing that a single rope could corral the entire herd. I quickly counted 30 heads, thinking it might be advisable to return in the morning with the same amount. That was a lot of horses for the crew size, but some saddle-pounders rode down four a day looking for renegades in rough country.

Tad opened the rope and mounted up. The herd calmly moved out. We went out about a mile before they started to graze. Much like cattle, horses are creatures of habit and soon learn the routine.

"Don't let them ramble too far from camp," the boss ordered. "Bring'um back at first light and a coupla men will help run um in the corral."

"What about rustlers...or worse yet, Indians trying to steal the horses?" I asked. By now, I'd heard plenty of stories of ranchers having whole herds of horses and cattle stampeded off in the darkness.

"You gotta rifle, haven't you?" he asked dryly, as if it was a dumb question.

I patted the stock.

"Well, Custer, come first light and these horses are gone, that damn rifle better be empty. It's a long walk back to the Rocking Bar P." With that, he galloped back in the direction of the chuck wagon. Friendly cuss, he was. I'd only been trying to make conversation. I didn't expect the job to include running gunfights. Later, I found Tad to be a straight shooter, but he wasn't my favorite at the time.

I soon realized sneaking up on a daylight barnyard rooster was easier than staying awake on nighthawk. Through the long hours, I rode Monty in a slow circle around the herd, singing and talking to myself. Couple of times, I almost pitched off headfirst. Coyotes yelped and flirted in the distance, stars sleepily blinked overhead. Wolves called from the high ground, but they seemed a long way off.

I considered what I'd gained with this new job: stay awake all night so I could get off chuck duty for a few hours in the morning. O-o-oh ya, what a smart move. Well, it was a start, and I was getting valuable experience.

There was no sign of the cattle herd in the dim light of dawn. The West's Second Greatest Scout cleverly located the tracks of 30 horses coming out from camp the previous evening. All I had to do was follow that easy track back to Coosie's campfire. With little guidance, the herd trotted back into the rope corral. Already, the chuck wagon seemed like home. I felt as if I'd lived on the range for years.

Chores waited before I could eat breakfast and then spread my bedroll under the wagon. I watered Monty at a nearby stream, gave him a good brushing, and then staked him out to graze. He was so happy to get rid of the saddle, he rolled completely over on his back three times before getting up with a satisfied snort and a good shake. Guess he wasn't used to night work either.

I was the last to eat and I filled my plate—biscuits, beef steak, and red beans. It hadn't taken long to get used to the Western habit of steak for breakfast, and it was lip-smackin' good. Saucer-sized oatmeal cookies too. Oh my, what Coosie lacked in personality, he made up for in cooking. Never had I tasted better pancakes than Coosie's. Oatmeal wasn't my favorite at home, but out here, I could live on it.

This nighthawking had to be Frank Pierce's idea. It looked as if it was some kind of game with him. I figured he wanted to find if I had enough sand to stick, or would I run up the white flag and head for the house. Well, fine. If I didn't prove I was serious about working cattle, he'd give me a dress and I'd be Mary Ann forever.

Several days slipped by, and I noticed the hands treating me with added respect since taking on the nighthawk job. It was just in small hints: they talked about the roundup and their own jobs as if I was part of it and would understand. Still, I wouldn't be a full member of the crew unless I worked cows. It didn't matter who the horse wrangler was; the job commanded limited respect.

Coosie was not so bad after all: after eating at noon, he gave me plenty of time to relax and jaw with the men who hung around for more coffee at the chuck wagon. They lit rolled Bull Durham smokes with brands from the fire.

That's when I learned about mavericking. If anyone found unbranded cattle on his land, he could claim them with his own brand. In the early 1880s, states passed Maverick Laws that only condoned what had been the practice for years. Of course, people abused the laws. Anyone could round up cattle and claim they found them on their property. Many of the large ranches got started with these so-called "maverick cattle." It explained why Frank Pierce wanted to brand as many as possible. By spring, anything not branded would belong to someone else. In 1876, he had cattle scattered over both Dakota and Wyoming territory, and eastern Nebraska—more than he could hope to prove he owned.

After a week of riding and sleeping in the saddle, Tad wandered over one afternoon while I was on my knees scrubbing Dutch ovens. Coosie used them to bake biscuits. "Getting tired of soapsuds, are you?" he asked. I figured he didn't give a damn whether I was or not.

"It's a living," I muttered, naturally adopting the short sentences that were common to the crew.

He chuckled in that deep voice of his and hunched down beside me. "How about taking over Coosie's job? Then I could run that grouchy old goat off."

I knew he was joshing. "Funny," I said. "Maybe you could join a circus and sell quack patent medicines."

He pulled off his big hat and slapped it on the ground, laughing again. "Maybe I'll do that. We'll all need a job once winter blows in. Anyway, fresh hands are coming tonight with the supply wagon. We need help branding. I'll set up a new Mary Ann, and you can join us each day after dinner. You'll still have the nighthawk job. Think you can handle it?"

Jerome A. Kuntz

Could I handle it? It proved I was coming up in the world by the fact that he would even bother to ask. The only soapsuds I ever wanted to see again were in a bathtub.

Naturally, I figured only some spittoon-polishing saloon swamper would take over as Mary Ann—the worse job on the crew.

Chapter 23

Even though ranch work had me dragging heels most days, I felt lucky to have experienced it before the "Great Die-up." Massive blizzards raked the high plains during the winter of 1886-87, destroying the great Western herds. A bad winter? When spring finally reached deep gullies in June of '87, they found cows in the tops of forty-foot cottonwoods. Well, by the middle of May anyway. No, not tree-climbing cows; this isn't the Speckled Loon Inn. Many ranchers reported 90 percent loss of their stock.

Remember cowboy/artist Charles Russell's world-famous watercolor, *Waiting for a Chinook?* He painted it while working in Montana in the spring of '87. It shows a lone, bony, starved steer—his luck played out and he's standing hip-deep in snow. Hungry coyotes, waiting for a meal they know is coming, surround the hapless animal. Charlie sent it to his boss in town to inform him of the condition of his stock. The rancher renamed it, *Last of the 5000,* and no amount of words could have better informed the horrified outside world what had happened to the great herds.

Never again would wild cattle roam the open prairie. More control was necessary. The ranchers built fences and stacked fodder to bring stock through lean winter months. With that came homesteaders, and Western beef raising became only another segment of the great engine of American food production.

I arrived back at the chuck wagon the next morning, hurriedly cared for Monty and staked him to graze. Sure enough, there was the supply wagon someone had driven out from the home ranch. I was anxious to see if my sucker replacement had arrived. Without someone to take the job, I'd have to stay on chuck duty. I headed for the cooking fire and got in the grub line.

Buck was helping Coosie!

"What the hell are you doing here?" I asked, flabbergasted.

He barely looked up from his work. "Why? Did you buy Wyoming since I saw you last?"

Smart alecky as always. Almost the same crack he used at the train station. "Buck, if I did have enough dough to buy Wyoming, know what I'd do?"

"Take acting lessons? Yeah, I know: nice shot, John Wilkes Booth."

"Plant trees, man. Wow, what do these people do for summer shade?"

"What people?" he said, swiveling his head to look around.

"By the way, if you don't mind my asking, why aren't you helping Robbie on his homestead?"

"I was until he lost it. He didn't prove-up and had it contested. In order to hold a homestead you have to live on it and build a house or anyone can file and move in. That's what happened. Robbie and Dirk stormed into the Hat Creek Claim Office, but it was too late. Robbie moved his family back in with Dirk."

Even though the crew had finished eating, it was the custom to hang around for another cup of Coosie's coffee. They called Buck "Mary Ann," but he paid little attention. He was always laid-back and not one to worry about what other people thought.

Buck held the huge coffeepot while filling the cowboys' cups. He grunted pretty good and wasn't having the easiest time of it. Coosie watched the green hand severely. I couldn't believe the kid had followed me. Still, I was secretly tickled to see him again.

"What about Jas? She still there?" I asked, acting nonchalant.

Buck looked at me blankly. "Who?"

"Have you gone deaf, you jackass?"

"Ah, keep your shirt on, lover boy. Ya, she's still there. Not for long though. There wasn't much call for teachers among the ranchers and homesteaders, so she's taking the coach to Cheyenne. Said something about The Tender T-bone restaurant."

"Egad, couldn't you find her a job in Hat Creek?"

"Damn, Custer," he said, finally stopping work and looking exasperated. "I might if I didn't so enjoy looking at the back end of two mules all day breaking sod."

"Well…did anyone try to talk her into staying on?"

"Of course, but you ought to know by now, Jas goes her own way."

He was too busy to visit, so I filled my plate and found a place on the ground to sit, Indian style. I idly wondered what it'd be like to use a chair again.

This was a bad turn of events. At least she wasn't going back to the Plains Saloon. I'd worn my welcome paper-thin in that place. Gosh, I missed her. When the job was over, I was riding straight for Cheyenne—Christmas at the latest.

I'd barely crawled into my blanket roll after breakfast when someone was kicking my feet.

"Dinner time, cowboy," Buck called cheerfully. "Cookie-man sent me to wake you."

I kicked back at him but he danced off to the side. "Watch it, buddy, or you'll get your old job back," he threatened.

"Uh-huh, then what would you do for a living?"

"Oh, I'd find something, maybe a sheriff's deputy again."

"Go ahead, fella. Just say what you want for supper before you leave and I'll eat it. Oh, and *your* share of chocolate apple dumpcake—forget it."

"Dumpcake? Yich-h-h! What the hell's that?"

"Never mind. Just more for me if you leave."

"Hum-m, that's big of you," he said, chuckling.

"Anyway, what do you think of Coosie?" I asked.

"Oh, he's kinda hokey. What does that Coosie mean?"

"Coosie is Spanish slang for *cosinara*. It means cook."

"This isn't Spain. Why don't they call him Cookie?"

"Hell if I know," I said. "This isn't Minnesota."

"I *know* this isn't Minnesota. I'll call him Chef."

"Isn't that French?"

"Yeah it's French. It means cook."

"This isn't France."

"AHA! It not Spain either, pal. Gotta go."

Danged kid, I thought. Getting tough as Sadie to get the better of.

I sat up and rubbed my eyes. Six hours sleep just wasn't enough. Still, most of the crew wasn't getting much more, and they were doing a lot of hard riding. I'd heard stories of cowboys staying in the saddle almost continuously for three days and nights. That'd be the end of me. I thought I was saddle-leather tough after the trip from Northfield. Now, I didn't believe I could match anyone on the crew—except Buck of course. At least I had some company. My belly brayed with hunger, so I tossed my bedroll in the hoodlum wagon and hurried to the grub line.

Tad strolled over while I ate. "You ready to brand this afternoon?" he asked.

"Sure, I'll saddle Monty after I eat."

"You won't need a horse. Your job will be to keep the branding fires going."

Back on the bottom again. I might have known. It turned out they had two branding fires. Lucas, the cheerful and willing supply wagon driver, had brought firewood, but that wouldn't last long. Later that afternoon I used the wagon and team to haul deadfall from a nearby cottonwood grove. Swinging an axe in Indian-summer heat made for a long afternoon.

I learned plenty watching the branding crew. As soon as the ropers dragged over a bawling calf, two men would slam it to the ground and hold it while the brander applied a red-hot iron. When another mark was called for, a fourth man stepped forward with a knife to make either an earmark or cut a dewlap, a slice in the loose flesh under an animal's neck. With no wind, the entire area stunk of burning hair and hide.

I'd never seen cattle with such horns—two feet or longer on both sides of the head! They were just like in the picture I told you about hanging over the dining table in the Speckled Loon Inn in Mankato. We couldn't allow that on the farm. Too dangerous and they wouldn't fit in the barn stanchions. The branding crew cautioned me not to approach longhorn cattle on foot, as they would charge, but it was perfectly safe on horseback.

Tad gave Buck additional work besides the chuck wagon. He had to keep the branding crew supplied with drinking water. Testing the kid out, likely. I could see on the Rocking Bar P, it was either get tough, die, or pack your freight. Take your choice.

By suppertime, nighthawking seemed like a dream job. In fact, it amazed me Frank paid for such cushy work. I couldn't wait to get off my feet and ride Monty in the cool darkness.

I didn't realize how dead-tired I was until I hazed the remuda a mile from camp. It was barely dark and my chin was already bouncing off my chest. I kept circling the herd, singing snatches of songs learned from the crew and from back in Northfield.

All of us kept track of time by observing the Big Dipper as it appeared to rotate around the North Star once in a 24-hour period—much like our smarter-than-average but exhausted, Mr. Moses, showed daylight time by rotating with the shade around the oak tree. Lordy, that was uphill work trying to keep awake! The last I could recall, it was about two in the morning. I woke to shouting voices. Now it was broad daylight.

Custer Van Winkle had slumped forward, catching his belt on the saddle horn with his head resting on Monty's neck. There was the high muckety-muck, Frank Pierce, yelling at me. Tad was by his side, looking slightly shocked. Two crewmembers sat their horses behind, fighting to keep grins off their faces.

"Where the hell are the horses?" Frank bellowed.

I quickly looked around but saw no sign of my charges. The herd was gone! Monty grazed without a care in the world. "They couldn't have got far, Frank," I croaked. I began circling, trying to pick up tracks. Just my luck Frank was back when this happened.

"You damn well better find them and then you'll draw your pay," he snarled.

"Now wait a minute, Frank," Tad protested. "What the hell did you expect? You got this growing kid working around the clock. He's on my crew and I say he stays."

Frank stared at him a moment in startled surprise. "Then, by god, you'll be responsible if he messes up again." With that, he whirled his horse and galloped toward the chuck wagon.

Tad watched him go, slowly shaking his head. "Banjo, you and Tall Slim help Custer," he said

I tried to thank him. "Thanks boss for sticking up—"

"Just find those damn horses!" He jerked a rein, pulling his horse's head around, and followed Frank back to camp.

I found the tracks so at least I knew the direction. Question was, how far had they gone?

"Hey Custer, don't get all head-up," Banjo called, laughing. "We all had time for a leisurely breakfast. First break we've had in a week."

I knew I'd be in for a lot of ribbing and figured I'd best get used to it. I could see for miles and there was no sign of the horses except hoof prints. Talk about worried! If wolves ran them down, even Tad wouldn't be able to save me. "Look Banjo," I said, "see all this good grass? Man, this is horse heaven. They wouldn't have gone far, not with water here too. Ain't that how you see it? Shoot, I'd bet they're close by, wouldn't you?"

He blankly stared at me for a few beats. "Custer," he said slowly, "maybe *you* feel this is horse heaven, but those broncs might think different. I'd bet they've run to hell and gone."

"Me too!" I shouted. "Let's ride!" We tickled the spurs and broke into a gallop. After about five miles, we skidded down into a deep gully. There was the remuda. They lifted their heads as if to ask, "What's all the fuss about?" Green grass snaked through the gully following a few trickles of water. They must have smelled it and moseyed off soon after I fell asleep. I was lucky; when those horses found that treat, they weren't about to move on.

We soon had them bunched and galloping hard for camp. The crew guided them into the rope corral. I noticed several grins among the men. A couple hours off work evidently improved morale. Frank, of course, was another matter.

I quickly stripped and brushed Monty and staked him to graze. Then I hurried to the chuck wagon. Good old Buck. He had saved a heaping plate of flapjacks for me. They were cold, but I was too hungry to care. I slopped on syrup while Buck poured scalding coffee.

That was one morning I was grateful he didn't tease. "*Danke*, buddy," I told him. "I owe you one."

"What'n hell happened? Tom Thumb was mad enough to pluck and cook."

Northfield

Trust Buck to come up with the perfect name for that old coot. "Yeah, he's a humdinger all right," I said, between mouthfuls. "Pure cussedness. I fell asleep on Monty. Six hours just isn't enough. If I'd fallen off, it wouldn't have happened. When I woke, Tom Thumb was yelling and the herd was gone. God, what a mess! I just want to crawl in and sleep."

Buck knelt on one knee, still wearing his bullet-holed cap, and his face was all sunburned. "If you leave, I'm skedaddling too. If you're not good enough, neither am I."

"Ya, okay, I know you mean well but everyone best go his own way." I didn't think Buck quitting would prove much.

"Oh, by the way," Buck said, "does ya feel guilty, hogin' all the bad luck in this ol' whirl?"

I couldn't help but laugh and then felt better. He went back to work and I dug my bedroll from the hoodlum wagon. Frank would now look for any excuse to nail my hide to the barn door. Likely, he hated being overruled by his foreman in front of the crew, and would blame me for it. Fortunately, he wasn't around that much.

As most people do all their lives, I fretted over the wrong thing.

Chapter 24

The next day at noon, Tad rode to the chuck wagon. I felt like I had hardly slept, but still got up to eat dinner. "Custer," he shouted, "from now on, get eight hours sleep and then help with branding."

"Thanks," I said, waving my fork at him. "For everything." He didn't answer, just spun his horse and headed back to the herd. Frank had probably chewed his ear a little more, putting him in a sour mood. Old Tad was turning out to be a square shooter. I told Buck to wake me at two and then I dived back into my bedroll.

Things rumbled on the same the next several days. The routine of it all made it easier. I only had to feed the branding fires a few hours before taking the horses out again. I didn't see how Buck could stand it, but he hung in like a trooper. Coosie had him busy from first light to sundown.

Rattlesnakes unnerved us all. Sometimes we came across hundreds, the prairie seeming to crawl before our eyes. Well, a dozen at least. Okay, High Pockets claimed he once spotted six …somewhere. As writer of this book, I wouldn't want you to think I exaggerate. The cowboys gave them a wide birth, not daring to shoot near the herd.

Have you ever had a snake dream while sleeping out? It seemed we all took our turn at that. Scary as a witches' nest. I was just glad to sleep in daylight. At least Coosie and Buck could keep an eye out for unwelcome critters.

I couldn't believe one man owned all those cattle. When branding was over, they planned to trail a herd of four-year-olds to Casper to sell to the army for distribution on Indian Reservations; that was the reason for the extra road brand put on some cattle. I had little hope of Tad picking me for that crew, but I didn't care. Now I would have extra pocket money and could spend more time in Cheyenne. The sooner I saw Jas, the better.

Over the years, I looked back on a rainy, lightning-blasted night as the beginning of the end. I expected an ordinary shift as I hazed the horses from camp, paying little attention to the heavy clouds on the northwest horizon. I had my slicker and was used to abrupt changes in the weather. Silent lightning forked a starless sky by the time the horses began to graze. Normally, the evening cooled, but that night it still felt hot and humid. It seemed strange weather so late in the year, but I was more used to Minnesota. The horses were restless and wanted to roam. I had to ride continuously to keep them bunched.

O-o-oh boy, at home with a storm like this coming, we sometimes took shelter in the hog barn. Heavy rain would pound the roof while the piled and snoring pigs grunted contentedly in their sleep. How a person misses things after leaving that you took for granted while growing up.

Those bad storms still failed to dampen Minnesotans' sense of humor, even the one I mentioned earlier that snatched the roof off the school's bell tower. Later, a story made the rounds and then came around again to make sure everyone heard it. Before it hit, the first neighbor had said, "Ya, that sky looks bad and the train whistle sounds like rain." The second neighbor replied, "Train whistle you say? Hum-m-m, now that's odd. They haven't finished the tracks into Northfield yet." First neighbor again, "Egad, no tracks? Everyone into the root cellar!"

By midnight on the prairie, I knew I was in for it. It was a slow-moving storm with the wind shifting every hour. Thunder rumbled a black warning. Twice I heard lightning-struck trees explode in the distance. A dangerous sulfur scent rode the breeze. I circled the remuda at a greater pace, talking and singing softly. When lightning flashed, I could see the entire herd and tried to make a quick count. Impossible I know, but if the bunch looked about the same, I figured none had bolted.

Rain and small hail came in great rolling sheets. Much colder now. The horses instinctively closed ranks, rumps to the onslaught and heads down. Now they'd stay put. Water poured off the front and back of my hat.

Just as I hunkered under Monty's neck, my back to his chest and reins in my hand—an old cowboy trick—I spotted four riders in a flash of lightning. They were riding in the direction of the herd. What the hell were they doing here? Never before had crewmembers ridden near my herd. I wiped rain from my eyes and waited. Monty's breath smoked white in the cold night air. Another flash. There they were again, farther away. They were looking back at me. Again, on the third flash. By the fourth flash, the prairie was empty, thunder howling like a mad dog over a black empty land.

Now what should I do now? Tad had told the crew several times to watch for rustlers. I couldn't leave the horses to report back, and I sure didn't want to return them in darkness. Too much chance of trampling sleeping cowboys. Besides, I doubted I could find the cow camp before daylight. Normally I could detect the far-off glow of Coosie's campfire until around nine; after that, all bets were off. No sound of the cattle herd either. During daylight, there was continuous bellowing, but in darkness they were quiet on the bed-ground. I decided to carry on like any other night. Maybe our men were looking for strays that bolted in the storm. Still, I doubted they would ride by without a "howdy."

Most of the storm blew over by four in the morning. Never had I stayed as alert as I did that night. There were no more nightriders, but I did get a visit from a couple of sleepy coyotes. I guessed heavy rain had driven them from flooded dens and they waited for the world to dry.

As soon as we had the herd secure in the rope corral at daylight, I sloshed over for a shot of Coosie's coffee. It had been a long cold night. The cook kept dry firewood in a rawhide pouch hanging under the chuck wagon for mornings like this.

The foreman was standing in the grub line. I ignored the usual joshing that came from crewmembers about bringing the horses back so early. "Tad, did you have riders out last night?" I asked, trying to keep the excitement out of my voice.

He looked at me strangely, already sensing something wrong. "Well, the night guard—"

"No…no, I don't mean the usual night guard. West of here, near the remuda. Four riders passed me about midnight, aiming for the cattle."

"Maybe they were Indians. You couldn't have seen much in that storm."

Other crewmembers gathered around. I figured he wouldn't take me serious. "Not a chance. I saw them in lightning. They wore cowboy hats, slickers and a couple carried lariats."

The crew stared at me, waiting for what was coming. Now I had their attention. I took my time, sipped my coffee. "Some outfit's watching the herd," I said flatly. I wasn't near that confident, but if I sounded wishy-washy, he'd ignore the threat.

"Damn," Tad swore softly, automatically looking toward the bedground. "Could be rustlers. Almost every year those yahoos hit one of the big ranchers. Whoever they are, they wait until the cattle are bunched to save rounding up. Then they start a stampede, usually on a moonless night, and make off with as many cows as possible in the confusion."

Tad waved the whole crew over. "Listen up, men," he said, "Custer here spotted nightriders. We gotta be ready in case they start a stampede. Banjo, you'll ride nighthawk with Custer. They might try for the horses too. I want every night-herd position doubled, starting tonight"—a groan went up from the crew—"and make sure you're carrying your six-gun. A rifle's too hard to use on a galloping horse."

It meant less sleep for everyone. I noticed a few sidelong glances. Still, no one questioned what I had seen. After all, even the greenest tenderfoot couldn't mistake four men on horseback.

Day and night, we watched and waited—the men grumpy from lack of sleep. Branding continued as before. Banjo joined me on nighthawk. Everyone went armed; some carried Winchesters in addition to their Colts. Chuck wagon meals looked like a war was on. Even Buck and Coosie were ready. Both packed six-shooters even while working, and Buck tied Cowboy to the chuck wagon next to gorgeous Sugar Babe. They were saddled, but with loose latigoes. They only had to snap tight the diamond hitch and were ready to run.

Worry gnawed at me. It was like Buck to be in the thick of things. Even when we kidded around, he seemed tense, as if preparing for action sure to come. I knew if I told him to stick with the chuck wagon, he'd be even more determined. Pa's note stated to keep Buck in school. There was more to it than that: he was making me responsible. It was my payment for Monty and the tack. The posse wages were mine either way.

Maybe those riders were only passing through. But at night? And in a storm? I couldn't convince myself and neither could the crew. Those birds could afford to be patient and pick the time and place to hit us. If they were watching during the storm, likely they'd make their play on the next bad night. It wasn't long coming.

It began like most nights. I was bored and sleepy. Banjo yawned and bellyached about the extra hours. By now, I felt the crew doubted I'd seen anything. Churchy even started calling me Mary Ann again. I paid no attention; that kind of gab never ended. The men teased each other mercilessly just to pass the time.

Around midnight, it clouded up. No sign of stars. Of course, I lost my space clock. If they were going to hit us, tonight was perfect. We wouldn't know they were here until they started the stampede.

It began an hour later. We heard gunshots and a drumming of hooves. The cattle were on the move! It had to be rustlers; no crewmember would ever be that careless. The back of my neck was a crawling anthill.

I stood in my stirrups, trying to determine which direction the cattle ran. Banjo raced his horse over to me and skidded to a stop. "Rustlers, Custer!" he hissed. "Bunch the herd and we'll push them back to the rope corral."

He was an experienced hand and I let him take the lead. Ten minutes tops, and we had them behind the rope. Banjo tied the gate while I ran toward the chuck wagon, calling for Buck. Too late—Cowboy was gone and so was Sugar Babe. Danged kid! He was out trying to save the herd.

More gunshots! I knew Buck would go after the rustlers. I only hoped he wouldn't shoot one of the crew.

"C'mon, Banjo!" I shouted on the run, "Help me find Buck!" We leapt into our saddles. "Hi-i-ya-a-a-a! Hi-i-i-ya-a-a-a!" we yelled. Bellies flat on our pummels, spurs raking, we raced in the direction of the shots, hoping to overtake the herd. It was risky running over unfamiliar ground, but we had no choice. I hated leaving the horse cavvy unguarded, but it would take us all to run off the rustlers and turn the herd in a circle.

It seemed hopeless. We caught the herd, but couldn't reach the leaders. I saw sharp flashes, which I assumed were gunshots, but I could hear nothing but pounding hooves.

Banjo and I stayed together, racing for the front. I figured he knew what to do and I would follow him. The most frightening times were dropping down into gullies, or cut-banks as they called them. Monty seemed to dissolve under me and I had no weight on the saddle. Only a death grip on the horn kept my seat.

We came alongside a rider. "Who are you?" I shouted. I was just trying to see his face. His head swiveled, trying to watch both of us at once. It was no one we knew and we both swung our pistols at his head. He folded off his horse. If cattle didn't trample that rustler, he would wake with scrambled brains.

I worried our crew might shoot us, thinking we were still back with the remuda. Cattle crossed in front of us, preventing our gaining the lead cows. I saw Banjo shouting and waving at me, but could hear only the thunder of pounding hooves and horns clacking like hundreds of ball bats. It was so dark, only a few cattle next to me were visible. I couldn't tell if I was gaining or dropping back. Soon, Banjo disappeared in darkness.

After traveling for miles, I heard more gunfire and saw flashes. Crewmembers had reached the front and were using six-guns to turn the herd. We raced along fast as ever, but I sensed a change of direction. Those boys in front played a dangerous game. If their horses went down, they wouldn't have a chance of getting out from under sharp hooves.

Now we slowed too. I was passing cattle beside me. With luck the entire herd would stay intact, and we wouldn't have to repeat the roundup. Banjo was again beside me.

We loped in a massive circle. The cattle heaved with exhaustion. No sign of any more rustlers. They'd counted on surprise, and wouldn't have any interest in a slowing herd surrounded by armed Rocking Bar P riders.

Jerome A. Kuntz

We came up on several of the crew and called their names, trying not to spook the herd. We wanted to let them know we were there. They waved back and we gradually slowed to a halt. I felt sick, ready to puke, from the pounding saddle and racing for miles without once seeing the ground. For some reason, I had a bloody nose and my saddle pummel was slippery-wet. How much worse it must have been at the front!

Long before daylight, those tough buckaroos were talking fast horses, Black Hills gold mining, and mail order brides. They softly sang, rolled cigarettes, and spat tobacco as if nothing had happened—just another night's work. Once again, I felt like a damn tenderfoot. With incredible skill and daring, they had saved the herd. Those cowboys rode for the brand, Tad and Frank expecting no less.

"Keep circling, men," Tad advised in a soft voice. "Calm um down. I think the worst is over."

Another thing I wasn't to forget.

Chapter 25

We spent the remainder of the night slowly circling the herd, singing and talking softly. Before long, they bedded down, completely forgetting the night's excitement. Coosie and Tall Slim rode back to the wagon camp to check the remuda and prepare a long overdue meal. Tad didn't send me because I'd been up all night and needed sleep before nighthawk.

I asked everyone if they'd seen Buck, but no one knew his whereabouts. Even Coosie had lost track of him. They'd left the chuck wagon together, but Buck had disappeared in darkness. Could he have pursued the rustlers alone? My mind refused to consider other possibilities. I was worried sick, but it was too dark to wander around looking for anyone. Possibly dangerous too—those remaining rustlers could be close by. We accounted for everyone else. No one could guess how far from the chuck wagon we'd come, and it was senseless to push the herd back before daylight.

We moved out at sunrise. Being the newest man on the crew, I rode drag—following the herd and breathing dust churned up by hundreds of sharp hooves. The cattle were tired so there were few troublemakers. I kept searching to the sides, watching for Buck or maybe Cowboy wandering loose.

We changed direction. The entire herd bowed left. Could they have misjudged the camp's location? I came up on a small group of riders standing in a circle. Why weren't they tending to business? A couple had their hats off and seemed to be looking back at me.

Oh, God, then I remembered something. My stomach knotted and I swallowed back acid.

No longer did I see my crewmembers. In startling clarity, the long-ago Kansas dream was back before me—Buck lying alone on the open prairie. It had been a terrible prophesy after all, just as I feared at the time, but had all but forgotten since. I knew exactly what I'd find behind those men.

As I rode up and slid off Monty, Tad hurried over, tears in his eyes. He clutched my shoulders. "Custer, don't go there," he pleaded.

I gently pushed his hands away. "He's my brother...and my responsibility," I said, wondering already how I could ever explain it to our parents. My world had crashed. The men respectfully parted and removed their hats.

Buck lay face down. Thankfully, the cattle hadn't trampled him. I knelt beside him for a time, trying to comprehend. Hours earlier, we'd teased each other at the grub line. Taking him by his shoulder and hip, I rolled him over. They'd shot him in the chest. His face was calm, as if he'd been riding to a picnic, skin white as our school chalk, even his lips. I closed his eyes for the last time and someone came with his silly cloth cap, the one he'd shown so proudly, and gently placed it on his face. I heard crying around me.

I pulled Buck's Colt and rotated the cylinder. He'd fired five shots; the gun was empty. He must have holstered it before falling. I looked back to where the herd had stampeded. Two bodies lay crumpled in the dirt. "Rustlers?" I asked, looking up at Tad.

"Yeah, Custer. Buck didn't go alone."

I remained surprisingly calm. Instinctively, I knew if I didn't hold up, neither could the crew. Someone was repeating my name. Then I heard Tad ask, "Custer, what do you want to do?"

I was in shock and could barely think. Hat Creek was the closest settlement, but I didn't know anyone there. "Bury him here," I said. "He loved this prairie as much as I do."

"Lucas," Tad said decisively, "ride ahead and bring back your supply wagon. Make sure the shovels are there. Get Tall Slim to help you cut out your team and hitch up so you can hurry back. Also, tell Coosie not to expect us until...oh, say two o'clock at the earliest. Got that?"

"Got it, boss." Lucas mounted up, whirled his horse and loped away.

Soon Tex rode up, leading Cowboy. "I found him, Custer. His reins had tangled in those bushes yonder." I nodded my head.

"Stay here with Custer, Tex," Tad ordered. "We'll hold the herd until Lucas gets back." Then I heard them ride away. The work went on.

My memories of the next few hours are surprisingly vague. It's probably nature's way of protecting the mind. Eventually, several of the crew took turns digging the grave. Tex and I waited by the wagon. By then, Tad had carved "Buck Compton" and the date on a board. It hurt—there was no lumber and no damn place to buy it for a coffin.

Someone always clutched my arm, even leading me to the grave for a simple ceremony. They had wrapped Buck in a gray army blanket and lowered him to his final resting place. We stood in a circle, holding our hats. Tad held a small black prayer book, but he looked over it, far out across the prairie. From the heart, he spoke this wonderful prayer. It was similar to funeral prayers at home but with a cowboy feel:

"Fellow travelers are we all,
From sweet birth to the long dark night,
Searching for our individual purpose in life.
Our good works are recorded in the great tally book of life.
At drive's end, Lord, help us to show a gain.
Vouch for the Rocking Bar P crew, Buck. Rest in peace.
Amen."

I shook Tad's hand and told him I was well satisfied with the ceremony. Then I thanked the gravediggers. I rode away leading Cowboy and with a crewmember always at my side. I'm eternally grateful for their quiet kindness. We left the rustlers where they fell for their families or friends to claim.

There was still a long trip back to camp. It was past noon when we reached the chuck wagon. I felt sorry for the crew. They'd worked all night, skipped breakfast, and were now late for dinner. Even then, a few had to stay with the herd until relieved. And I used to think farming was a hard life!

It was good to see again the horse cavvy. From habit, I made a quick count. Coosie had his cooking fire going and looked ready for us. Tad rode over while I watered and brushed Monty and Cowboy. The poor horses stood with lowered heads, too tired to nibble the trampled grass.

"Custer, someone else can take over nighthawk," he said.

"Thanks, but I won't be able to sleep anyway." I knew I had to go on with the work.

"Well...make sure you eat and get some rest before you go. Coosie's rustling grub now."

"Don't worry, I can smell his biscuits from here."

"Lucas is driving the supply wagon back to the home ranch tomorrow," Tad said. "No one will fault you for going back early. The branding will be done in a few days anyway."

I had plenty of time to think this over on the way back, even deciding what to tell Pa, Ma, and Sadie. "If Lucas will take my letter to Hat Creek and send it by stage to the Cheyenne post office, I'd like to finish the job," I said. My best friend was gone, and now I hated leaving the crew. Then I'd be truly alone until reaching the Bradford families. Besides, my leaving would put a strain on Coosie, and someone else would have to take over nighthawk.

I didn't cry in front of the men, but I blubbered most of that first night on nighthawk. The wolves were much closer now, sending their mournful wails into the blackness. Over and over, I howled back as it gave me some relief. My charges knew me well, but still they lifted their heads and stared curiously, sharp ears pointing. By daylight, it seemed much of my grief had drained away. Besides, I'd hadn't slept much in two days, and I was numb with fatigue. How could it happen? All Buck had to do was stay with the chuck wagon.

Of course, everyone was subdued while continuing the work. Still, the job went well and we finished in three days. I rode nighthawk and helped Coosie in the afternoons. He hardly asked anything of me, but I still kept busy. If he wasn't too proud to work chuck, neither was I.

I came to understand more in those three days than I had in the past five years. Now I saw the swiftness of life, its terrifying limitations, and how easily one could lose it. Don't you imagine most everyone reaches that enlightenment at some time? Then we chide ourselves forever for not loving life enough.

It was time to leave. I saddled Monty and Cowboy, and tied Buck's few belongings on his saddle, along with his pistol and belt. It was about the only thing of his that I carried back to Northfield. The crew stood around the cooking fire, pretending to warm themselves. They had scarcely looked at my face since that terrible day; cowboys never look at the pain in another man's eyes. I shook everyone's hand and thanked them. They had all told me that Buck played a large part in saving the cattle and maybe even their own lives, so that made me feel better.

Part of the crew was leaving soon for the home ranch with the hoodlum wagon, gear, and most of the remuda. The rest of the men, along with the cook and chuck wagon, would trail the herd of four-year-olds to Casper.

Tad walked over, extending his hand. "Come back anytime, cowboy," he said, smiling. That was kind: he called me what I'd told Frank I wanted to be. Then he handed me an envelope. "That's your wages and Buck's. I talked it over with Frank; you both deserve this and our thanks." I later counted much more than we were due.

"Thanks," I stammered. I tightened the girth on Monty and mounted up. The men stood with arms folded over their chest, their faces expressionless.

You know this: people sometimes give you things that can't be bought anywhere for any price. That's how I felt about those cowboys. Even now, I can't explain how I so easily felt their kindness when they said so little. A tough bunch, but I never met finer men. I touched my hat brim with two fingers, mouth-clicked to Monty and loped south. The job was over.

Late that night, I reached the Bradford homestead. I'd made some decisions on the way. The best thing I could do was return to Northfield—at least for a while. Besides, I needed to sell Cowboy and that money, along with Buck's wages, belonged to Pa and Ma. Lucas would mail my letter explaining what happened, but they would have a lot more questions. I'd been foolish and Buck had paid the price. For the rest of my life, I new I'd never forget Jasmine's warning at the hotel in Council Bluffs. I'd just have to live with it.

You can imagine the Bradfords' shock when I rode up leading Buck's horse. In cowboy country, a rider-less horse under saddle is like a loud pounding on a lone prairie cabin door after midnight—a sign of alarm or tragedy. The women and children especially were so grief-stricken, I knew I couldn't stay long. Besides, Jasmine had taken the stage to Cheyenne two weeks earlier and I had to see her.

Do you remember when I told you how Phoebe and Elliot followed Buck around but were shy with me? Again that bond and understanding among twins. They cried uncontrollably, no matter how much Judy and Libby tried to comfort them. They all loved him as much as I did. It was as if they had lost one of their own.

My clothes were dirty and ragged. Judy and Libby washed and patched them as best they could, but I needed new ones for the train ride home.

I would have to sell both horses and tack. Dirk purchased Cowboy along with the saddle and bridle. I knew Robbie and Judy wanted Monty, but couldn't afford him until later. We agreed on a price, and they promised to send the money on to Pa. I would leave Monty at the Cheyenne Livery and Feed, and Robbie said he'd take the stage south in a few days and pick him up when he came for supplies. At least I knew our mounts would have a good home. Even the children loved both of those fine horses. Cheyenne was tugging hard on me, and I had to be going.

Three days later, I rode slowly down Cheyenne's dusty streets. Quite a town. Saw a sign as I rode in, "No Gunplay on the Streets" shot full of holes. It's a fact: give a cowboy a beer and he'll empty his shooting iron. People came out on the boardwalk to watch. They knew who I was. Streets were quiet. Monty's hooves sounded like the West had gone hollow—it surly had for me.

Once again, I was reminded how fast news travels in a lightly populated area, long before phones and radio. Lucas must have told passengers at Hat Creek, and they carried it south to Cheyenne on the daily stage. Naturally, a good share of the town already knew about our ruckus at the Plains Hotel.

Jas told me much later all the stories she heard working at The Tender T-bone: the Compton brothers taking on a saloon full of men; bullets flying around the hotel lobby and down the street; dancehall girls beating a man senseless. Most of it was poppycock. Once again, people telling a good story to put spice in their lives. Trouble is, a lot of folks believed.

Northfield

Worst of all was Marty, The Plains Hotel Saloon owner. I don't know how he got our names, probably from Jasmine's ex-roommate, but he told anyone who'd listen—the Compton brothers were outlaws and ought to be locked up. That day, I didn't care if I saw him or not. After what had happened, he would only be as bothersome as a housefly.

People on the boardwalk didn't wave or call to me; they merely stared. I wondered what to make of it. Later, I learned how sympathetic they really were. Cattle were the lifeblood of Cheyenne, along with the railroad of course, and people admired and respected cowboys. Damn well still do from what I hear. It wasn't at all like the great trail drives from Texas to Kansas railheads. After losing the Confederacy, those Southern drovers little respected Northern law or its peace officers.

A tall thin gent with a hatchet face came from a saloon, wiping his hands on his apron. I rode over. "Can you tell me where I might find The Tender T-bone restaurant?" I asked.

"Down yonder and across the street," he said, pointing. "They gotta a sigh hanging out front, and you can't miss it. She's expecting ya, Custer."

Imagine my surprise. Everyone in town must know, I thought. I nodded my thanks and rode in the direction he had indicated. Now I was scared. My clothes were faded and patched, the fancy new boots were water stained and pooched-out from hard service. My sweat-stained black hat resembled the collapsing roof of an old barn. Those days on the branding field were long and hot. I found out, cowboying was a weedy row to hoe. I had to punch new holes in my gun belt. Even Monty thinned down considerably from the endless riding. He needed grain and a good rest. I was in a sorry shape to see my girl. That's how I now thought of her. I wasn't sure how she felt.

The Tender T-bone looked spanking new. The owner had built a ways off the street with a large wood patio stretching to the boardwalk. People would probably eat out there on nice days. I rode up and dismounted. Jas came out, along with customers and co-workers. Her hands covered half her face, eyes brimming. "How are you, Custer?"

I just stood twisting my hat, feeling empty as a drum. "I rode a silent trail," was all I could think of in way of an answer.

She acted as if she intended to hug me.

"Don't...please don't," I held my hands out before me. I knew I'd break down if she did. She nodded her head while wiping away tears. She understood. So many people watching. I looked at them and nodded my thanks and they hurried inside as if busy with something.

"You looked starved," she said, her voice wavering. I didn't remember her eyes so dark and face looking that strained. Can you imagine the shock the poor girl received when first hearing from strangers the news about Buck. She couldn't even be sure I hadn't met the same fate.

"Oh...I reckon so. Not much appetite lately." How would I ever get through this?

She took my hand and led me into the friendly warmth of the restaurant. "This is your lucky day, cowboy," she said, smiling. "The T-bone's brand new and the best eating place in Cheyenne."

She got no argument from me. I hadn't seen hot food in days. Two of Jasmine's co-workers hurried over to wait on us. It was quite a change: other than the Bradfords, several weeks had passed since I'd even seen a girl, and now I was surrounded by three pretty waitresses.

It seemed I ate everything on the menu, but o-o-oh, was it good! A bit embarrassing though. Nearby customers sneaked quick peeks in my direction as if not believing anyone could pack away that much grub. A Manitoba raider couldn't have done better. Those were the biggest dumplings I'd ever eaten and the first since leaving home. Have you seen them as big as your fist? And chicken gravy on mashed potatoes! Oh hey, I could have made a meal of that alone. The T-bone would likely put all the other restaurants out of business. I told Jas how the Bradfords were faring, and that they bought Cowboy and Monty.

"But what will you do without a horse?" she asked.

"I'm taking the train back to Northfield," I said, between mouthfuls of apple pie.

"You are? Okay if I tag along?" Just like that. It wasn't what I was expecting, but she had thought long and hard about it and made up her mind. She already guessed I'd be returning to Northfield.

"Of course not. You don't mind leaving your new job?" I asked.

"No, I didn't come to Wyoming to wait tables. I'll try again to find a teaching job in Minneapolis. Wyoming is nice, but with so few people, they don't hire many teachers. Mom wrote, new families are moving into Minnesota every day. She said there could be 60,000 people in the Twin Cities alone."

I think we were both feeling better by then, and Jas made us all laugh with her family story. Truth or childhood fantasy, I couldn't say. Her ten-year-old younger sister decided to bake a sponge cake with chocolate frosting for grandpa's birthday. She set it to cool on a chair in the front porch. Grandpa came in from chores in the dark and sat down to pull his boots off. He yelled, jumped up, and hurried into the kitchen with cake all over the seat of his pants and chocolate on his hands. "What is this?" he demanded. They all began to sing, "Happy birthday to you. Happy birthday dear Grandpa."

Two days later, we rode the Northern Pacific across eastern Wyoming, aiming for Omaha. It was much like a week earlier when thoughts of Jasmine had pulled me back to Cheyenne; now the soothing peace of Northfield was calling me home.

Oh, did I feel better. All the way from the Bradfords' I'd been numb with grief, guilt, and worry over how Pa, Ma, and Sadie were handling this. Now I wouldn't have to face them alone. Jas had a knack for cheering up everyone around her. I loved her for that and realized I'd felt that way since our first meeting on the Sioux Falls/Council Bluffs stage. Once again, I felt a ray of hope, as if life still had something to offer; and I determined to make Miss Jasmine Bodecker part of my future.

Epilogue

Jas traveled with me to Northfield before going on to spend the holidays with her family in St. Cloud. All the way I had that someone's-missing feeling. My brother had always been part of our relationship. Maybe that's why I was already writing this story on the train ride home; it was my way of holding onto Buck. Nope, I won't say "his memory." I mean Buck. He was a lot closer than that. By telling you my life, I again experienced what I hold dear, at the same time realizing the transience of youthful pain.

It was a homecoming filled with tears and hugs, and we might not have made it without Jas. Especially Sadie. Even though she kidded Buck mercilessly, they were so close. Within hours, she and Jas were like sisters and remained so until Jasmine's passing in her seventies.

Of course, we had a memorial service at church—filled to capacity and overflowing down the steps to the lawn. All of Buck's friends from school came, and they were stunned to learn he was an ex-deputy sheriff, killed by cattle rustlers in Wyoming Territory. They came to me and silently shook my hand, seemingly unable to speak.

There was so much healing warmth in our home. Northfield too had that feeling of undefined security I desperately needed. Uncle Roy and Millie practically lived with us as long as Jas continued her visit. People were always dropping by, bringing cakes and pies. They just wanted us to know they cared.

I wonder if you remember my telling you it was a miracle to find Buck in that vast Kansas prairie, kidnapped by buffalo hunters. I didn't realize it at the time, but that was the second miracle. The first was meeting Jas on the Sioux Falls/Council Bluffs stage. She generously claimed Buck and I were heroes and saved her in Cheyenne. The truth was quite the opposite: she saved all of us from hopeless despair so we could go on with our lives.

It was Sunday, a week before Christmas. Jas would leave in two days for St. Cloud.

The day before, Sadie and Jas rolled and kneaded bread dough under Ma's watchful eye, and then left it to rise overnight near the warm kitchen woodstove. You should have seen those two girls—elbowing, shoving, and giggling while Ma tried to keep a sober face. I doubt she ever considered bread making a contact sport.

Our farmhouse was tight and snug against the latest Arctic blast. Deep snow blocked the front yard, and wind sang under the eaves. I could see a high sharp drift, like the prow of a great ship, out the kitchen window—snow swirling off the top like smoke blowing from a stack. Stark box elder branches reached for an ash-colored sky, heavy with promise of more snow. We didn't have a tree in those days, but Ma and the girls had decorated the house with bright ornaments and popcorn strings and hung evergreen branches over the doors. The crib scene, stable and small figurines on straw, occupied the center of the dining room table.

The night had been brittle cold with drifting snow. Exploding sap-filled branches echoed in the darkness. Sadie, not trusting the warmth of the cow barn, sneaked out after midnight and brought in Bubbles and Mr. Moses. A safety wire ran from house to barn, and she held it all the way. Our mournful bloodhounds sat by the stove with their heads lowered, hoping to stay inside.

For Sunday dinner, we had heavenly baked chicken along with fresh-baked bread, burned on top the way I liked it. Like old times, Sadie and I fought over the end crust (she cheated and won).

With dinner over, Pa and I had hitched Prince and Jack to the sleigh and we gave the girls a bundled ride into Northfield. Sadie wanted to introduce Jas to her friends and they planned to play cards and checkers. The horses' breath was like tumbling steam around them. I enjoyed the trip, especially the proud white jackrabbits loping effortlessly over frozen drifts.

It would be dark again in two hours. We had to leave soon to pick up the girls. My parents and I sat around the kitchen, the largest room in the house. Our nickel-trimmed cast iron cook stove kept us warm and we never allowed it to burn out. I began a clumsy apology for not keeping Buck safe. First, I mentioned the note Pa wrote and that Buck passed on to me.

"Note? What note?" Pa asked, his face showing confusion. "He left Roy and me a note pinned in his deputy sheriff badge on the wagon seat, which we read the morning after finding that rascal gone."

Now it was my turn to be confused. "No, Pa, I'm talking about the note you wrote telling me to watch Buck, and make sure Jasmine got him back in school. He gave it to me at the Omaha train station."

My parents exchanged looks and began to laugh—the first real laugh since Jas and I had walked through the front door. What was so funny? They both had a wonderful sense of humor, even during tough times. I could only wait until they stopped.

"What Pa? Gee willikers, what did he do?" I asked helplessly.

Pa wiped his eyes and struggled for control. "Oh, Custer," he said, "it's too much. I never wrote you a note. That boy ran off, knowing I'd never let him follow you."

I didn't know what to think. Pa looked at me as if I'd gone stupid. "Don't you see, boy? Buck must have forged the note you read. In the note he wrote us, he said to keep his posse wages to pay for Cowboy, and he would send more later. He was going with you to Wyoming."

I couldn't believe it. Imagine Buck fooling me like that! Danged kid! He was going to owe me. Then I remembered.

"I know he would have sent wages, Pa," I said. "He was a go-getter. Neither Coosie or Robbie, that homesteader I told you about, had any complaints."

I should have guessed Pa wouldn't allow Buck to go. If he did, he would have made sure he had the money. Buck only added that part about school to convince me that Pa wrote the note. Well, it worked. Those twins, Buck and Sadie, were of the same mold: if they said it was a full moon, you best go look out the window.

Later, I watched Ma bustling around the stove. A roast and stew happily bubbled on the stovetop in a green metal roaster pan. It would be ready by the time we finished chores. Pa contentedly returned to his *Rice County Journal.* I wanted that day to go on forever. Oh, was it good to be home.

Best of all, Pa never drank again. He did it for Buck; I know that for sure. Nothing else would have kept him from it. We told him often how proud he made us.

By now, you likely guessed it. Jas and I were married four years later, July of 1880. That gave her time to follow her dream as a teacher in Minneapolis, while I continued my education and helped the folks farm. I couldn't have found a better wife.

The wedding was in our Northfield family church, but the reception and polka dance took place at the farm. We had a beautiful day for dancing on the lawn. It was said that during the shindig, only a couple of stray dogs were left in town.

Families each brought a dish, and long tables strained to hold salads, casseroles, baked chicken, homemade buns and loaves of golden-brown bread, mashed potatoes topped with butter and paprika, peas and carrots in thick cream sauce, sponge cakes and fruit pies, and gallons of scalding coffee.

Oh, did we party late into the night, confident of the future, happy with the future. Lanterns glowed in the trees and stars sparkled overhead as the famous barn dance band, Northfield Polka Kings, played until we could dance no more.

Jas looked so-o-o beautiful. I wish you could have seen her in her snowy-white satin-and-lace wedding dress. Ma, Sadie, and Jas made it together. I look at that photograph often. It's a wonder she held up; she must have danced with the entire male population of Northfield.

The other pictures are a kick too. Even now, I can't stop laughing while going through them. What a grand day for Jas and me!

Several of Pa and Uncle Roy's army buddies from the Minnesota 1st Regiment Infantry came, and were still there the next morning, sleeping it off under our apple trees. (Bubbles and Mr. Moses joined them, grateful for the company, such as it was.)

Both her parents and mine helped us buy a farm northeast of Osakis, Minnesota. In fact, our acreage bordered the great walleye fishing lake named after the closest town: Lake Osakis. It was practically a wilderness when we moved there. The clearing of land and raising of three sons wouldn't have been possible without Jasmine's spunk and courage—the same courage she had showed traveling alone to Cheyenne. Buck was with us as an important element in our mutual love. Tough to explain.

We were proud of our part in helping to build a church in an idyllic country location. That's the best place to have a church, not in some noisy, busy town loaded with distractions. It became a popular meeting place for the entire surrounding community. A wonderful picnic spot after church services.

Of course, we returned often to Northfield to visit "Papop" and "Grandmop." I would show my boys where the James Brothers robbed the First National Bank. Even now, the bank remains the same as the fateful day of the robbery. I also showed them Joseph Lee Heywood's grave, the incredibly brave bank clerk who lost his life, giving residents time to organize and destroy the murdering James Gang.

Our boys wondered how anyone could ride horseback into town in broad daylight, rob the bank, and manage to escape. I could only tell them, regardless of what the James Gang did, they were Civil War veterans and some of the toughest men that ever lived. How else could you explain it? Townspeople had severely wounded several, but the Gang had still managed to elude statewide posses for weeks.

The locations mentioned in this memoir are also familiar to our sons and grandchildren. They traveled the same trails we passed over so many years ago, even visiting Uncle Buck's grave. With cars trundling down paved streets of Cheyenne, airplanes passing overhead, and radios playing, they couldn't visualize Buck, Jasmine, and me racing down those same streets of dirt on horseback with bullets whistling overhead. I didn't blame them. I'm just as dubious when they talk of future space travel, organ transplants, and pictures sent through the air much like radio signals.

I'm so old now. Everyone's gone from my youth, even Jasmine, and I miss her dearly. Only Sadie remains. She taught school for many years in Sauk Centre, and people still come from around the world to interview her concerning her most famous pupil, Sinclair Lewis. I always meant to read *Main Street,* but now my eyesight is too weak.

Sadie and I get together often, and no matter where we meet, we're kids again. The years are whisked away and we're back on our Northfield farm, following coveys of bantam chicks or searching the haymow for all-too-rare calico kitties. She never really changed—still telling endless outrageous stories without the slightest burden of proof.

Of course, everyone at times feels the world is cold and heartless. It's happened to me often. Then something usually occurs to shame my self-pity. Over the years, I've been in contact with the crusty gentleman who owns the land where Buck rests forever. He built a powerful fence to keep cattle from violating the grave and sent me a photograph. I estimated the cost and sent him a check. A few weeks later, I received his answer:

> *Buck is buried on our land and the legend of the fifteen-year-old ex-deputy sheriff who lost his life riding for the brand and sent two rustlers to meet their maker belongs to my family too—not to mention the state of Wyoming.*

He returned my voided check.

Life is like that: all of us pulling each other along toward...I won't say happiness. It's too strong a word, and as elusive as a hummingbird. I'll say contentment—something no one can put a price on.

Other relatives and friends have visited the gravesite and reported to me. A faint, unmarked two-wheel track breaks from the public road and appears to wander without purpose into a vast open prairie. It stops at Buck's grave. It's on private land, but the owner installed gates, believing people have enough sense to close them. Now there are cattle guards. What a beautiful spot under the constant watch of hunting hawks and eagles! So silent except for the whirr of homeless wind and whisper of waving buffalo grass.

Complete strangers, lawmen, Northern Pacific railroad workers, ranchers, Fort D. A. Russell soldiers, cowboys and cowgirls visit the site. Even Cheyenne dancehall girls when they still existed (stories got around). They leave things too: fancy cowboy belt buckles and spurs, bottles of beer, military medals, card decks, crucifixes, railroad

Jerome A. Kuntz

buttons, and deputy sheriff badges. Sadie sent along her own remembrance: *Don Quixote*—her picture for a bookmark.

This is pure speculation of course. I treasure an ancient tintype of our family. Everyone smiles forever except Buck. He stares back expressionless at a cold world as if in sad acceptance of a fate not to his liking. I always felt I'd meet someone like Jasmine and live a long happy life, and that's how things turned out. I suspect many people lack those expectations, and with good reason.

Buck still comes to me in dreams. In my youth, I never tired of staring at the saints portrayed in our stained-glass church windows. That's where I see him—made of shapes of colored glass, but alive and moving. He's the same light-haired, freckled boy I remember in my youth. He never aged. He stands with head tilted down, staring back at me. "Buck," I ask, "why didn't you stay with the chuck wagon?"

He slowly looks up to respond, tight as ever with words. "I was part of the crew, Custer. It was my job."

It's a good answer, and exactly the one I'd give. You didn't know him like I did. No matter what, he'd do what he considered his duty.

Then he silently shatters into countless shards of colored glass, streaming off into blinding sunlight. I wake with my arms extended, trying to hold him together. It's the end of sleep for the night, but that's all right. Old men need little sleep.

Dreams of my brother, Buck, are just dusty old memories pushed to the surface like frost-heaved boulders in the long Minnesota winter; but my love for my brother, even after sixty-five years, is still love.

THE END

Acknowledgements

Characters in "Northfield" arrived on the frontier by way of my own daydreams. Any resemblance to actual persons, living or dead is coincidental.

Special thanks to my wife, Connie, and my sister, Debby for their gentle encouragement to continue the journey and for their professional editing. Grateful thanks also to Bob Flynn, friend and computer guru, for his generous high-tech assistance.

NORMANDALE COMMUNITY COLLEGE
LIBRARY
9700 FRANCE AVENUE SOUTH
BLOOMINGTON, MN 55431-4399

Made in the USA
Lexington, KY
25 April 2011